Against The Wall

"What happened last night?" I asked, coming to believe that this was more than just a hangover. Something was seriously wrong with me.

Had I taken something last night without my knowledge?

Faces of college basketball players floated past me, spinning and laughing. Christ, had I been roofied?

"Seriously," I said, shaking the bed now as I made my way up along his side. I batted at his hand that hung out from underneath the sheet. "What the hell happened last night? The last I remember was meeting you at Distill."

Batting at his hand again, I was surprised at how cold it felt. It was late June in Vegas, and though I could feel that the air conditioning was on in his apartment, it was still warm in his bedroom. And he was under the covers, too.

Slowly, I took his hand in mine. The word *lifeless* came to mind, and though my fuzzy brain was three steps behind, I knew that I meant the word in the literal sense.

Oh, God. Lifeless. Dead.

I pulled myself up to my knees, not wanting to, then pushing the sheet down to see his face. So handsome. I'd thought so since the first time I met him. I placed a hand on his cheek. So cold. His eyes were closed, and I sent up a silent prayer of thanks for that.

I knew it was too late, that he'd been gone for a while, but I pulled down the sheet to bare his chest, thinking I could do CPR while I called for an ambulance.

But once I peeled the sheet lower, I knew CPR would do no good.

There was a bullet hole right through his heart.

OTHER TITLES BY MARA JACOBS

The Worth Series
(Contemporary Romance)
Worth The Weight
Worth The Drive
Worth The Fall
Worth The Effort
Totally Worth Christmas
Worth The Price
Worth The Lies
Worth The Flight
Worth The Burn

Freshman Roommates Trilogy
(New Adult Romance)
In Too Deep
In Too Fast
In Too Hard

Anna Dawson Series
(Mystery)
Against The Odds
Against The Spread
Against The Rules
Against The Wall
Against The Grain

Broken Wings

Instant Replay

Countdown To A Kiss
(A New Year's Eve Anthology)

Against the Wall

Anna Dawson Book Four

Mara Jacobs

Published by Mara Jacobs

ISBN: 978-1-940993-15-7

For more information on the author and her works, please see www.marajacobs.com

To my nieces—Kendyl and Taylor.
I'm so proud of you both!

One

MY HEAD ACHED AS I WOKE UP. CAME TO, MORE THAN woke up. Was that bourbon I drank last night? I didn't think so. I couldn't imagine drinking so much of that stuff that I'd get blackout drunk. What I *could* remember was beer. But I'd never felt like this after a beer-drinking night.

I moved slowly out of the bed, careful of the sleeping body next to me.

Jesus, what happened last night? It wasn't entirely unexpected that I woke up next to him, but the way the evening had started last night, if I had to have guessed whom I'd wake up next to, my money would have been on the other horse in the race.

It wasn't unusual for all of us to get a little out of hand, but this? I looked down at my naked body, expecting to see, what? Scars and blood?

But no, it was just my normal body, though it felt so alien to me. And the fact that I was naked was a bit of a surprise too.

I moved off the bed and grabbed his shirt, which was still on the floor. I'd been to his apartment before last night, but never here in the bedroom. The shirt let me know for sure whose bedroom I was in. After buttoning up the long-sleeved white cotton shirt, I gently padded into the bathroom and did my business, then used my finger and some toothpaste to brush my teeth. I spied some Listerine in his medicine cabinet and swished that around a few times, trying to clear my mind as I cleared the foulness from my mouth.

It didn't work.

It was as if my thoughts were at the back of a foggy tunnel. I could see them, hovering, mocking me, but I couldn't get to them. They were always slightly out of reach.

I splashed cold water on my face, and it helped a little, but I still couldn't quite bring my brain into focus.

God, how did a drinker like Jack do mornings like this on the regular? And then get up and go catch murderers? At least when I binged on my particular vice, my head and body were just fine physically. I was just broke. Or in debt. Or paralyzed with shame. Okay, yeah, we all had our cross to bear.

He hadn't moved from the bed when I left the bathroom. I walked across the room and grabbed my phone from on top of the chest of drawers by the small window. Almost noon? What the hell happened last night?

Not sure if he needed to be woken—I assumed he would have set an alarm if he had—I let him sleep on. Quiet and unmoving, I watched the back of his head, wondering if we hadn't made a huge mistake last night. How would things play out now?

I took my time getting dressed, not trying to be quiet any longer. If I had to deal with this nightmare of a hangover, so could he.

I pulled back the curtains, letting in the midday Vegas sun. Mistake. I shielded my eyes before my retinas burned off, if that was even possible.

It felt possible. It felt like the sun could melt me where I stood. And like the Wicked Witch, I would shrink to the ground, leaving behind nothing but cargo pants, a Henley, and pockets full of discarded bet slips.

Not just in my pockets, but on the bedside table, too, apparently.

Holding my head in my hands as if it would fall off if I didn't, I moved back to the bed and sat down on my side, not being careful about landing too softly, though I was more worried about my state of being than waking him up.

Like most people would look for a condom wrapper after a night they couldn't remember—whether hopefully or regretfully—I was looking at the pile of bet slips that were scattered on the nightstand by where I'd slept.

What the hell had I done last night?

Apparently I'd thought that LeBron was going to have the game of his life if the amount of money—and the number of different bets—on the Cavaliers was any indication.

It was June, and the NBA was deep into playoffs, but I hadn't bet on any of the games thus far.

Hell, I hadn't even been following it other than how I'd happen to see it on the front page of the papers. I'd even avoided papers for the most part over the last couple of months.

Had any of these bets won?

Still holding my phone, I clicked on the ESPN app and went to the box score, as I gathered up all the slips and fingered through them. Game winner, over/under, prop bets…Jesus, I'd made over ten different bets on one game.

Then had gotten too drunk to even watch it?

Something wasn't kosher, as Ben would say.

Mishegoss, Saul would say.

"Hey," I said, bouncing a little on the bed, my back still to him as I matched up the different bets with the stats I was reading on the phone. "Wake up and tell me what the hell happened last night."

Nothing from him. Dead to the world. Lucky bastard.

Winners. Every single one of them. I went an astounding ten for ten on bets in last night's game. That had never happened to me before. Would never again. Simply unheard of.

Even the obscure bet of which team would score the most

free throws was a winner.

But why would I have bet on something so stupid?

I very seldom made prop—proposition—bets. Oh, sometimes Lor and I would do the fun ones for big games together, like would a safety be scored in the Super Bowl, or something like that. They were just for fun. Fifty-dollar bets, max.

But the ones I held in my hand were for a shitload of money.

I couldn't recall how I'd gotten the money to bet them all, but as of this morning I was getting it all back, plus another eighty-six thousand dollars in winnings.

Not bad for a night I couldn't remember.

What was the saying about God watching over drunks and fools? Add in gambler, and I was the trifecta last night.

"Hey," I said again, placing my phone on top of the now neatly stacked bet slips, setting them all on the nightstand. "I need to get going. Where did I leave my car?"

I didn't drive to his place, did I? I wouldn't be that stupid to drink and drive?

Ha! A glance at the bet slips assured me that my stupidity level was off the charts last night.

I left the bed once more and went to the window, the sun still stabbing into my eyes, but this time I looked down, to the parking lot below his apartment. My Porsche wasn't there and I sighed in relief. So, not *that* stupid. I vaguely remembered getting an Uber at some point. From my house? That didn't make sense. It'd be more likely that I'd gotten one from the Red Rock, where I'd placed the bets.

"I've really got to get going," I said, more loudly this time. Still nothing.

Now I was starting to get pissed. If I had to deal with this massive hangover, he shouldn't get to skate by and sleep it off.

I turned from the window, a little too quickly, because I had to place a hand on the wall to balance myself. Then the whole room started to spin and I sank to my knees, crawling around the bed to his side.

"What happened last night?" I asked, coming to believe that this was more than just a hangover. Something was seriously wrong with me.

Had I taken something last night without my knowledge?

Faces of college basketball players floated past me, spinning and laughing. Christ, had I been roofied?

"Seriously," I said, shaking the bed now as I made my way up along his side. I batted at his hand that hung out from underneath the sheet. "What the hell happened last night? The last I remember was meeting you at Distill."

Batting at his hand again, I was surprised at how cold it felt. It was late June in Vegas, and though I could feel that the air conditioning was on in his apartment, it was still warm in his bedroom. And he was under the covers, too.

Slowly, I took his hand in mine. The word *lifeless* came to mind, and though my fuzzy brain was three steps behind, I knew that I meant the word in the literal sense.

Oh, God. Lifeless. Dead.

I pulled myself up to my knees, not wanting to, then pushing the sheet down to see his face. So handsome. I'd thought so since the first time I met him. I placed a hand on his cheek. So cold. His eyes were closed, and I sent up a silent prayer of thanks for that.

I knew it was too late, that he'd been gone for a while, but I pulled down the sheet to bare his chest, thinking I could do CPR while I called for an ambulance.

But once I peeled the sheet lower, I knew CPR would do no good.

There was a bullet hole right through his heart.

I CRAWLED AROUND THE BED and grabbed my phone from the nightstand, then continued on my hands and knees into the bathroom, where I shut and locked the door.

My hands shook as I pulled up my contacts. I could have just called 911, but something in me told me not to. It was the voice in my head that I listened to, even though most times I didn't want to.

It was JoJo.

"Hello? Anna?" the man answered when my call went through. "Are you okay? Is it Jack?"

"Frank? I need your help." I could hear the panic in my voice, the fear. "He's dead, and I was right next to him. He's cold, so I think whoever did it is gone, but I'm not sure. I—"

"Whoa, Anna. Where are you?"

I told him where I was, and he said a patrolman would be right there, and that he would be there shortly.

"Stay with me, Anna. Talk to me until the patrolman gets there. Tell me what happened."

"I don't know what happened. I was…"

"Asleep?"

"Unconscious, I think."

"As in passed out?"

"I think I might have been drugged."

I could hear someone next to Frank asking questions but then they stopped abruptly, like maybe Frank had put up a hand or given them a look or something.

Frank Botz was a cop, and sometimes partner to *my* sometimes partner (of a different kind), Jack Schiller.

Not only a cop, but a homicide detective. So I figured calling him instead of 911 was just cutting out the middle man.

I could also tell that Frank was in a car, so I knew he was on his way, though I wasn't sure where the car was in proximity to the bathroom where I now huddled.

I checked the lock of the bathroom door, then scooched

along the floor to the shower, where I climbed into the bathtub.

Memories of doing the same thing months ago to protect myself from a killer with a gun flashed through my mind.

But that time I knew who was outside the door. This time I wasn't sure of anything.

Frank asked me questions and I told him what I remembered, and what I knew, but it wasn't much. Soon, I heard the sirens wailing and the patrolmen enter the apartment. It was either unlocked or they had a way of entering without busting down the door, because there was no splintering of wood sounds, no loud crashes, just a knock on the bathroom door.

"Ms. Dawson? I'm Officer Adam Fisher with the Las Vegas Metro Police Department. Remember me? I was assigned to watch your house a few months back."

I did remember him. Back after Danny had been killed. He'd watched Jimmy's house, too. I'd even brought him and his partner some of Lorelei's cooking. He was blond and fresh-faced, probably in his mid-twenties.

"Yes, I remember you," I said through the locked door.

"We've been through the whole apartment and it's clear. It's safe for you to come out now."

"Okay," I said, lifting myself from the tub, the porcelain cold against my skin. Almost as cold as his hand had been.

I opened the door, and Officer Fisher was there, reaching a hand for me, which I gratefully took, my feet still unsteady, though I wasn't sure if it was from shock or from whatever had entered my system last night.

"We'll take you to the living room to wait for Detective Botz. This whole place is now a crime scene."

"Okay, let me just get my shoes," I said, moving toward my side of the bed. Fisher's partner nodded at me from the other side as he looked down at the body.

I pulled on my socks and grabbed my shoes. Quickly looking to see if either cop was watching me—which they weren't, both of them looking at the lifeless man—I slipped the bet slips from the nightstand into my pants pocket.

Cold to be thinking about money at a time like this, but I didn't want the paper to be caught in an evidence bag, never to be seen again. If I was going to fall off the wagon for those bets, I was damn well going to cash them in.

They led me to the living room and we all sat down, waiting for Frank, who arrived a short time later.

Faxon was with him, and both men made their way into the bedroom, stepping carefully, scanning every detail of the apartment.

A few more cops showed up, as well as what I guessed was a forensic specialist, given the large case he was carrying. I could see an ambulance pull up from the window.

It wouldn't be needed.

Somebody placed a cup of hot coffee in my hand and I started to sip, but Frank had just come back out of the bedroom and stopped me. "Don't put anything in your system just yet, Anna. Let's get you to the hospital and run some tox tests."

"I don't need to go to the hospital," I said.

He squatted in front of me, resting on his haunches. Taking the untouched coffee from my hands, he set the cup on the side table, then took both my hands in his.

"I'm sorry, Anna."

"Thanks."

"Are you up to talking a little bit before we get you checked out?"

I nodded. "But I don't know how much help I'll be. I really don't remember much."

He squeezed my hands. "That's okay. Just tell us what you do remember." He moved from his squatting position to sit on the coffee table in front of me.

"Why don't you start at the beginning."

Two

Six Weeks Earlier

My name is Johanna Elizabeth Dawson. I'm thirty-four and have lived in Las Vegas since I turned twenty-one and came here from my home state of Wisconsin to play poker professionally.

I got into a little trouble a few years after arriving, and was helped out by Ben Lowenstein, a septuagenarian (now eighty-two) retired odds maker who took me under his wing when we met during physical therapy. He had just had his hip replaced. My foot had been broken by Paulie Gonads, the enforcer of my loan shark, Vince Santini.

It wasn't the last time I owed money to Vince, but it was the last time I'd taken a beating for it.

The other times, I became JoJo and would fix college basketball games to get out of debt.

A victimless crime (or so I told myself) with the player having no knowledge that they'd been involved.

I would slip them a roofie or a sleeping pill or something so they'd be out of it the following day and play like shit. It would have to be one of the star players on an otherwise vulnerable team.

I'd do this in their hotel rooms, gaining entrance in a variety of ways—and a variety of disguises—where they would be safe to sleep the night away after the drug hit.

I'd make sure they were comfortable and locked in, and would come to no harm other than having what would feel like a hell of a hangover or the beginnings of a powerful body flu the next morning.

I didn't do it a lot, maybe six or seven times total, and I'd never been caught. Never even saw the player again after JoJo would mix him a special drink, except once.

But that was all over.

Paulie was dead, as was Vince. And I hoped like hell that JoJo was, too.

For the past ten years, Ben had lived with me. Six years ago, Lorelei Samuels joined our household to help with Ben. And me.

She definitely helped with me, hiding my money so I couldn't gamble it all away. Investing for me, making sure I didn't have access to easy cash, and basically running the household.

The household that had expanded a couple of months ago when Raymond Joseph came to live with us.

Raymond was one of the college basketball players that became involved with a JoJo scheme. Needing money for his little sister's drug rehab, Raymond approached me about point shaving in another game.

And then he got caught.

The investigation was dropped, and Jack and I went to Chicago and brought Raymond back to Las Vegas with us.

Which brings me to Jack. Jack Schiller, homicide detective with the Vegas Police Department. And quite possibly my soul mate.

If shared bad habits and self-destructiveness were the prerequisites of soul mates.

Who knew, maybe they were.

In a weird twist, it was revealed that my Ben was Jack's

biological father. Jack had been given up at birth and adopted by the Schillers in the Bay Area of California. Neither Jack nor Ben knew any of it. The only one who did was Saul Greene, Ben's best friend since childhood. Saul let something slip on his deathbed that led me to uncovering Jack's paternity.

The two men couldn't have been more thrilled, having already formed a bond while Jack and I had been together. And even when we hadn't.

Jack had been shot a month ago, while trying to protect me. He'd been convalescing at my house, which made sense and also was completely crazy.

It gave Ben the chance to be near Jack and help. And with Lorelei, Raymond, and me all in the house, we were able to care for both Jack and Ben—who seemed like he'd aged five years overnight when Jack was shot—around the clock.

Raymond was planning on attending UNLV in the fall to complete his degree in sports medicine, so he really jumped in and helped out with the medical stuff. Which was just as well, because Jack didn't want me anywhere near him.

Oh, and the gambling. Yeah, I guess I need to mention that, as it's at the center of everything.

At the center of me.

The reason I'd get in debt to a loan shark in the first place was because of gambling. And not poker playing, which I was good at and where I won more often than I lost. My beautiful home and the cars in the garage attested to that fact.

But the same couldn't be said of my betting on sporting events. Although I probably won more than I lost with those, too. But when I lost, I lost *big*.

I knew it was affecting my life. And my relationships. Basically everything.

I quit. For a while. Okay, for twenty-nine days. That was all I could do. Until now. I haven't placed a bet in thirty days.

Unlike last time, I didn't kid myself that I was cured. I knew better. I could place a bet at any time.

But maybe not today.

And then maybe not tomorrow.

One day at a time.

WE HAD PUT JACK IN THE WING with Lorelei and Ben, thinking Lor would be the most help and Ben wouldn't have to walk as far to spend time with his recuperating son.

I knew he hated coming here, but he was so weak when he was discharged and still needed complete bed rest, so there was no way he could go back to his apartment alone.

At first we had home healthcare for him, but at some point Raymond started taking over and Jack said he'd rather just deal with the group from our household than outside help.

So, Raymond got instructions from Jack's medical team—as did Lor and I—and took over his care.

When Raymond moved in, we'd all thought he'd be instrumental in helping a male member of the household with simple tasks that were no longer simple.

We all just thought it would be Ben.

I quietly made my way down the wing, which held three people I loved in various ways.

I passed Ben's room first, looking in on him, opening the door slowly. There was a soft glow from the nightlight in his en suite bathroom. I knew another one would light up along the floor if he got up to use the bathroom.

I was tempted to go in and watch him sleep, but I didn't.

Next was Lor's room, and her door was open so she could hear Ben if he needed her or fell or something. There was a space where her drapes didn't quite meet, and light from the outdoor patio area spilled into the room and across her cherry sleigh bed. Her red hair shone in sharp contrast to her white pillowcase.

Ever the light sleeper, she lifted her head and blinked at me. "You okay?" she asked.

I nodded, moving a few steps into her room. "Just got home. I was with Monty. Everything all right here?"

She let her head sink back into the pillows. "Yep. All's quiet on the Summerlin front."

"That's good," I said. "Sorry to wake you."

"'S'okay. I wasn't completely asleep. I think Jack's having a restless night."

"Yeah?"

"I've looked in a couple of times, but he said he was fine. Maybe you should check, just in case."

"Lor…" I said with warning in my voice. She was definitely a Jack and Anna shipper, and I wouldn't put her past pulling out a false concern.

"No, really. Whatever." She pulled the sheet up over her head, and I concluded that our conversation was over.

"Night," I said, stepping out of her room.

"Night," she answered.

Further down the hall was Jack's room. All three rooms were on the same side of the building, all with their own bathrooms and sliding doors leading out to the pool area and backyard.

The door to Jack's room was closed, but I didn't knock in case he was asleep. Like I had done with Ben, I slowly opened the door.

"I'm awake," Jack said before I'd even opened it enough to see him in his bed.

Except he wasn't in the bed—he was sitting in the little alcove next to the sliders. He had the lights off, but the drapes were wide open, and dim light from outdoors easily showed Jack sitting in one of the two chairs, his feet up on an ottoman.

My eyes first went to his hand on the arm of the chair, looking for a glass of bourbon. Empty hands. "I heard you talking with Lor," he said.

I moved into the room, closer to the seating alcove, but not quite to the empty chair opposite Jack. "She said you had a bad night?"

A hand came up, made some halfhearted motion, then dropped back to the chair. "Not so bad. Just couldn't get comfortable."

I motioned to the chair. "And that's more comfortable than the bed?"

"I'm sick of that fucking bed."

I was sure he was. Jack had been thrown off a big case because of his involvement with me. That had driven him crazy, not being in the thick of it all. He'd ended up being there at the end, even bringing the killer down, but nearly died himself.

Which had nearly killed Ben. And me.

But the month since being shut out—and completely inactive—was almost a different kind of death for Jack.

And as far as I knew, he was doing it sober. No drinking at all.

It had been a long month for both of us.

I sighed, moved to the empty chair, and sat down. I put my foot on the ottoman, and Jack moved his over to make room for mine.

"I'm sure you're pretty tired of just lying around. I have to say, though, Ben has loved it. You're a captive card player, puzzle doer, and listener. He's been in heaven. Apart from the you almost dying part."

"Apart from that," he said, a tiny grin tugging at the corner of his mouth. God, I missed that smile.

"You need to listen to the doctors. Rest, rest more, rest. Then PT."

He nodded, but it was clear he hated it.

Three

I HAD A MAMMOTH BREAKFAST THE NEXT MORNING. It used to be the gauge of how well I'd played poker the night before. Now it was just love of good food.

The Corporation—the group of retired odds makers that met each morning for breakfast—was now down to three members. Ben Lowenstein, whom I'd brought to the Sourdough Café at Arizona Charlie's. Jimmy Mancini, a behemoth of a man with a full head of raven-black hair. And Gus Morgan, a charmer with sparkling blue eyes and beautiful white hair, reminiscent of Paul Newman. Except with a lot more marriages.

There had been five members originally, but we'd lost Danny and Saul months ago, bringing our daily table to just four, with me joining the boys.

We didn't pull out odds sheets and talk about that day's games after breakfast, as we did most mornings.

We hadn't for a month, mostly for my benefit, though it was May and college athletics were done for the year—at least those you could bet on—so there were fewer things on the board.

Instead we talked about the old days, the boys telling stories I'd heard a hundred times and could listen to a hundred more.

Ben was mostly silent on the drive home, which was, sadly, our new norm.

When Jack was shot, Ben had been scared shitless—as we

all were—and lashed out at me. I understood it. I, too, blamed myself and the life I led for putting Jack in a position to be shot at.

For a while I thought Ben might move out, but Jack needing to recuperate took that off the table.

At least for now. Me not gambling helped as well.

"I love that story about the betting on the first Super Bowl," I said, hating the silence, so stating the obvious just to say something.

"Yes, that's a good one," Ben said.

It hadn't been a month of the silent treatment, and Ben had actually apologized for what he'd said at the hospital. No, not really. He'd said he was sorry he'd said what he had while I was hurt myself. Not that his words weren't true.

Because they were.

I didn't push it any further, driving the rest of the way from Arizona Charlie's to my house in silence.

When we turned the corner in my subdivision to my lane, I saw several cars parked at the curb in front of my house.

"What day is it?" I asked. It was a question that was bandied about quite frequently in my home with everyone having off-hour and off-day jobs.

"Wednesday," Ben answered.

"Right," I said, sighing. I maneuvered past the cars and into my large driveway, opening the garage door, though I usually parked outside.

Today I wanted to go in through the kitchen, not the front door.

"Another one?" Ben asked.

"Yes. But it's the last one, I promise."

"It's your home, Hannah. You can have whomever you choose over."

No "Hannah, dear," like he normally called me. When we'd met ten years ago he'd misheard me when I told him my full name was Johanna but everyone called me Anna. I hadn't corrected him when he'd called me Hannah, thinking I'd never see him again.

A month later, I'd moved in with him.

And had loved when he called me Hannah darling or Hannah dear.

At least he was still talking to me.

"Monty got a lead on some office space, I guess. He's going to check it out."

Ben waved me away as I tried to help him out of our Lexus SUV, but I brought his walker around for him from the back.

I opened the door and let Ben in, following him as far as the main hallway that opened to the large bottom bar of our U-shaped house. I made my way past where Ben turned to go to his room, coming to the living room.

Quietly I peeked my head around the corner to see my living room full of five strangers and Monty Westerfield, who was speaking.

I was in his line of vision, the others with their backs to me. My movement must have caught his eye, because he looked right at me as he finished his sentence. "…and this is an intervention."

A chill ran through me and I slid back out of sight, keeping my back to the wall like I needed to dodge bullets.

I knew he wasn't talking to me—that I'd just let him use my home as a safe place for an intervention—but my palms seemed to leave a trail of sweat behind me as I kept them plastered to the wall, making my way to the kitchen.

Lorelei was at the small table with a coffee mug in front of her. At the stove was Raymond Joseph flipping over what looked to be a monster omelet.

They both looked up at me as I came in, and I guessed that my face was showing exactly how freaked out I was at the thought of an intervention that wasn't meant for me.

"Relax," Raymond said. He went to one of the cupboards

and pulled out two plates.

"I can't," I said, walking fully into the room and going to the fridge to pull out a bottle of water. I could smell the coffee Lor was drinking, but I'd had enough at breakfast and was trying to cut down on my caffeine.

Trying to cut down on a lot of my bad habits. Some were working, some not so much.

Raymond offered me some of the omelet, but I declined, so he cut it in half and brought it over on two plates to the table, sliding a plate in front of Lorelei and taking a seat with his own portion.

"Looks good," I said.

"It is," Lor said after taking a bite. "Thanks again," she said to Raymond.

"Anytime. You shouldn't have to do all the cooking around here. I can help out with that."

"I like cooking," she said. "Especially when the boys come over and I can do something big."

"You've been getting a lot of that lately," I said, and she nodded then returned to her eggs.

"When did Monty and his group get here?" I asked.

"About twenty minutes after you and Ben left. I made a few pots of coffee for them all, but they've basically been just waiting for the guest of honor to show up. From your face when you walked in here, I'm guessing that happened."

"Yeah, somebody was having the ball dropped on them."

"It's nice you let him use your place," Lor said. "Especially since it can't be easy for you to see other people going through their own stuff."

I shrugged. "Monty's been good to me, so if I can give him a space that doesn't sound off warning bells to a prospective intervenee, then that's cool. I just hope it doesn't inconvenience you too much."

She shook her head. "It's not. Besides, he said this morning that he had his eye on some office space."

I nodded and took a drink of water. "He told me that."

She looked at me as if waiting for more, but I just took another drink of my water. She sighed, then said, "He also said you were helping him out with the deposit and first few months of rent."

"Can I not swing that? I know I should have told you about it first, but I didn't know he'd find something this quickly. I can—"

"It's not that you can't swing it. Yes, you can. And you certainly don't need my permission to spend your own money."

"I was going to tell you before he came to you for money, I swear. I've just been too busy," I said.

"It's not that either. I just wish you'd told me because…you know…it's really great that you're doing this for him."

Oh.

Yeah, Lor was used to me coming to her for money to play poker, not seed money for a counseling service startup.

"Like I said, Monty's been good to me."

"I know," she said, reaching out and taking my hand and giving it a squeeze. Before I could squeeze back, she released me and returned to her omelet.

Raymond sat back in his seat, his half of omelet completely demolished while Lor gushed over my good deed.

"Well, he needs to keep his mouth shut, even if it's not part of his oath, or whatever," I said.

"He's just proud of you," Lor said.

"And was grateful about you helping. I think today's victim is just a kid," Raymond added.

"That *kid* is your age," I said to Raymond. "She has her whole life ahead of her. Parents who care, who want to help. She doesn't need to piss it away because she gives in to her vices."

"Like you did?" Lor asked gently.

"Exactly. Ben came to my rescue. Monty came to this girl's.

Here's hoping she can get whatever help she needs."

"The help who needs?" Jack said as he entered the kitchen. He walked slowly, not quite shuffling, but not his sure, confident, pre-shooting stride.

Raymond explained about the intervention going on in the living room.

"Booze," I said before he could ask. He nodded, got himself a bottle of water from the fridge, and came over to join us. I fought the instinct to jump up and help him—he'd hate that.

He took a long swig from the water, recapped it, then tipped it up in a mock toast. "May she have better luck than I."

Four

"ANNA, DO YOU HAVE A MINUTE?" MONTY SAID AS HE entered the kitchen. He nodded at everyone else in the room, receiving a wave from Raymond, a chin nod from Jack, and an enthusiastic smile from Lor.

Lor, more than anyone, was happy I was working with Monty, since she was the one who first brought him into my life.

But I wasn't ready then, hadn't sunk as low as I had a month ago, having dragged Raymond into point shaving and Jack nearly dying—not all my fault, but the guilt and shame were enough for me to contact Monty and ask for help.

"Sure," I said, following him out of the kitchen and down the hallway to the main entrance. A man and a woman from the intervention were in the foyer speaking in hushed tones, the woman dabbing at her eyes with a Kleenex, the man gently patting her arm.

"How'd it go?" I asked Monty quietly. The tears and comfort could be signs of either success or failure.

"Great. Jessica is being driven to rehab now. Her mother and stepfather are grateful to you for the use of your home."

I slowed down my pace. "They don't want to talk to me, do they?"

I was too fragile for that, and didn't deserve it. Not after all I'd done in my past.

"They wanted to thank you in person, but," Monty said, then took my elbow and swerved me into the dining room before we reached the foyer, "I'll tell them that I passed on the message."

Monty got me. Then again, maybe he got all degenerate gamblers, which was why he was the right counselor for me.

"But stay here for a sec while I see them out? I want to talk to you about something."

"Sure," I said, and took a seat at our large dining room table while Monty ducked into the foyer and presumably passed on my good wishes to Jessica's parents.

I really did wish the best for her, but I knew I needed to focus on myself. On my own recovery.

Recovery. Such a strange word to me. As if I were the one who'd been shot and was now strengthening my muscles day by day.

Some days it felt like that.

"So, yeah, thanks again for the use of your house," Monty said, reentering the room and sitting at the table across from me.

"Of course. I hope it helps."

Monty was nodding. "It will. She's getting some help. She's pretty young, so hopefully she can start her life over."

"Yeah," I said, not expanding. The truth was, even if I had stopped gambling, I *liked* my life. I wouldn't want to start it over in another direction.

Which was something Monty understood about me. He knew I missed the thrill, the adrenaline from gambling. The Hummer, I called it.

"I wanted to talk to you about a group I'm putting together."

Ah, so he was trying to come up with ways to fulfill my need for a Hummer with some other activity. Group activity, apparently. Visions of an Expendables- or A-Team-style group flashed through my mind. We'd rappel down buildings, swinging through windows, plucking junkies out of opium dens and whisking them off to lovely rehabs nestled in the forests of Minnesota or the beaches of Malibu.

"I'm in," I said.

"Great. It's all gambling, no other addictions."

Okay, so the opium den in my mind was quickly swapped out with a casino in Macau. We'd slide down ropes to land on a craps table, swoop up our target, and be lifted out by an awaiting chopper.

"Fine," I said.

"I'd love to have our meetings here, but that wouldn't be appropriate with you being a member of the group. It would feel like you had home court advantage."

I nodded out of habit, not really understanding what he was saying. Meetings? To discuss capers, maybe. Different escape routes and stuff? Yeah, probably best not to have those here. Lorelei would worry about what was the appropriate meal to serve while doing recon.

"I mean, ideally, I'd like to get my own space. Meeting space. Dedicated to working one on one and group therapy sessions.

"Wait, what?" I asked, my mind now fully out of search and recovery mode. "Group *therapy*?"

"Yes. It's called GREET. Gambling Recovery through Emotional Exchange Treatment. The theory is to find the emotional reasons why you gamble, through discussion, therapy, exercise, meditation, and other resources, then re-channel those emotions to a healthier lifestyle."

I stared at him blankly. Not *greeting* his idea with any emotion, re-channeled or otherwise.

"We talked about this when you first called me a month ago. That it was one route of treatment."

Treatment. Recovery. Therapy. I hated those terms; they all felt like…failure.

"A route to which I quickly said no," I reminded him. It took a lot for me to call Monty, to admit I needed help to stop gambling—at least for longer than a few days at a time. Mostly we just talked, and he gave me some tips, I called them, on ways to avoid making bets. Yeah, I guess you could call that therapy and treatment, but I didn't let my mind go there. To me, I was just…hanging out with Monty.

And now he wanted me to hang out with a bunch of people just like me? A group full of Annas, each with their own stories of their falls from grace and rock bottoms.

Uh, no.

"Yeah, no," I said. "I'm glad you're branching out, but count me out."

"You just said yes."

"That's before I really knew what you were talking about."

"What did you think I was talking about?" he asked.

Too embarrassed to share my visions of the Destroyer (as I'd formerly named myself) becoming the Savior, I only shrugged.

"This is a small group of people I've been working with who I think would really benefit from hearing each other's stories."

"My worst nightmare," I said, too late realizing it was out loud.

"There's a reason why people do group therapy, Anna. It works and is a helpful tool."

"And I said I preferred to work with you one on one, not go to any kind of meetings." At the time I'd meant twelve-step program type meetings, but this GREET thing sounded just as unpalatable to me. I knew twelve-steps worked for lots of people, and I had all the respect in the world for them and people who went to them. I just didn't think it would be a good fit for me.

Monty was pretty good at not showing his frustration with me. He was still new to all this, but he was a quick learner, and one of the things I imagined he'd caught on to right away was having a good poker face.

Especially with the degenerate gambler types like myself.

But, even though he hid it well, I knew he was frustrated

with me.

Which made me feel like shit—a feeling I was certainly accustomed to, but never *used* to.

Monty had been good to me, coming when I called for help and basically holding my hand for the past month as I dealt with Jack almost dying, Ben being blunt about how my gambling was affecting our little family, and the fallout of being involved in a very high-profile murder.

All while not placing a bet or playing a hand of poker.

"How small of a group?" I asked, and, much like I knew when someone was trying to bluff, Monty knew he had me.

"I THINK IT'S A GREAT IDEA," Lorelei said later that night at dinner, sitting at the same dining room table where I'd sat with Monty. "We could hold them here. I could do a brunch. Or maybe just bagels? What do you think—"

I held up a hand, stopping her from what I knew she would do. "Monty doesn't think it'd be a good idea to hold them here. Like the others would feel I was the one in charge or something."

"Level playing field," Raymond said. "Makes sense." Ben nodded his agreement. Jack only watched me as he pushed around the food on his plate.

"I think it's a good idea," Ben said. He'd been warming up to me ever since Monty had been coming around. I hated to admit how much the opinion of an eighty-two-year-old retired odds maker mattered to me, but it did.

Almost as much as that of a forty-year-old homicide detective.

But ultimately, it wasn't for their approval that I was trying this—trying to stop. It was for me.

And if Monty thought this would help… "God, I'm going to have to listen to every sob story under the sun, aren't I?"

Everybody chuckled except Jack.

"You never know, you might get a bunch just like yourself, no sob story to tell," he said.

"Jesus, I hope not. That'd be even worse," I said, and everyone chuckled again. This time even Jack.

Five

“WHAT IS THAT SMELL?” I ASKED MONTY TWO DAYS later as he let me into the space he was using for our first group meeting. Our meet and GREET, if you will.

“I’m not quite sure,” he said. “It was an Indian takeout place a while ago, but hasn’t been used in about a year.”

“That’s not curry.”

“No,” he said, and left it at that. I propped the door open with a large rock, hoping to get some air circulating in the small space.

The room was in a small strip plaza, the kind that populated Vegas. It was between a smoothie place and a bakery. Total, it was about the size of my dining room. It maybe had had room for a couple of small tables where Monty was now setting up folding chairs that he’d brought in the trunk of his late-model Ford Taurus.

“It’s not permanent, but it’s all I could find in my budget on short notice. I didn’t want to wait any longer to get this group started. I’ll keep looking for a better spot, but it’s fine for now.”

“You’re right, it’s fine.” I didn’t want to be a prima donna. I knew that degenerate gamblers were used to some pretty nasty places, either to play cards at, or because they’d sunk so low they now inhabited them.

I was guessing not everyone I’d meet today lived in a six-bedroom, eight-bath home in Summerlin.

I helped him place six chairs in a circle. "Why not go to a municipal building or a church or somewhere like that where they're used to hosting this kind of stuff?"

Monty went around the circle, shifting the chairs a little here and there, making the circle exactly as he wanted it. Finally, he looked up at me and said, "I think doing that would feel too much like twelve-step meeting to these people. Gamblers Anonymous is a great organization, but I don't want anyone feeling like I'm pushing that on them."

He was right—it would have felt like that. The closest I had come to attending a GA meeting was the night I'd met Jack, who was poised to attend an Alcoholics Anonymous meeting in the same building.

Neither of us had gone in.

And here we were, months later, living under the same roof, but apart. So, so apart.

But how many of the people coming today had gone into that building? Had done the steps and the meetings? Found the sponsors and carried the chips in their pockets? And, for whatever reason, were working with Monty. Exploring GREET.

"Good call," I said.

He checked his watch. "Thanks for helping me set up. Why don't you go next door and grab a coffee or something until the others arrive at three?"

"Want me to grab you something?"

"No. And don't come back until you see others arrive."

"Why?"

He shrugged. "I don't want the others to know you were here earlier. That you helped me."

"Why?" I asked again.

Another shrug. "Nobody likes a teacher's pet."

Feeling a little thrill that was pathetic beyond belief, I left Monty to it and went next door and ordered the first healthy smoothie of my life.

I watched from the smoothie place as people arrived and went into the space Monty had rented for the meeting.

All men, of course. Not that women couldn't have gambling problems, too—it was an equal-opportunity vice. But, much like I would usually be the only woman in a full sports book room watching games, it seemed I would be the lone female today as well.

The first man pulled up in a Nissan that looked like it had seen better days. Better years. The guy who got out was probably in his late fifties, maybe early sixties. You'd think spending most of my time with octogenarians I'd be better at guessing people's ages, but I wasn't. He was balding a little, his hair longer where it wasn't, a kind of black turning to grey. Not a clean salt-and-pepper way, but more like white with patches of black undergrowth. Kind of like Debbie Harry back in the early days of Blondie. But this looked natural, and not at all edgy like Debbie, but like he just hadn't quite turned the page into greyhood yet. He wore a wrinkled tee shirt from the Rio and khaki shorts with running shoes. It was May, and hot most days, but you would see all types of dress in Vegas due to the air conditioning in the casinos.

I had a year-round uniform of cargo pants (all those pockets to store all those odds sheets) and a Henley or some other kind of long-sleeved knit shirt. In the summer I ditched my denim or leather jacket, but always had a hoodie in my car to take into the casinos with me.

The next guy drove a newer Prius, and was as put together as the guy before him was bedraggled. His shorts were pressed with a collared shirt in a powder blue. He could have stepped right off the golf course, but, given his destination, it was more likely he'd come from a casino or card game. He was younger, too. Probably late forties. Dark blond hair, a good haircut, very handsome.

As soon as he was in the doorway, a car screeched up to the door and idled at the curb. An older Camaro, I could hear the bass coming from it even though its windows were closed and I was inside the smoothie place with the doors closed. I should have made my way over, but I waited and watched, and after about thirty seconds the passenger door of the Camaro opened and a scrawny leg in skinny jeans stepped out, then the next leg, then, reluctantly, it seemed, the rest of the guy—boy, really—unfolded from the Camaro and stood at the curb, looking back in at the driver. He was most likely over twenty-one, but he looked younger. His hair was longer, and swoopy, with waves going in several directions. He looked like a swift wind would blow him down the Strip.

He was saying something to the driver, looking like he wanted to get back in the car. I knew how he felt.

Finally, he closed the door, the Camaro swiftly drove off, and the kid ambled through Monty's door.

It was three right on the dot, and even though I wanted to wait and watch the last person arrive, I didn't want to be late for Monty's first group session.

"We'd better make our way over," came a deep voice from behind me.

I turned to find a man about my age holding a carrier containing five smoothies. "What?" I asked.

"Time for the healing to begin," he said. When I still continued to stare at him, he nodded next door to where Monty and the others were waiting for me.

Waiting for *us*, apparently.

I tried to remember if the guy had been here before me, or if I'd watched him come in, but wasn't sure.

He motioned for the door, and I opened it for him, since his hands were occupied with the smoothies. Grabbing my cup from the table where I'd people-watched, I followed him through and the seven steps over to Monty's place.

He had on jeans that fit him like a glove, not the skinny kind the kid had on, or lush designer ones that casino guys often wore with longer shirts untucked and exquisite loafers.

No, this guy had on plain old Levi's. And I had to admit, they looked good. His shirt was white cotton with the sleeves rolled up. Running shoes that looked like he actually used them for running. His hair just barely touched the collar of his shirt, and was a chestnut brown with a tiny bit of wave in it.

He waited at the door—which someone must have shut after I'd left—for me to open it for him, which I did.

"How'd you know?" I asked quietly as he walked past me.

He shrugged. "The same way you knew when you saw those guys get out of their cars."

"They could have been going to any of the businesses in this plaza," I said.

We were in the room now, the others all having taken seats in Monty's Circle of Life. He waited for me in the entrance. "Yes, they could have. But you knew where they were going the moment they got out of the cars, didn't you?"

It was disconcerting to know he'd been watching me watching the others, but I guessed it was all part of the same game.

"Yes," I said.

"We all have that look," he said—the same thing I was thinking.

I wondered if he could put it into words, label it somehow, for we all—on the surface, anyway—looked very different. Before I could ask, Monty said, "Good, we're all here. And it looks like the Smoothie Fairy has brought treats."

The guy I was standing with laughed and passed the carrier to Monty, keeping one out for himself. Monty did the same, taking a smoothie out and passing the carrier around.

"I would have got one for you, too, but it seemed like you were covered," he said, nodding at the cup in my hands. He moved to one of the two seats left available.

"Thanks anyway," I said, and sat down in the last seat, between the older guy and the kid, and across from Monty. The smoothie guy and the golf course guy were on Monty's sides.

Everybody nodded or said thanks to the man for the smoothies. Monty took a sip of his, then set it on the floor next to him and picked up a stack of large index cards. All the others, including myself, held on to their smoothie with both hands and looked around nervously, or straight down at the floor.

Good, I wasn't the only one that was a first-timer, then.

"Thank you all for coming," Monty said, looking up from the cards as he spoke and making eye contact with each of us. Or at least those of us who would look at him. The kid kept his head down and was cutting his thumbnail into the foam of his smoothie cup.

"Some of you have done group sessions before. Many of you have done a twelve-step program and those meetings as well. We're going to do things a little differently here with GREET, but I think a couple of those tenets are worth carrying over for our purposes."

Monty had come a long way from the guy who had nervously done one of his first interventions on me months ago.

One that hadn't worked.

Or maybe it had, but just on a time-release delay.

"First, we'll only do first names here. Second, though the word *anonymous* is not part of our group, the idea remains that what is said here stays here. That you don't speak about other people from the group with outsiders."

There were nods from everyone, and we looked at each other, then back to Monty. "Particularly," he said, "if you happen to recognize or know of someone here in the group. Las Vegas can be a small town in gambling circles, I've been told."

True. And I may even have been the one who said those exact words to Monty. But I didn't recognize any of the men that sat with me.

But apparently they knew me, if the look they were all giving me was any indication.

"Like, we're not allowed to tell anyone we met the Black Widow?" the kid said, mentioning the name I was known by in professional poker circles.

"Exactly," Monty said. "Or at least you shouldn't say how or where you met her." He looked at me, and I shrugged. If the kid got bonus points by telling someone he'd met me, that was cool.

"Okay, those are really the only two rules. First names only, and you keep what is said here by others to yourselves." He leaned over, took a sip from his smoothie, and turned to his next card. Here he spoke about the theory behind GREET, basically repeating what he'd told me the other day. "Let's just go around the circle, introduce yourself, and tell us in a couple of sentences why you're here—what it is you're trying to work on."

He looked to his right, to the golf guy, who nodded, took a deep breath, and began. "I'm Mark." He took a quick glance at Monty. "We don't do the 'and I'm an alcoholic' thing here?" Monty shook his head. "Yeah, so I'm Mark. And I guess I'm here because the gambling has gotten out of hand. I really need to cut back a little bit, but it's been hard to do that."

We all nodded, I gave a smile to convey understanding, and Mark relaxed a little in his seat.

"I'm Herb," the older man sitting next to me said. "I need to stop gambling or my wife is gonna leave me."

Well, that seemed pretty straightforward. Herb knew what was going to happen if he didn't stop. No ambiguity there. No "cutting back" like Mark had mentioned.

I forgave Herb for his shitty need-a-cut-to-get-it-all-grey hair, and warmed up to him.

We didn't all do the "Hi, Herb" or "Hi, Mark" ritual, for which I was glad.

Herb looked to me and I realized I was up. Concentrating

on the others' responses, I hadn't taken a second to think about what I would say, which maybe was a good thing.

"I'm Anna," I said, and they all nodded. Herb was near the end of his smoothie already, and he took a sip that turned into a draining sound. "Sorry," he whispered to me, but I just gave a tiny shake of my head and continued.

"I'm here because…because…"

Because gambling got me into so much debt that I would break the law and drug college kids so they'd play like shit and my loan shark could make money betting against them and pay off my debt.

Because the man I loved was a highly functioning alcoholic and even his issues didn't affect us like mine did.

Because I had pulled a good kid into my point-shaving schemes and gotten him kicked out of school, put in danger, and uprooted from his home and family.

Because the people with whom I kept company were ruthless and hard, and had tried to kill me, *had* killed others, and I had to watch as the man I loved struggled for his life.

Because even though I had done all this, had been through all this, I *desperately* wanted to leave this hole-in-the-wall and go place a bet on any team that might happen to have a game today.

"I'm here because my gambling has started to affect my relationships," I said.

Everybody nodded, and the focus moved to my right.

"I'm Jordan," the kid said. "And I'm here because I can't stop playing poker online."

The others all nodded, but I didn't. I understood the obsession, of course, but had not gotten into online poker for that very reason: it could become an obsession.

I'd had Lor put a block on my computer so that I couldn't do anything where I'd have to put a credit card in. And she hung on to all my credit cards.

I had, once upon a time, put lots of self-preservation stops in place with Lorelei's help.

But they hadn't been enough. Enough so that I didn't have huge credit card debt from playing online poker fifteen hours a day. But really, was I any better off than Jordan sitting next to me? Probably not.

"I'm Sebastian. Seb," said the smoothie guy. "I'm here because…" He took a deep breath, rubbed his hand across his face, looked at the floor, then looked up at all of us. And it felt like he was looking directly at me when he said, "Aw, hell, I'll just say it. Gambling has completely fucked up my life."

I felt my breath hitch a little, like someone had just slapped me. Maybe, in a way, Sebastian just had.

Six

"HOW'D IT GO?" LORELEI ASKED ME WHEN I FOUND HER in the kitchen after I got home.

"Okay. Good, I guess," I answered. I went to the fridge and pulled out some of Lor's homemade chicken salad. She put grapes and walnuts and I don't know what in it, and it was tremendous. She was standing by the large pantry and went inside and brought me out a box of crackers, which I took from her with a nod of thanks.

Pulling out a knife from the drawer and a small plate, she said, "Do you want to take this in the book room? Jack and Ben are in there watching the Yankees."

I shook my head. "Nah. Ben will feel like he needs to turn off the game, and I don't want him to do that." Lor had gotten a special sports package so that we had all the New York channels and Ben could watch his teams play. He never missed a Yankees game if he could help it.

I went back to the fridge, grabbed two cans of Diet Coke, and took them to the table, where Lor joined me, handing me a plate as I handed her one of the pops.

We dug into the chicken salad, spreading it on the crackers. "This is outstanding," I said. "Best batch ever."

She laughed. "You say that every time I make it."

"You keep getting better," I said, and took another bite,

careful to keep my mouth over my plate for the cracker crumbs.

"Do you want to talk about it? Your meeting? Or are you not supposed to?"

I took a drink of Diet Coke, setting the can down on the blue and gold placemats that I thought might be new. "We're not supposed to talk about the other participants at all. It's okay to talk about the stuff I said; that's only privileged to me."

"Do you *want* to talk about it?"

There wasn't much to say. After introductions, we each talked a little bit about how we started gambling, whether it was family card games when we were kids or neighborhood craps games or whatever. That had pretty much taken up the whole hour.

"Monty did give us an assignment as we were wrapping up," I said.

"Yeah?"

"We're supposed to start journaling," I said, my obvious distaste coming through in my tone. At least I'd held my groans in during group when Monty had brought it up—not necessarily the case with all of us.

"Have you ever journaled?" she asked.

"Never. Not even a diary with the little lock on it as a kid."

Lor beamed. "Oh, I had one of those. Mine was purple with pink fuzzy stuff on it. God, I loved that thing."

I smiled with her. "My older sister had one, too. I used to want to break the lock to look at it, convinced she was letting Robbie Kurkowski feel under her bra."

Lorelei laughed. "And was she?"

"I never got the damn thing open. But yeah, I'm pretty sure she was."

"Little tart," Lor teased.

"At least that's who she ended up marrying."

"No? Really?"

I nodded. "Yep, Robbie is now my brother-in-law and

father to my two nieces."

She smiled and we ate chicken salad in silence.

"I think…" I said between bites. "I think maybe even back then I knew I didn't want to put my thoughts down on paper."

She studied me. When she did that, I usually started getting nervous, knowing she'd see more than I'd want her to. More than I'd want anyone to. But today I didn't duck away, neither literally nor figuratively. I let her look. I let her *see*.

"Did you think you would write something incriminating back then? Did the fact that you'd try to break into your sister's diary prevent you from, I don't know, trusting in the system?"

I shrugged. "Maybe. I mean, I wasn't doing anything that needed to be redacted or anything."

"Other than invading your sister's privacy."

"Other than that. But that's basically my job as a younger sibling."

"True. Go on."

The thoughts were coming clearer to me now. Maybe it was talking during group about early stages of gambling. Maybe it was just that I was so damn tired of being in my head all the time, so, *so* guarded. Whatever it was, I went on when Lor asked me to.

"I think it might have been—how do I say this? Intentional lack of self-awareness."

She let that sink in, as did I. It was the first time I'd put that thought together, but it felt true somehow.

"Jesus, I thought group was over for the day," I said when Lor's probing eyes got too much for me. Or maybe it was my own words that put me over my self-help quota for the day.

"Anyway," I said, "that's our assignment for next session. Bring our journals to group." I started wrapping up the unused crackers and putting the Tupperware lid back on the chicken salad, though I'd made a sizeable dent in it. "We meet again on Wednesday. We're starting three days a week at first."

"At first?"

"With the idea that we might go more. Or less, I guess, if needed."

"But everyone there was thinking more, rather than less?"

"That was the general feeling I got," I said.

"Where do you meet? Am I allowed to ask that?"

After putting everything on my plate, I got up from the table and put the crackers back in the pantry, the chicken salad in the fridge, and the plate and knife in the sink. "I don't see why that would be under the anonymous blanket. We're at some empty former takeout place in one of the little plazas over by Durango and the 215. Total dive. Monty said he's looking for something better, but he got this place cheap, I guess."

"Do you know where he's looked?"

I shook my head as I leaned against the sink, facing Lor where she still sat at the table. "Not a clue."

"Maybe I could help him look for a place."

Yes, Jack had been with us recovering, but with Raymond now fully in the house and helping out with both Jack and Ben, and with me not gambling and thus around more and not out of town on a JoJo errand, I supposed Lor had less to do than normal.

And Lor didn't like it when she didn't have a project.

I was her project most of the time, and now that I was working with Monty, I was guessing she figured she'd passed the baton.

"He could probably use some help with a lot of things," I said. "He's really bought in to this GREET program. He mentioned something about hanging his own shingle out. I think he's getting enough clients now that he could do that. But I'm not sure if he'd even know how to go about that."

Her eyes were skimming across the room, and I knew she was looking for— Yep, there, she had her tablet and pen in her sights and was out of her chair, grabbing them from the counter and taking them back to the table. Flipping to a fresh sheet, she looked to me. "Do you mind if I offer to help?"

"I think it's a great idea. I don't mind at all. Why would I mind?"

"Well, you are working with him. Would it get too incestuous if I helped him get his business started? Or would that feel like some kind of conflict of interest?"

I waved an arm in the air. "Not at all. Go for it." I started to leave the room, but thought of something and stopped. "Actually, when you talk to him, if he needs startup money, seed money or whatever, and we can spare it, I'd be happy to help out."

She smiled as she nodded, then ducked her head to write something down. Her red hair was back in a high ponytail today, and I could clearly see the flush of excitement that rose up her neck to her cheeks as she scribbled.

"Like a donation, or an investment?" she asked.

"I was thinking a donation. What would I know about being a partner in a—what would it even be? A home for wayward gamblers?"

"A treatment center," she said quickly. "And you wouldn't need to know anything about it. You'd be a silent investor. Monty could handle the treatment stuff and I—" She stopped herself and looked up, a little embarrassed.

"Could handle all the business stuff," I finished for her. "It's a great idea."

"I don't know if he'd even be interested in taking on a partner."

I pushed away from the sink. "Only one way to find out. Ask him. I'm cool with him coming to dinner anytime you want to invite him."

She was reaching for her phone as I left the kitchen, nearly running into Jack as he entered.

"Sorry," I said, stepping wide around him.

"No worries," he said. "Time to start practicing my zigging and zagging."

"Have you been given clearance for zigging and zagging?" I asked, trying not to smile at just the sight of him walking so well. And upright.

"Not specifically. But then, the doctors don't know about all the moves I've got."

I rolled my eyes and walked past him. But I silently agreed that Jack Schiller had moves in him that defied modern medicine.

"SO, THOSE POKER GAMES. The ones you play in?" Raymond said that night at the dinner table. When Monty's head jerked up from his plate, Raymond added, "*Played* in."

"Yeah?" I said, watching as Monty relaxed and dove back in to Lorelei's pot roast.

"How do those work? I mean, can anyone set those up? How does Carla make them happen?"

I looked around the table. Jack and Ben were there, as well as Jimmy, Monty, Raymond, Lor, and myself. I assumed Gus had been invited if Jimmy had, but he wasn't with us this evening, which wasn't unusual. Since whatever *thing* Gus and Lorelei had been having petered out (as I was guessing it had), he was about a fifty/fifty show on the nights we did a big family dinner. But he would always be considered family, and thus invited.

I looked at Raymond. "I don't really know how the private games work. I met Vince at a poker game once in a casino and he invited me to play."

"And then some," Jack said from the opposite end of the table.

"How *do* they work, Jimmy?" I asked, ignoring Jack. "Not just backroom games at holes-in-the-wall, but the kind Vince ran?"

After swallowing down a huge amount of potatoes, Jimmy wiped his mouth on the cloth napkin (Lor had gone all out this night) and said, “It can be done a few ways. You can apply for a license to actually run your own game. Lots of hoops to go through with that, which can be done legitimately, or not so legitimately. Or you can grease the palms of some of the folks in the nice hotels so they look the other way when they know you’re hosting your own poker game when they got perfectly good poker tables right downstairs that they’d prefer you to play at.” I nodded. That was my guess as to how Vince had hosted his games in the nicest suites in the nicest casinos in town. “Or,” Jimmy continued, “you could just take a chance you wouldn’t get caught. Say you were hosting a bachelor party or something to account for the bar and food. Smuggle a poker table in somehow. Make sure your dealer don’t say nothing.”

“Vince probably greased palms to look the other way,” I said. Both Jimmy and Ben nodded their agreement.

“And do you think that’s what Carla’s doing, too?” Raymond asked.

“Probably. She’d know what palms were greasable from working for Vince. Hell, she was probably the one who applied the grease. She or Paulie. And Paulie’s gone now, too,” I said, sneaking a look at Jack, who was watching me.

Still a touchy subject for Jack and me—Paulie’s death, Vince and Carla, and the part I played in it all unfolding.

Probably even more touchy than Lion LaGasse’s death and the part I played in that. (Which, in my mind, was purely coincidental. In Jack’s mind, nothing was coincidental when it came to me, gambling, and a body count.)

“Why you asking, kid?” Jimmy asked Raymond—the question that I probably should have had.

“Just wondering. Seems like a pretty easy setup. Pay your dealer, pay your bartender, order some food. And keep a percentage of any money people may borrow.”

"Looking for some after-school work?" Jack said to Raymond. "Maybe a paper route would be a better choice."

"I'm not starting UNLV until fall," Raymond said. "And I ain't got a bike to deliver papers."

Jimmy and Jack snorted at his response, and I smiled. I liked that Raymond fit in so well with my boys, that he showed respect to Ben, Jimmy, and Gus, but also didn't take any shit. Especially from Jack.

"The thing is, kid," Jimmy said, "you gotta have a good bankroll to start out, since the way you make money on those games is by having people borrow from you. You could always take a percentage of the pot. But then why would people bother playing in your game? They'd just take their game downstairs, where they take a rake on each hand. So, to really make some money, you need to have a good nut to lend, and some degenerate gamblers who need to play poker so bad, they're willing to pay your vig at thirty points."

"Which," Jack said, "is, of course, illegal."

"And immoral," Monty added. "To knowingly prey on the weak like that. Hope people become in debt. Invite them to games you know they can't leave, or say no to."

Everyone's eyes were on me as Monty spoke. I chewed my pot roast slowly, the flavor turning a little bitter, though I knew it wasn't the food.

The whole night seemed to turn a little bitter as I realized just how intertwined my life was in gambling, with Raymond, Jack, and Monty all being pulled into my world of lies and deceit.

Finally, I swallowed the lump in my throat and took a drink of water. Avoiding Jack and Monty's stares, I said to Raymond, "We'll get you a bike."

Seven

THE NEXT MORNING AT BREAKFAST, I MENTIONED TO Gus what a good dinner he'd missed the night before. He only gave me a wink and said, "Next time." I didn't press him on it any more than I would have pressed Lor, which was not very much.

Lor and Monty had disappeared into our shared office after dinner, presumably to talk about his business and how—if—Lor could be involved. Raymond and Jimmy had gone into the book room, presumably to watch games, but probably so Raymond could pump Jimmy about details of how to run an off-the-books poker game. And Jack and Ben had gone to their wing of the house, presumably to rest, though it was more likely they were playing cards.

Everybody doing their own thing…without me.

I'd have to remember to ask Monty where self-pity played into all my "work."

But it brought up a bigger question to me: if I wasn't a gambler anymore, who was I?

Jack was set—he was a cop until the day he died… hopefully a long, long time from now. Lor was looking at ways to branch out as our little family expanded, grew, and needed her in different ways. Not less, certainly, but definitely different, especially if I wasn't out until all hours of the night playing poker or away from home for days at a time with my extracurriculars. Raymond would get his degree next year at UNLV and begin a career in sports therapy. If he wasn't in jail for running loan sharking and illegal poker games.

What the hell was I going to do with the rest of my life if I wasn't playing poker?

I had investments, and everything we owned I'd paid cash for, so no debt. (The debt I accumulated was a different kind altogether.) Lor had put the money aside for Raymond's education, and, though she wouldn't give me exact figures (smart!), she told me I didn't really have to work again for the rest of my life and I'd be okay.

But I knew myself. Even the parts I tried to deny. And I wasn't going to be okay not doing anything for the rest of my life except hanging with my posse. Especially since half of them were in their eighties.

So, if not gambling, what?

I saw Ben to his room when we got back from breakfast. Always an afternoon napper, Ben had recently added a midmorning nap to his routine. Though he was still up and ready for breakfast every morning at seven, I thought that the added stress of Jack being shot and me trying to stop gambling probably wore on him.

Or it could just be that "being in his eighties" thing.

There was no sign of Jack or Lor on their side of the house, or in the living room or dining room. Probably in the kitchen. Instead of going to join them, or looking for Raymond to hang with, I went to my office and got online.

With my approval, Monty had instructed Lorelei to clean out all my desk drawers of gambling-related items, such as college sports media guides, season preview editions of the sports magazines, old betting slips (God, just the feel of them made me crave), and the like. He'd also done a clean sweep himself of my phone and laptop, removing any apps or bookmarks and blocking some sites. It probably wasn't needed, as I'd never been an online gambler—probably the only reason we still had a roof over our heads.

Today, though, I wasn't looking for scores or point spreads or any of those glorious things I could find online. Today I opened Google and typed, *Interesting jobs in Las Vegas.*

Umm, yeah. No. You can only imagine what came up for that search.

Trying again, I typed, *What do former gamblers do for a living?*

"Got a sec?"

I jumped at Jack's voice, and he held a hand up in a calming manner as he stood in the office doorway.

"Yeah, sure," I said, quickly putting the lid of my laptop down lest he see my pathetic attempt at finding a life beyond the only one I knew.

He eyed me—and the hastily closed laptop—suspiciously, but didn't say anything as he entered the room and sat at Lor's desk, across the double desk from me. It was then I noticed he held a high-end shopping bag in his hand, which he put on the desk and slid toward me.

"What's that?" I said, the suspicion in my voice matching that of his eyes moments ago.

"Open it," he said. "I didn't have time to gift-wrap it."

I tried to cock an eyebrow at him, but it only made him chuckle—a sound I had sorely missed hearing. "Just open it, Anna." Still Anna, not Johanna as he would sometimes call me when our relationship was different. When we were an *us*.

Curious, I pulled the bag across the desks, sliding easier now that there weren't shoeboxes full of losing bet slips and odds sheets cluttering up my side. It was heavy, and wide, but thin, like maybe it held a couple of hardcover books. I stifled a sigh. Monty had lent me a few self-help type books about compulsive gambling, and though they were good—okay, enlightening—I wasn't in the mood for more of them today.

And especially not from Jack. He didn't see me getting him any *Stop Drinking Now!* books.

"It's not that," he said, reading my mind. "Just open it."

Ignoring him, I opened the bag and saw, indeed, two large books. I pulled them out, and they weren't self-help, or anything published. They were two—beautifully bound—leather journals. Empty and waiting for me.

"I overheard you with Lorelei yesterday," he said, not even bothering to look guilty for eavesdropping. Guilt was not in Jack's nature when it came to anything remotely investigative.

"And you had her run out and get these for me?" I stared down at them. "Thanks, but you—and she—didn't need to do that. I was going to just use this until I got something." I pointed to a stack of yellow legal pads over by the printer.

"Now you don't have to. She was happy to do it," he said, rising from the chair. The movement was slow, and I could tell it caused him pain, though he hid it well. "Think I'll head to my room," he said.

"Thanks again," I said, nodding at the journals. He gave me a wave and slowly walked out the door.

I set one of the two identical journals to the side and pulled the other one in front of me on the desk, cracking the pages. They were really nice, with beautiful lined paper that I could tell was a fine quality. The leather was soft and aged, with a little toggle tie that came around the front. Much easier to break into than my sister's diary, but I wasn't worried about that in this house. I was the only one who didn't respect boundaries.

"Oh, good, he gave them to you," Lorelei said, making me jump once again. Why was I not hearing anyone approaching me today?

"Yeah. Just now. Thanks for doing this, Lor," I said.

She came in and sat in the chair Jack had just vacated. "All I did was drive."

"Yeah, well, they're really nice." I looked at the bag—even it was nice. "I mean, these aren't something you picked up at CVS in the office supply section."

She chuckled. "God no. He knew exactly what specialty stationery store he wanted to go to. He must have found it online."

"Jack?" I asked, kind of confused. At her nod, I continued, "You mean he went with you?"

"Went with me? It was all his idea."

"Right. To get me a journal. But he didn't just mention it to you and you did it?"

She brushed her hair away from her face as she shook her head. "No. No. Not at all. And he didn't just *mention* it to me. He asked me to drive him to a specific store. He went in, took forever picking out what he wanted, and even asked about having them embossed with your initials, but we wouldn't have been able to have them this morning, so he skipped that."

"This morning? This all happened this morning?"

She nodded. "He asked me last night to drive him this morning. He found the place he wanted to go to, but they were already closed, so we went while you and Ben were at breakfast."

He wasn't supposed to be out and about, but he'd obviously survived his adventure with Lor, though that was probably why he'd quickly retreated to his room—too much activity in his weakened state. My hand fluttered over the soft leather. "And he picked them out?" It wasn't really a question. The journals were totally Jack's style. Totally *my* style. Though they still would have been nice, Lor would have picked out something different, I was sure.

"I was looking at ones that were much cuter. More feminine. But Jack went for these. No argument. It was his show from the get-go."

I traced the stitches along the outside binding with my finger. "Thanks for taking him."

"Of course. I argued that he shouldn't, of course, but he was pretty insistent."

"Hard to argue with an insistent Jack Schiller," I said, knowing of what I spoke.

"Got that right," she said. She nodded once, as if she was satisfied that her work was done, then got up and left the office, leaving me alone.

Alone with the journals Jack bought me.

Eight

"SO, I'VE WORKED WITH EACH OF YOU SEPARATELY," Monty said at our next group session. "That's how I was able to put this group together—I think you all could benefit from each other's experiences."

We all looked around, probably trying to figure out what the common link was that made Monty decide we were the right fit.

Besides being degenerate gamblers, of course.

There we all sat, with our fresh new journals on our laps and smoothies in our hands. I was acquiring a taste for them.

Hadn't quite acquired a taste for journaling yet. I had tried, but the voice in which I wrote sounded so much like JoJo that I had to stop myself from throwing the damn thing across the room.

"But there is one thing that Anna brought up when she and I spoke that no one else mentioned, and I thought it was interesting."

Great. I was the freak among the group of freaks.

"I hope this is okay if I paraphrase something you told me, Anna?" Monty asked, but he wasn't really asking. One of the ground rules to this group was that anything we had previously talked to Monty about was up for discussion. He felt we could cut through a lot of time that way.

Like I had any clue what the best way to fix any of us was. I waved Monty to continue and took a deep drag from my smoothie.

Damn. A monster case of brain freeze.

"Are you sure it's okay?" he asked, mistaking my look of pain for reluctance.

I nodded. "Brain freeze," I said, holding up the smoothie.

"Put some of the smoothie on the roof of your mouth," Mark said.

Herb added, "No, put your tongue on the roof of your mouth."

"I thought it was pinch the tip of your thumb," said Jordan.

I looked at Seb for words of wisdom, but he only smiled and shrugged, then took a sip of his drink.

Before I could try any of the methods, the feeling passed and Monty continued.

"She said that there were two—I'm going to call them entities—that drove her when she gambled. A voice and a feeling. They were very specific to her; she seldom confused the two. One was the feeling she got when gambling, the other was the voice in her head that rationalized, even encouraged, her behavior." He looked at me. "Did I sum that up correctly?"

I nodded and cleared my throat. "Yes. A little too correctly." The others chuckled.

"And you even had names for them both, yes?"

I nodded again. "Yes." I took another sip from my cup, more slowly this time.

"I'm not asking you to share those names with us," he said. A tiny shiver of relief went through me, and I was surprised. Why should I care if these guys knew I called a Hummer a Hummer and JoJo was regularly whispering sweet nothings to me?

"If you get to a point where you'd like to share the names, that's fine," Monty said, probably reading my body language. "But the *idea* of it is what I want to ask the group. Has the feeling you get when you gamble, and the rationalization that you come up with, become so strong, so singular, that you could put a name to them? Even if perhaps you haven't?"

No hesitation at all. Four heads all bobbed up and down in agreement. Only Monty and I abstained.

"Fascinating," Monty whispered more to himself than to us. He scribbled something down on his cards and Seb looked at me with a soft smile of understanding. Yeah, he was trying to help, but we were like lab rats for Monty, too.

"Sin," Herb said, and all eyes moved to him. "That's what I call the feeling you're talking about. Sin."

"Wow," I said, then wished I hadn't. "I didn't mean for that to sound judgmental. 'Cause, like, who am I to judge? It's just… really powerful. Sin."

"I like it," Jordan said, keeping his head down, his floppy bangs hanging in front of his face, not allowing me to see if he was yanking Herb's chain or was serious. He looked up then, as if knowing we were assessing him. "It sums it up perfectly," he said to Herb, who, I think, was also trying to tell if Jordan was playing him.

"It's like sex, and drugs, and fattening food, and you know it's wrong, but it's going to be so fucking good, you know?" All heads nodded with Jordan. Up until now, he hadn't said much unless Monty had asked him something directly. "Yeah, man." He looked at Herb. "Sin. That's fucking genius."

"A little fire and brimstone, though," Mark said, and I found myself agreeing with him.

"Yeah, like, where's the joy? There is joy in that feeling, too," I said.

"You don't think there's joy in sin?" Sebastian asked with what I thought was maybe too pointed of a stare at me. "Maybe you're not doing it right."

Laughter from everyone, and a tiny smirk from Seb, which made me smile. I waved my arm around, encompassing the group and our surroundings. "I think this whole thing is a testament to just how right I was doing it."

More laughter, and Monty sat back while the rest of us were off and running, talking about our common interest. The names we placed on our vices.

Sin from Herb. The Hole from Seb, which I thought was also a little joyless, but he seemed to feel it wasn't necessarily a dark place. Oxygen for Jordan. "Because I need it to breathe, you know?" We all nodded. We knew. Caviar from Mark, which made me take a second look at him. Subtle, but very expensive watch and clothing. The guy had taste. "It's not for everyone, costs me, and makes me feel like I made it." Smaller nods, but I got it. Status was important to Mark. I couldn't necessarily relate, but I got it.

All eyes were on me, and I realized that even though my idiosyncrasies started this ball rolling, I hadn't divulged my name.

"The Hummer," I said, and watched as sly smiles came across each of the men's faces. Even Monty, who had heard it before. "Not *that* kind of hummer," I said, with enough disgust in my voice to make them all turn from smiles into outright laughs. "It's like when all of those things—Sin, Caviar, Oxygen—swirl around and rush through the Hole, then explode through your body. Makes it Hum."

"That's exactly what *tha*t kind of hummer is, too," Herb said, and they all laughed, and this time I joined in.

We talked about the feeling for a while, what it did to us, how we tried to re-create it with non-gambling things to no avail.

"It can be done," Monty said, "but that's also risky. Many former compulsive gamblers replace gambling with other things that also take over their lives. Running or exercise, for example."

"Not likely," Herb murmured, and I nodded in agreement.

"Work. Treatment. Shopping. Whatever it is, they find the

same feeling, maybe to a lesser degree, but they do, so they keep doing that new activity until it becomes a compulsion as well."

"So you're saying *don't* take up jogging? Because I'm good with that," Jordan said. Mark rolled his eyes, and I took a closer look at him.

As well as the expensive taste in watches and clothes, his body was lean and fit. Where he'd been wearing shorts our first session, now he was in jeans, which had been ironed, if the razor-sharp crease was any indication. Never having gotten near an iron myself, I wouldn't know for sure.

"I'm saying it's better than gambling," Monty said. "To find something that gives you…Oxygen, or Sin. But that isn't detrimental to your finances, work, and relationships. That's all well and good."

There was some feet shuffling, and Herb was trying to slurp every last drop from his smoothie. I made a mental note to get two for him next time.

"But that just replaces one compulsion with another, albeit healthier, compulsion." Herb set down his empty cup, and we all tensed a little, sensing we were about to hear something from Monty we didn't really want to know about ourselves.

"Ultimately, though, the goal is to learn *why* you need that feeling, and if you can achieve it without compulsive behavior. Or if you can live a healthy, happy, productive life without that feeling."

"But I need it to breathe, man," Jordan said quietly, again staring at his beat-up Chuck Taylors.

Yeah, definitely not something we wanted to hear.

Nine

LORELEI WAS WAITING IN HER BMW IN FRONT OF THE plaza when our session ended.

We'd never even gotten to the names we called our rationalizations.

"Is everything okay?" I asked as she got out of her car when we started to leave the building. The space had windows all along the front, which wasn't a great thing in what should be an anonymous setting, but I had been facing the other way and hadn't seen her pull up, so wasn't sure how long she'd been there.

"Everything's fine," she said. "I'm sorry to worry you. I would have called if there was anything wrong."

I pulled my phone out of my pocket. "We keep our phones turned off when we're in there."

"Right, of course. Everything is fine. Raymond is with Ben and Jack. Ben and Raymond were playing cards when I left, and Jack was in his room on the phone with his son."

Jack's son Casey was supposed to have visited right after Jack was shot. The visit had been postponed until Jack was better. I knew Jack spoke with his son often, but I wondered if they were trying to reschedule Casey's visit.

I wasn't sure how I felt about meeting Jack's son—Ben's grandson—while things were so shaky between Jack and me.

No, not shaky. Nonexistent.

"Anyway, I'm not even here because of you," Lorelei said, pulling me from my thoughts. "I'm meeting Monty to look at this space and see if it's one we want to keep."

"You're a 'we' now?"

She smiled, and the sight was almost blinding. And we were standing in Vegas sun. "Looks like it. We have some things to discuss. I spoke with Gary and he's on board. He thinks it's a good idea, actually."

Gary was my business manager and accountant. Between him and Lor, they kept me solvent. Or perhaps rich. It was in my best interest not to entirely know for sure.

"He's setting Monty and me up with an attorney to talk about the legalities of us setting up an LLC or maybe an S-corp, because—"

I held up my hand. "Whatever you guys think is the best way to go. Just tell me where to sign when you're ready. And make sure that we still have money to live on if it doesn't work out."

"I will," she said.

Blind trust. Faith. Stupidity. Whatever you wanted to call it, I let Lor handle the things that I knew she was good at, loved, and that I couldn't stand.

No Oxygen for me in learning about LLCs or S-corps. Whatever the hell they were.

"Hello," Mark said to Lorelei as he and Seb left the take-out place. Perhaps the new home of Whatever & Whatever, LLC?

"Hi," Lor said. We all looked at each other. Lor at me for introductions, me at Mark and Seb for protocol.

"Um, do we…" I floundered before Mark saved me, sticking his hand out to Lorelei.

"Mark. I'm a new friend of Anna's."

"Lorelei. An old friend of Anna's," she said, smiling at Mark.

"Not possible. You're too young to be an old friend of anyone's," he said, still holding on to her hand.

Seb and I shared a look and tried to hide our grins. "Dude, you did not just say that," Jordan said as he stepped around Mark.

"Bad?" Mark asked Lorelei.

"Cheesy," she admitted. "But effective."

"That's all that counts," Mark said.

Jordan nodded at Lorelei, then a chin bob to the rest of us, and walked to the curb where the Camaro pulled up. Hopping in, he flicked a wrist in wave to us, and the car peeled out of the parking lot.

"Chatty," Lor said.

"I'm Sebastian," he said, shaking Lor's hand. His eyes stayed up top, not skimming down her knockout body, as most men's did. Even Jordan, in the nanosecond he'd looked at her, had spent as much time on her bust and butt as anything else. Mark was still looking her over. Lor was used to it, of course, reveled in it sometimes. But today she was all business.

"Lorelei. My roommate," I said, waving a hand between Lor and myself. That statement had both Seb and Mark looking back and forth at Lor and me with interest.

Men.

"Along with Ben and Raymond; don't forget them," she added, giving me a wink and a sly grin to Mark and Seb.

"Can't forget them," I added.

The addition of our "boyfriends" killed the light in the men's eyes, and they relaxed, as if they wouldn't be called upon to be male any time soon.

"Nice to meet you both," Lor said, then excused herself to go into the shop and meet with Monty.

"Does he do another meeting right after ours?" Mark asked, his eyes following Lor as she went into the meeting place and greeted Monty.

"No. Lor and Monty are doing some business together," I said, then wished I hadn't. I wasn't sure what would come of their conversations, and if they would want their business connection known.

Me, who never said a peep to anyone lest a secret of mine could be leaked, was now apparently spilling info left and right.

That was what came from therapy—learning how to tell people stuff.

I'd have to watch that. I might have turned over a new leaf, but JoJo's deeds were still on the tree.

"Do you guys have to be anywhere?" Seb asked. Both Mark and I shook our heads, Mark after taking a quick glance at his watch.

"This is about the time I'd usually head to the casino, to catch the games that started on the East Coast and Midwest. Wouldn't mind hanging out somewhere non-casino for a couple of hours if you want to join me."

"That's cool," I said. "Do we need to find a place without televisions, or just someplace where you can't bet?"

He looked at me gratefully. "Without televisions altogether would be best."

Both Mark and I nodded. "Are you hungry?" Mark asked.

"I could eat," I said. I'd had breakfast with the boys, and that was always pretty big, but had had nothing since. I'd been busy writing in my journal, thinking we might have to show our work today.

"Pretty hungry, yeah," Seb said. "Amazing how much my appetite increased when I stopped gambling."

"Right?" I said. "I get what Monty was saying about replacing one compulsion with another."

"I know a place that has one of the best steaks in town, and they do an early bird special. Kind of a cool place, actually. You can't get a table after six; even right now might be crowded."

Vegas never slept. No clocks. So a steak place that was crowded at four in the afternoon had to be damn good.

"Let me just tell Lor I won't be home for dinner," I said.

I ducked my head into the shop and told Lor I was going to get something to eat with the guys and not to hold dinner for me. She nodded, used to me making alternate plans.

Used to me not showing at all.

Monty looked beyond me and saw that I meant Seb and Mark. "Is that against the rules?" I asked him. "Should we not be gathering outside of sessions?"

Monty shook his head. "No rules. We're trying a different form of group therapy here, so whatever feels right to you. I think it's great that you spend time with others that are also trying not to gamble."

"And this way, the boys can play cards after dinner without fearing they'll poke the bear," I said.

"Everybody just wants to help," Lor said. "They can do something other than play cards. Those old men have played enough cards for three lifetimes."

I laughed. "You got that right. Okay. We're off. See you later, Lor. Thanks, Monty."

They both nodded to me, but their heads quickly turned back to whatever papers Lor had brought with her and now had spread out along the counter where people had ordered their Indian takeout.

"Mom says it's cool," I said to Mark and Seb when I got back outside, causing them both to chuckle. "And Dad says he's happy we're playing together."

Mark rubbed his hands together. "Great. Because since I mentioned it, I've been craving a big slab of red meat."

That did sound kind of good.

"This place is on Sahara, between Valley View and Arville." He gave us the name, and we all got in our cars and made our way to the restaurant.

It kind of felt like we were working on an extra-credit project together after school.

One that came with a baked potato on the side.

Ten

"IT'S NOT CAVIAR, BUT DAMN, IT'S CLOSE," MARK SAID as he put another bite of his steak in his mouth. I knew he wasn't talking about caviar in the literal sense.

He'd been right: it was one of the best steaks I'd had in town, and I'd had a few with Jimmy.

Besides the tremendous slabs of red meat, the place was cool as hell. With pictures of the Rat Pack in their heyday on the walls—along with red velvet fleur-de-lis wallpaper—it had a cool retro vibe. The bartenders were dressed up like they could have been doing a stage presentation of *Guys and Dolls* later that night.

And their drink menu was seven pages thick, with stories about the history of fun drinks like Pimm's Cups and Harvey Wallbangers.

I even had a Gin Fizz, joining Mark's martini and Seb's Tom Collins.

Apparently none of us were also dealing with drinking on top of gambling.

"To good food," I said, raising my glass, which the men quickly clinked with their own. The place, early as it was, was loud due to the small size and boisterous crowd. It was a long, narrow bar area with cool round booths along the wall. They all had high backs and tufted upholstery.

It was just as well deep, private conversation was hard to come by in the loud place, because it occurred to me that maybe we shouldn't be asking too much about each other.

There was a benefit to talking with those that understood, sure. That was the whole idea behind group therapy. But without the safety net of Monty, would we tread into dangerous waters?

After we'd eaten, we decided to walk down to a Jack in the Box for a shake for dessert. We had all finished our huge steaks, and there was no way any of us could be hungry, but Seb had suggested it and I thought that maybe we hadn't killed enough time at the restaurant. That he'd be tempted to go to a casino if we split up now. Mark must have been thinking along those lines, too, as he was the first one to agree.

So we sat in Jack in the Box where no games were on, and you couldn't place a bet, and stared at shakes that we were too full to drink.

"Thanks for doing this with me," Seb said. "Both the dinner and this." He lifted his cup, which sweated beads of condensation around his fingers. "I'm not sure why today was harder than others. I just know when I walked out of that door, I wanted to get in my car and drive right to a casino."

"Maybe it was talking about our feelings?" Mark said.

"Yeah, I hate talking about my feelings. Always makes me want to place a bet," I said.

"I meant feelings as in…what we call the feeling we get when—"

"Oh! Yeah, right, that too," I said, ducking my head while the guys chuckled.

"It stirred up some shit for me, too," Mark said. "So, I'm glad we're doing this. Less time away from my place."

"Things bad at home?" I asked, and then regretted it. "I'm sorry. That's none of my business."

"It's okay," Mark said. "I guess we're making that kind of stuff the others' business by agreeing to do group sessions, right?

But that's not what I meant by not wanting to go home. I'm single, live alone."

"Oh. Don't trust yourself not to gamble?" I totally got that. I'd had Lor set up my computer and phone, and everything else, so that I couldn't place a bet from home. No bookies I could conveniently call. That, at the very least, I'd have to get in my car and drive a mile and a half to the Red Rock or the Suncoast—Summerlin casinos—to place a bet.

He laughed, but not a gleeful one. This laugh was full of scorn. And believe me, I knew from scorn. "Yeah, kind of. I mean, I can't even turn on the lights without it all staring me in the face, you know? The truth is, I haven't completely stopped gambling; I've just cut way back. For me, that was a huge step."

I didn't know recovery procedure, and I certainly wasn't going to throw stones from my huge glass house. "Every step is a little closer," I said, then cringed.

Mark sighed and Seb barked a laugh. "That bad?" I asked.

"Let's just put it this way," Seb said as he took his hand from his shake and patted mine, which was on the table. His hand was cold, and should have been wet from the cup, but was smooth and dry. "You're no Monty."

"That's for sure," Mark said.

"Whatever," I said, waving my other hand, but leaving the one Seb had patted where it was. Was I hoping he'd touch me again?

"It's a process, I'm guessing," Seb said to Mark, who nodded, his head down.

"A long fucking process," Mark said. "And I know I should get rid of my equipment, but I just can't. Like the thought of it even makes my chest start to hurt, my breathing get tight, you know?"

"I know," I whispered. There must have been something else in my voice, or maybe it was just the lack of volume, but both Mark and Seb looked at me then, sadness in their eyes as they watched me.

Sadness, but not pity. Like me, they had no pity for degenerate gamblers.

Because they each were one.

"Wait. Equipment? What equipment?" I asked, throwing the attention off myself.

A brightness swept across Mark's face, transforming him. He had been good looking before in a very kept-up kind of way. But at the mention of his gambling "equipment," a softness overcame him and he became heart-stoppingly good looking.

Did I get pretty when I thought about gambling?

If that were the case, was JoJo a Lorelei-caliber knockout?

"Wanna see?" Mark asked us, like a ten-year-old who wants to show off his new bike.

And like fellow ten-year-olds, Seb and I quickly nodded in agreement.

"Um, yeah, so...equipment," I said when we entered the large living room of Mark's apartment.

Living room, or NASA mission control center, I wasn't exactly sure.

There was an alcove in the large room that was wall-to-wall computer screens. Large, small, and in between. They were placed on tables that were leveled like risers, with keyboards all on one level, and monitors, two or three for each keyboard, on another level. The sea of black monitors was broken up by swaths of yellow sticky notes attached to the sides of each monitor, creating an almost bumblebee effect of yellow and black. There were two state-of-the-art ergonomically correct office chairs on rollers, but only one was seated at command central; the other was tucked into the corner.

A seat for a copilot, but one that seldom made an appearance.

"Holy shit," Seb said—exactly what I was thinking. "All of these are for poker?"

Mark nodded, not able to hide his pride at the elaborate—and I was guessing expensive—layout.

I wasn't one to talk. I had no idea how much Lor had spent on the book room at our house, but it was probably more than what Mark had spent here.

He sat in his chair and started moving quickly along the table, turning on monitors. The floors were hardwood, I guessed by design, and his chair easily wheeled from machine to machine, his legs pushing off and stopping short with amazing accuracy.

I had thought he had the lean, lanky look of a runner, but now I knew how he stayed fit, at least in his legs.

"Jesus," Seb said with reverence as the monitors came to life, each showing an online poker game. He stepped closer, on the side of the room where Mark had stopped in his chair.

"How many games have you been in at one time?"

"Thirty-two," Mark answered without missing a beat. "I can easily see four games per screen. Eight screens. Anything over that and they get too small for me to see when it's my turn from any kind of distance." He pushed his chair to one end of the long table and pointed at the screen furthest away from him. "I can see one game really well from here. Enough to see the cards. If I split that into four games, I can only tell when I'm up, but I have to move down to know more."

"But you have to move anyway, to be able to take your turn."

"Yes and no," he said. Leaning down, he pulled up a keyboard from under the table. "I have this wireless one hooked up so I can use a function key to flip from screen to screen. So in theory, I can access every screen from right here." He placed the wireless keyboard on his lap and toed himself back in his chair to the wall leading to the hallway. "I *don't* play this way, but I could. I usually only play ten or twelve games at a time."

They talked about Mark's setup—Seb with envy, Mark with pride—but I sat down in the other unused chair in the corner and mentally tuned out.

It was an impressive setup, to be sure. And it was obvious that Seb was an online poker player too. Or *was*. Given Mark's admission that he still played, had only cut back, I wasn't really sure about anybody else's level of continued gambling in the group.

Maybe we'd get to that at our next session.

Maybe that was something we would work on with Monty at our individual sessions.

But online poker had never been my thing. For one, I knew on some level that perhaps it would be my undoing if I became addicted to it.

Not that Vince's games and JoJo's birth weren't my undoing in another way.

Also, I liked facing a player, seeing their movements, their tics, looking for tells. Seeing their eyes when I trapped them. Basking internally when they knew they'd been had. You didn't get that online.

"Yeah, I do this too," Seb said to Mark, pulling my attention back. "Though I'm not as detailed as you. Man, you know your shit." He was looking at the rows and rows of sticky notes.

"What's on those?" I asked, still staying seated. Curious, but not enough to get out of my chair and take a closer look.

"Stats," Mark and Seb both said.

"You need stickies to know if you're winning or losing?"

They shared an "aw, how do we explain it to the dumb girl?" look, which should have pissed me off, but didn't. I had always found it to my advantage to be underestimated in gambling. I didn't play dumb, but I didn't correct people who thought I was.

"Not *my* stats. Other players'."

"Other online players?" Well, duh. Maybe their shared look was justified.

"Oh, yeah, you have SharkSnake. I search for his tables," Seb said, studying one of the stickies closely.

"Me too. Guy is an idiot who doesn't care that he's an idiot."

"My favorite kind," Seb said.

"So, you keep stats on other online players. And then search for them?" I asked. It probably wasn't much different from me trolling poker games that I knew would have a lot of tourists in them. Always looking for a fish.

"I keep all their stats. How often they raise, call, re-raise, fold. All that stuff. Winning percentage. You see a lot of the same players over and over. When you know someone's a fish, you join their table. When you know a player can be bullied, you look for them. Someone with a great win percentage…"

"You stay away from?" I asked. Sometimes I liked playing with great players; they were more likely to play good poker. Idiots could get lucky, and then you never knew what they were going to do.

"Mostly. But sometimes it's good to be on a table with a whale because they'll do the aggressive stuff for you and you can sit back and glide in."

Yeah, that sounded a lot like how I played with the groups I knew in Vegas. In Vince's games. Mr. Chow was not only a whale, he was my white whale.

They looked at the stickies for a while, comparing notes on players they both knew. The screen names they tossed out varied from mundane, to ridiculous, to profane. I was trying to think of a graceful way to leave—this held no interest for me, but the glee in Seb and Mark's faces as they talked reminded me of how much I missed gambling.

"So," Mark said, indicating the rows of stickies. "Who are you?"

"Like I'd tell you," Seb said.

"But you're on here, aren't you?"

"Taking the fifth," Seb said.

They went on some more, and I resigned myself to the fate of sitting there until I could find an excuse to leave. It was an odd feeling. These two men and I shared so much. And yet, right then, sitting there listening to them, I felt completely alone.

Eleven

"THANKS FOR LETTING ME KNOW YOU WEREN'T GOING to be home for dinner," Lorelei said when I got home. "How was your night?"

"Okay, I guess," I said. "How'd your meeting with Monty go?"

She was sitting at the dining room table, a few papers in front of her, as well as one of her tablets for list making. Her face lit up as she filled me in on the strides she and Monty were making toward going into business together.

Well, actually, Monty and me going into business together. But this silent partner would be extremely silent.

I sat with her at the table and went over some of the things that she wanted my approval on.

"So this is really a go? Something you want to do and you think would be a good investment?"

"I do. I love the idea of all the business stuff of it, and you said Monty is good at what he does."

I shrugged. "He seems so to me. I'm not the best one to ask. Monty's my first, you know, so I don't have a lot to compare him to. But yeah, I think he's certainly committed."

"And there will probably never be a shortage of people who need help with gambling. At least not in this town."

"Sadly, no."

She gathered up her papers, stacking them in one pile that she then straightened, tapping the edge against the table. "We talk with a lawyer on Monday. And the landlord of a new place on Tuesday. That place you were in today was fine to get started, and we'll make some small improvements to it for the short term, but if we're going to grow, we'll need a better space."

And I was just getting used to smoothies.

"Sounds good. Anything in this new venture that would work for Raymond to be involved with?"

She thought for a minute, her pretty face scrunching up. "Not really. We'll eventually want an office manager of some sort who can deal with the different insurances, payments, and that kind of thing. Part time at first, I'm guessing. I don't think Raymond would like that. And he couldn't keep up with it in the fall when he goes back to school full time."

"No, that doesn't sound right for him. Or for the treatment center."

"Why did you ask? Are you worried about him?"

I ran my fingers along the smooth wood of the table. "I'm not sure. I know he's doing some games still for Carla, but I think she'll ultimately find some permanent staff. His asking about how to set up a backroom game just made me realize that we need to keep that brain of his occupied."

"Idle hands are the devil's workshop?"

"Yeah, something like that. A lot of temptation in this town."

"He's been really great with Ben and Jack," she said, and I nodded my agreement.

"But Jack is on the mend."

"I am," he said from the doorway, making both Lor and me jump in our seats. "Sorry to scare you. I'm moving pretty well now."

"Well enough we'll have to put a bell on you," I said.

He motioned between Lor and me. "You guys discussing

something private, or looking for company?"

"We're just discussing Anna's financial venture into a treatment center for compulsive gambling."

Jack had started entering the dining room, but at Lor's words, he stopped short.

"Excuse me?" He started moving again, sitting on Lor's side of the table, next to her and across from me. I tried not to read anything into his choice of seats.

A girl could go crazy trying to read any kind of motivation from Jack Schiller.

I might think of myself in my alter ego at times, but I wasn't crazy.

"She's going to be Monty's partner in the new treatment practice he's opening."

"A silent partner," I said.

He studied me, but I didn't flinch. "I think that's great," he said quietly.

"It's not final or anything. Lor's doing all the work on it; I'm just the money. It's really her baby."

"Still…" he said.

"Exactly," Lor said. "Your investment will hopefully help a lot of people who need it."

They were both looking at me, Lor with happiness in her eyes, Jack with…well, like I said, I could never read Jack, and I'd be crazy to think I could start now, when we weren't even seeing each other.

Even though we saw each other all the time.

"Congratulations," he said to me. Turning to Lorelei, he said, "Monty's lucky to have you in his corner. I can't imagine him being in better hands."

"Thanks, Jack," she said, beaming. He was right: Lor would be an incredible asset to Monty trying to make his way. Much more so than any money I put up.

"I'm glad you're together, I need to ask you both something.

And feel free to say no," Jack said.

"What do you need?" Lor asked, already pulling her tablet from her pile and getting her pen ready.

"Casey doesn't have school on Monday. So, I asked Lisa if she could bring him down here for a long weekend. They'd fly down Friday when he's done with school and leave Monday afternoon. She would come with Rick—that's her husband—and drop Casey here, then they'd spend the weekend in town. I'm putting them up at Caesars. But I think it'd be better if—"

"Of course Casey can stay here," Lor said, getting where Jack was headed before I did. "With his dad and his grandfather. It makes perfect sense."

"I'm strong enough that I could move back to my apartment for the weekend, and we could just stay there."

"Nonsense," Lor said, waving that suggestion away while already writing in her notebook. "What kinds of things does he like to eat? Or not eat? Is there anything he's allergic to?" She looked up at him. "Maybe I should move to the other wing for the weekend, so he can have my room and be near you and Ben? But then what if Ben needed someone in the night? Or if you did? We wouldn't want to put that on Casey."

"Whoa, whoa," Jack said, holding up his hand. "No allergies. He'll eat anything, and lots of it. You're not moving out of your room. He can sleep with me in my room."

"I don't know if that's such a good idea," Lor said. "He could kick you, or hurt you in some way. You're still recovering."

"The guest room in Anna and Raymond's wing, then. Or just crashing on my floor. We'll let him decide."

Lor nodded while she continued to write.

"I just don't want this to be a lot of work for you, Lorelei," he said. "Especially now that you're taking on this Monty thing, too."

"Oh, pish, this is nothing. Having a kid around will be fun."

"Thank you. I just think it'd be easier for him to be here than me try to deal with him alone at my apartment. And when Lisa told me about this long weekend, well, I just..."

"Of course you want to see your son, Jack," I said. "He must have been really scared when you had to cancel spring break because of being hurt."

A look I could finally read crossed his face. Regret. It wasn't an emotion that haunted Jack Schiller. Unlike me, who was filled with regret—and shame—Jack lived his life with few regrets.

Except where Casey was concerned.

He rose from the chair, his movements slow and deliberate, and I knew he was trying to hide the pain the small actions caused him.

"I'll go call Lisa and tell her it's a go for her to bring Casey here Friday night. And I'll let Ben know. Thanks. Both of you."

Lor was still head down, writing, but waved to him. He stared at me and I only nodded, then he made his way out of the room.

"Well, this ought to be fun," Lor said, looking up from her lists.

Jack's son staying in my home. Possibly meeting Jack's ex-wife.

All while I was Hummer-less.

Yeah, a lot of fun.

BEN WAS GIDDY WITH EXCITEMENT over Casey's visit. It definitely added the zip in his step that had been missing since Jack had been shot.

Thursday at breakfast, that was all he talked about, to the point of Jimmy and Gus's eyes nearly glazing over, though they were happy for their friend.

Monty came over for the afternoon, again sequestering

himself with Lor in the office while they went over plans, only asking me in when they had an estimate of the initial investment I'd need to make. I asked Lor if I could afford it, she said yes, and I gave them my blessing.

Honestly, the startup money wasn't all that much when I put it in JoJo terms. I'd lost that much on a Manning brothers parlay one Sunday a few years ago.

Not that I'd let Monty and Lor know that.

I helped Lor get the spare room ready for Casey. It had seen some use over the past few months with Saul, and then Gus, staying with us at various times. It was in the wing that Raymond and I shared, with Jack, Lor, and Ben on the other side of the house. Jack was going to give Casey his choice of that room, or crashing on Jack's floor in a sleeping bag. A Star Wars sleeping bag that Lor must have picked up while I'd taken Ben to breakfast. And the sleeping bag wasn't the only little-boy thing she'd found, if the pile of juice boxes in the fridge were any indication.

We had a small dinner Thursday night, with just Ben, Lor, and me. Jack was sleeping and we didn't want to wake him, and Raymond was working a card game for Carla, so he wouldn't be home until early the next morning.

On Friday morning, Ben again talked about Casey arriving that evening and how Jimmy and Gus would come over for dinner. Jimmy asked what was on the menu, and Gus said he'd be there.

All through breakfast, I waited. Which wasn't unusual. Most times, though, I was waiting for the talk and eating to be done, and to start talking about that day's games being played and the point spread. But today I was waiting for something beyond what was part of our morning ritual.

I was waiting to get back to group session. That realization both pleased me and scared me to death.

Twelve

"SO, ON WEDNESDAY WE TALKED ABOUT THE FEELING you get when you gamble," Monty said. "The other element to that, which Anna told me about—and I'd like to ask you all if you feel the same way—is the voice you hear in your head. Whether it's chastising you for gambling, or rationalizing your behavior. Does anyone else hear this voice?"

Nobody said anything for a second or two, and I started thinking that perhaps I was the only one that bitch JoJo haunted.

"Yeah, of course," Mark said. "I don't know that I actually use the term 'voice in my head,' but of course there is rationalization. Otherwise…"

"Otherwise what?" Monty asked.

"Otherwise we'd either have quit, or gone insane," Herb said.

"So the voice keeps you from quitting?" Monty asked, leaning forward in his chair, sensing he was onto something.

Maybe he was. But I couldn't help but think that if you pitted JoJo against Monty, she'd eat him for breakfast.

"I just think of it as angel on my shoulder and the devil on the other one," Seb said. "Two separate entities. One for encouragement, one for regret."

"And shame," Herb added.

"Yeah, don't forget shame," Jordan said.

You could feel the air in the room change as our shoulders slumped, bodies shifted in the hard folding chairs, and some heads were hung.

Once again, JoJo had brought the house down.

"DRINK?" SEB ASKED MARK and me as we stepped out of the meeting place when we were done.

"How about five of 'em," Mark replied, and I nodded.

"Herb, would you like to join us?" Seb asked the older man, but he shook his head.

"Thanks, but no. Got to get home or the wife will think I made a pit stop to play cards."

We all nodded knowingly. "Jordan?" I asked as the kid came out of the building. "We're grabbing a drink. Want to come? You are twenty-one, right?"

He snorted. "Twenty-three. Can't tonight, but maybe some other time?" The Camaro pulled up then and we all nodded to him and said goodbye. He got in the passenger side and the car roared off.

"Interesting kid," Mark said. "Wonder what his story is."

"Probably not that much different than ours," Seb said.

"Yeah, probably not," Mark said. "Where to?"

When we agreed on a place, again not in a casino and without a lot of televisions with games on them, we met up, each taking our own cars.

One drink turned into two as we talked about the angels and devils on our respective shoulders and how we'd tried to listen to one and silence the other throughout our lives.

Around six, Seb checked his watch, and I knew he was thinking about packing it in. It was time to go home, but I thought about the big family dinner with Casey. And whether Lisa and Rick had already been there and dropped him off. If she had come into the house and seen where Jack had been staying while he convalesced.

Probably. Any mother would want to see where her son would be sleeping for the next three nights. She'd met Ben when he and Jack had gone to Portland to have Ben meet Casey, and I was sure Ben made a great impression—he always did. I wouldn't put it past Lor to invite Lisa and Rick to join us all for dinner, though they'd probably want to have a little alone time in Vegas after dropping off Casey.

"You have any plans for dinner?" I asked the men. "We can keep this going if either of you want."

They looked at each other, Seb checked his watch again. "Yeah, I can do dinner. I need to make a call first."

"Me too," Mark said, reaching for his phone. "Why don't you order another round and ask for menus," he said as both he and Seb stepped away from the table, going in different directions and starting to make calls.

I motioned to the waitress for another round, then pulled out my phone and texted Lor that I wouldn't be home for dinner.

I pressed send, waited for it to go through, then, coward that I was, turned my phone off.

THIS TIME WE ENDED UP at Seb's apartment. It wasn't as large as Mark's, and was more sparsely furnished. I was guessing that Seb had either lost more than Mark had, or never won as much.

"What do you guys do for a living?" I asked, curious for the first time. It probably should have occurred to me to ask before now, but for us, gambling was our *real* profession. The other was just what we did to survive. Gambling was what we did to Live.

"Everything," Seb said. "Right now I'm picking up work driving."

"Like for Uber?" Mark asked.

Seb shrugged. "Them. Car services. Wherever." It felt evasive, but then we gamblers could be a slippery bunch.

"How about you?" Seb asked Mark. "Your place, and setup, was pretty sweet."

"Financial management," Mark said. We both looked at him, and then all three of us burst out laughing.

"I'm serious," Mark said.

"I'm sure you are," I said, with a smile still on my face.

"I'm very good with money. Other people's money."

He was probably telling the truth about what he did—and his apartment's location, size, and decor said that he'd had money, either now or at one time.

But there was something about his face when he said it… My poker-playing senses kicked in and I knew—would bet the house on it—that he was bluffing.

But why bother with just Seb and me?

"Yeah, well, you'll excuse me if I choose not to put my life savings in your hands," Seb said. Mark flipped him off, and we all laughed again.

"Like you have any life savings," Mark said, not unkindly. "Or maybe you do, 'cause it sure as hell wasn't spent on this apartment."

"Screw you," Seb said, though he didn't seem offended. "Beer? It's all I've got."

"Sure," both Mark and I said, then we made our way into the small living room. Not much on size, but it was clean and uncluttered. A large TV and a computer with two large monitors took up one wall. A black leather couch and matching recliner sat facing the electronics, with a glass coffee table in front.

I sat in the chair and Mark took one side of the couch, crossing one leg over his knee. After handing each of us a beer, Seb took the other end of the couch, slouching low and sticking his legs out, crossing them at the ankles.

I studied the men who had become friends of a sort. Both

good looking—Mark in a pressed-jeans, expensive-shoes way, Seb in a comfortable, slouchy, favorite-pair-of-sweats way.

Though I didn't really think of them as *men*, there was no denying they were equally attractive. I had a flash of Jack and Vince Santini in my brain—the comparison of those two men reminding me of the differences of Mark and Seb.

Except Vince was now dead and Jack was barely speaking to me.

Jack, who was right now entertaining his son in my home.

"So, Anna, we know you play poker professionally," Mark said, then glanced at Seb as if maybe he'd spilled the beans, but Seb nodded his agreement. "Did you have another profession before you made it to that level?"

"No," I said. "I started playing at twenty-one. Around Jordan's age, I fell into a group of gentlemen that looked out for me, taught me the ropes, how to spend—and not spend—my money. If it wasn't for them, I wouldn't have survived this long."

"Sounds like a good life," Seb said.

"It was. It is. But..."

"Now you're trying to quit," Mark said. No questioning tone in his voice, and for that I was grateful.

"Yeah, the poker was never the problem. I'd win, I'd lose, but I could usually walk away from the table."

"Usually?"

"Unless I was trying to win enough to place a bet," I said. We hadn't really delved deeply into the nuts and bolts of our gambling in group yet. From Mark's setup at his place, I was guessing online poker was an issue for him. But I didn't know what other facets their compulsion encompassed.

"I hear ya," Seb said, and a little breath I didn't realize I was holding went out of me. "Like when you *knew* some team was going to cover and your pockets were empty."

"Right," I said quickly. "That's when I'd stay at the tables too long, to get the stake for a bet."

"Why not just call a bookie? Get on a tab?"

Because I had a unique way of paying off my tabs.

But I didn't say that. I trusted these guys in the way condemned prisoners on death row trusted each other—like, what's the point now, I might as well tell the truth. But it wouldn't just be my secrets I'd be giving up.

"One of the things those gentlemen taught me was to not run up tabs. Not saying I never did, but I stayed away from bookies. Only bet when I had the cash to do it at a casino."

"Wow, that's willpower," Mark said.

"Not enough, apparently, because here I am."

There was silence, then Seb said, "So, the betting was really the problem for you, not the cards?"

"Right," I said.

"So you're still playing?" Mark asked. Both of them were watching me intently, I thought hoping I'd say yes. It'd make it easier for Mark to turn on those computers once he got home.

His rationalization voice was probably already warming up with choruses of "But Anna's doing it" in his head.

"I've stopped playing poker," I said. Yeah, I was right, because their shoulders drooped a little with my answer. "Monty said it'd be better to stop it all, since one usually led to the other."

"He's right," Seb said. "I mean, alcoholics don't just stop drinking the hard stuff, but keep drinking beer."

"Yeah, I guess," I said, figuring the analogy was pretty spot on.

Monty's take on the whole thing was gambling being more of a compulsion than addiction, and thus to be treated differently. It was true, there was no physical withdrawal if you stopped gambling as opposed to drugs or drinking. Unless you counted loss of Hummer as a physical reaction. Which I did, rightly or not.

"So, if playing poker is all you've ever done for a living, and you intend to give up all forms of gambling…" Mark led me to a place I hadn't really wanted to think about, though of course I needed to. "What are you going to be when you grow up, little girl?" he said, smiling at me.

It was soft and understanding and made it easier for me to say, "I have absolutely no idea."

Thirteen

WE WATCHED TWO MOVIES, THOUGH I WASN'T REALLY paying attention to either one, and the second had been at my suggestion to keep going and not call it a night, as it appeared Seb and Mark were willing to do.

In the back of my head, I wondered what time six-year-olds usually went to bed, and whether bedtime would be pushed due to visiting Daddy and Grandpa?

When it was obvious my new buddies weren't up for a triple feature, we said our goodbyes and Mark walked me to my car in the parking lot of Seb's apartment complex.

"I'd ask if you were okay to drive," he said, "but I know you barely finished that second beer hours ago."

"I'm good, thanks," I said. "You?"

He nodded. "Fine. I stopped a while ago. Only had two beers total." I guessed I would have known that if I'd been paying attention to my surroundings instead of counting down the time until I felt it was safe to go home. To my own house, dammit.

When we got to my Porsche, I leaned against the driver's-side door, but didn't open it. Mark came and leaned against it as well, crossing his arms and standing next to me, our bodies not quite touching.

"How are you feeling about all this?" he said. "Monty's group, I mean."

I took a deep breath and let it out. The night was still warm, even though it was near eleven. I had on my denim jacket, though I really didn't need it. "I'm not sure. I like the theory behind GREET. I know Monty's committed, and that he wants to work with gamblers exclusively, so I feel like I'm in good hands."

"Young hands," Mark pointed out.

"True."

"I mean, even if he has gone through his own shit—and I'm not sure how much he has—he hasn't been around long enough to have gone through the stuff you, me, and Seb have, you know? Not to mention someone like Herb."

"That's true," I said. "But look at Jordan. You don't have to be old to hit rock bottom."

"Yeah, I guess. But how well do you know Monty?"

"Do you have to know your therapist well to be helped? Isn't it better not to know much about them?" His question did have me wondering if Lor and I should do some kind of background check on Monty as part of our due diligence on the investment. Knowing Lor, she was probably already all over that.

"How long have you been working with him?" Mark asked.

"Just a few weeks. This time," I said.

"This time?" Mark asked. He turned so that he was leaning his hip against the car and looking down at me. "Never mind. You don't need to answer that; it's none of my business."

"No, it's okay," I said. I wasn't willing to incriminate myself, or anyone else involved in JoJo's doings, but I wanted to be as honest as possible where I could be. "I met him a few months ago for the first time when he did an intervention that my roommate arranged."

"An intervention for you?"

I nodded, looking at him. He was taller than Jack by a bit, and given his proximity, my chin was tilted up toward him.

"Arranged by the same roommate I met the other day?"

"Lorelei, yes."

"And how'd that go?" he asked.

I rubbed my hands along the legs of my cotton cargo pants, the feeling of them suddenly clammy as I thought back to that day months ago. "Let's just put it this way—if I'd gotten help then, a whole lot of things might be different than they are now."

Would Vince still be alive? Possibly. Would Raymond still be in school in Iowa, finishing up his degree after completing the basketball season? Probably. Would Jack and I still be together? Who knew, but I would never have played poker with Lion LaGasse, which inadvertently led to Jack and me being shot. I walked out of the hospital the next morning, whereas Jack had been on tubes for a week and was just now able to see his son.

"A *whole* lot of things," I added, more to myself than to Mark.

"So, it took a second intervention to stick."

"Actually, that was about the seventh intervention that Lor threw for me, though the first one that involved Monty. And it wasn't another intervention that finally got me to get help."

"No?"

"No, it was almost losing someone I loved."

"Loved? Past tense?" His eyes skimmed over my face, spending a little more time on my lips, before returning to my eyes.

"It doesn't matter," I said, telling the truth. It didn't matter how I felt about Jack—he'd made it clear how he felt about us having a future.

Even if he did pick out journals for me. Hell, they were probably just a thank-you gift for letting him convalesce at my place. As if Ben would have let Jack go anywhere else.

"That ship has sailed," I said.

Mark nodded, and we stayed like that, quietly watching each other. I wasn't going to reach for him, but if he did dip his head to kiss me, I wasn't going to stop him.

Mark was attractive, and though not quite my type, I liked

him. And to be honest, seeing a man look at me in the way he was now felt good. No judgment, no regret, no knowing that it couldn't possibly work. Nothing like how Jack looked at me lately.

"Probably not a good idea," he whispered softly, still only inches away.

"Probably not," I said, though I stayed where he was.

I thought, in the end, neither of us wanted to be the first to change the dynamic of the relationship. Yeah, it would have felt good to have some basic human contact, but it probably wouldn't help when seeing each other in group the next time.

Plus, the whole "where does Seb fit into this" thing.

"Have a good weekend," he finally said, and pulled back.

I fought the urge to reach out and grab his fine cotton shirt. Instead, I turned to the car and pulled out my keys. "You too," I said.

He waited at his car for me to get in mine and drive away, watching me as I did.

When I thought about going home to the Lowenstein men's retreat, I almost circled back and beeped down Mark, but I didn't.

I drove home to face the music.

Fourteen

THE LIVING ROOM AND DINING ROOM WERE BOTH empty and dark when I got home. Making my way to the kitchen, I saw a light and joined Lorelei, who was sitting at the table writing in one of her tablets, a cup of tea still steaming at her side. She wore athleisure wear (as she called it), hair pulled back in a braid. Sensing my presence, she looked up.

"You're pissed," I said, getting to the point. I moved to the fridge and got myself a bottle of water, then joined her at the kitchen table.

"Kind of," she said. "Was it something that couldn't be helped?"

"No," I admitted.

"Then yeah, I'm pissed." She returned to her tablet, and I was reminded of what Mark had said.

"Lor, beyond the lawyer that you're working with, have you done anything about checking out Monty himself?"

"Why do you ask? Do you know something about him that I should?"

"No, it's not that. I just realized I know very little about him. And I think that's good for the situation I'm in with him—I don't want to know him on that level, you know?"

"Right. I get that."

"But as investors, we probably should—"

She held up a hand then placed her pen down on the table. "I have a private investigator discovering all things Monty Westerfield, starting from the time the kid was in diapers. I'm doing my due diligence, Jo."

I slumped, both in relief and embarrassment. "Of course you would. Sorry."

"I'll give you that one. But I'm still pissed you missed dinner tonight."

"I know. I'd say I was sorry, but I'd probably do it again."

"Are you, what? Threatened by a little boy? Didn't want to run into Jack's ex-wife?"

All of the above. Plus I knew that if I'd been here, I would have felt the outsider. That the Jack and Ben circle was wider, but still didn't include me any longer.

None of which I could say to Lorelei. Hell, I wouldn't even really admit it to myself.

"I don't know," I said. "Partly. Just didn't want to have to deal with Jack's life right now." That was true, too. "I've got enough on my plate." Also true, but I was starting to sound a little whiny, and so I just sat back in my chair, unwilling—unable—to go any further.

Lorelei looked at me, tilting her head, as if she were trying to read me at a poker table. Realizing she'd get nothing more, she sighed and returned to her notes. "Well, you missed an awesome dinner. Plus we had a sundae bar for dessert."

"Bet Casey loved that."

She smiled. "He did. He's a pretty sweet kid."

"I'm sure he is."

"You'll be around tomorrow to meet him, right? No more running?"

I couldn't promise there would be no more running, but I could make it through breakfast with a kid. "Yeah, I'll be here in the morning," I said.

Rising from the table, I went to her side and placed a kiss

on the top of her head. "What was that for?" she asked.

"Thank you for making this household work. Despite my actions." I walked to the door, but stopped when she called me.

"You make it hard to stay pissed at you, you know," she said.

I couldn't quite smile at that, but I tried for her sake. "That's what's kept me alive this long," I said. I heard her chuckle as I left the kitchen, but I didn't laugh with her.

I wasn't joking.

Hoping they were both asleep after a big day, I quietly walked down Ben and Jack's wing of the house. Ben's room was dark with the door opened just a crack—something we insisted on so somebody could hear if he called out. I peeked in on him and heard his gentle snoring. Moving down the hallway, I saw Jack's room was open, soft light filtering out.

Shit.

"I know you're out there, Anna," he said. Quietly enough not to wake Ben down the hall, but strongly enough to know I had to show my face.

He was sitting in his chair when I entered the room. "How's Casey settling in?" I asked, standing in front of him. He nodded to the empty seat next to him, but I hesitated. I was hoping this could just be a quick check-in, not another picking of fresh scabs, like my conversation with Lor.

"Sit down," he said, his voice firm. I sat. "He settled in fine. Thank you again for having him stay here. It's a much better solution than me trying to manage on my own at my place."

"No problem," I said. "Ben's *casa es su casa*."

"But it's not just Ben's casa, it's yours, too. And I know this isn't easy on you. I need you to know that I do understand that."

Jack Schiller understood me too well. That was part of our problem.

"I know you do," I said.

"So, you no-showing for dinner was not a surprise."

"No? Because it was a spur-of-the-moment decision for me."

He looked at me with such skepticism that I had to wonder if it really had been a spur-of-the-moment decision.

"Whatever," he said. "I just don't want you feeling that you have to stay away from the house the whole weekend. Not it if puts you…at risk."

"At risk?" I asked, though of course I knew what he was talking about.

"In the past, if you weren't here, you were typically at a casino, either playing poker or watching a game you bet on."

He was right, but that didn't stop me from getting a little riled. "That's a pretty narrow view of my life. You don't know how I spend my days, just because I spent a fair share of my nights in bed with you."

He winced, but I wasn't sure if it was from my words or the fact that he'd leaned forward. "You're right. There was also all the time you spent being questioned in murder cases."

"Ha ha. You're a riot, Detective Schiller," I said. But there was no bite in his words. He wasn't trying to pick a fight.

"I'm just saying, I don't want to be responsible for you trying to kill time away from home for the next two days. We can make ourselves scarce, stay on this side of the house. Hell, the kid will be in the pool all of tomorrow if his eyes when he saw it were any indication."

"It's fine. Really. I'll meet Casey tomorrow and even grill the hotdogs on the patio during the pool party."

He watched me carefully, just like Lor had just done in the kitchen.

"I'm not sure what's on Lor's menu," he said.

I laughed, and he smiled in return. "I was with some of the people from Monty's group therapy," I said. "We decided to get a drink after, and that turned into dinner."

"You don't need to explain to me," he said.

"I know. I'm not telling you as my… As someone I used to… I'm just explaining why I wasn't here to meet your son. I'll happily play in the pool tomorrow with him."

God, I couldn't even remember the last time I was in our pool, though I was pretty sure Lor kept it heated year-round. I had no worries that it would be pristine and ready for Casey—that was how good Lorelei was.

"So, you're liking Monty's group? That's great."

"You sound surprised."

He sat back in his seat, steepling his hands, elbows on the armrest. "Yeah, I guess I am. I wasn't sure how you'd respond to a group situation."

I rose from my chair. "Christ, Jack, you sound like a shrink. How I'd 'respond' to it?"

"I'm just happy you found something you seem to like, that's all."

I liked spending time with other degenerate gamblers who understood the Hummer, even if they called it something different.

I didn't like that I *needed* any of that.

"Well, it's early days, but yeah, the group is interesting."

"That's all I'm saying, Anna. I'm glad you seem to like it, though maybe *like* isn't the right word."

I nodded. "I'll let you get some rest. Big pool party day tomorrow and all that. Do you need any help?"

He shook his head. "I'm good." As I started to leave, he called my name, and I turned and looked at him. "Would it be condescending to say I am proud of you?"

"Yes," I said. "And extremely hypocritical."

He nodded once.

"But thank you," I said, and left the room.

On my wing of the house, Casey had the first bedroom and his door was open. I didn't want to, but I couldn't stop myself from tiptoeing across his room to take a look at him.

I'd seen pictures of him, from both Jack and Ben. Lots of them from Ben when he'd gone with Jack to Portland to meet Casey. But to have this little ball of flesh and bone right in my home was an odd feeling.

The drapes to the patio were open—no doubt so he could see the pool area—and the outdoor dusk-to-dawn lights cast a swath across Casey's bed, allowing me to see his little body. An arm, small and gangly, stuck out from the covers, dropping off the side of the bed, as if he'd fallen asleep while reaching for something on the floor. I carefully moved his arm, surprised at the warmth emanating from his body, and put it back under the covers. His brown hair covered his forehead, and his eyes were obviously closed, but the brow and mouth were Jack's. And Ben's.

A rush of emotion whistled through me. It wasn't a Hummer, but it was powerful nonetheless.

If things had been different, would I be a stepmother to this little boy?

Because he was Ben's grandson, it didn't matter that Jack and I were over—Casey would be in my life.

It was time to suck it up and not be afraid of the bogeyman, whether he be in the form of a first grader, or JoJo.

I left Casey's door open when I exited, just in case the kid woke up in the middle of night disoriented.

Raymond's room was next, and he was sitting in his chair with the television on but the volume low. He was wearing track pants and a Central Iowa tee shirt. Waving me in, he took his feet from the ottoman and clicked off the television.

"Wanna talk?" he asked.

I shook my head, but sat in the chair opposite him. Each of the six bedrooms had the same basic layout—bedroom, sitting area, en suite bathroom—but different decors. Raymond's room was done in soft navy blues.

"Not really," I said. "Kind of all talked out."

"Yeah, sure, I get that," he said. Putting his feet back on the ottoman, he turned the television back on. He was watching the movie *Hoosiers*, which I hadn't seen in years.

"I love this movie," I said, and made myself more comfortable in the soft chair. I looked behind me, grabbed the throw that sat on the back of the chair, and wrapped it around myself.

We watched mostly in silence as Gene Hackman led his team to glory.

When it was over, it was nearly two in the morning. I knew Raymond had been keeping Vegas hours because of working games here and there for Carla. And, of course, my internal clock was always messed up between playing cards late, getting up for early breakfast with the Corporation, and catnaps here and there. Thinking about Raymond staying up to work Carla's games reminded me about his questions the other day.

"Hey," I said, and he looked from the screen to me. "What you were talking about the other day? Setting up your own card games?"

He waved a hand, as if that was all in the past. "Don't worry about it. I was just thinking out loud. It seemed like a pretty easy deal, but if all it really is is a way to get people in debt, yeah, that's not for me."

"Good," I said.

I must have been looking at him too closely or too long, because he snorted, then said, "I'm serious. I let it drop."

"Yeah, I know. I just worry about you, you know."

He pushed the ottoman away and leaned toward me, elbows on his knees, hands dangling. "You need to stop that. Worrying about all of us. You need to take care of yourself right now."

It was my turn to snort. "Are you serious? It's my selfish behavior that got you thrown out of school. Got Jack shot, got—"

"Shut up. Just shut the fuck up." His voice was stern, though not raised, I was guessing for Casey's sake. "Enough with the pity party. Yeah, you fucked up. Get over it. Start doing what needs to be done, and stop worrying about everyone else. What? You think Lorelei is going to stop taking care of us? You think I'm going to let Ben fall behind so his hip isn't supporting him? Or mess up Jack's recovery?"

I shook my head. *No, not for one second.*

"We are not going to drop the ball. We've got it covered on the home front. So if you need to stay away to do you, then do it."

I nodded. "Thanks," I said.

He shrugged. "No big thing."

"It is," I said. "It's a very big thing to only have to concentrate on getting better."

"And are you? Getting better?"

I took a deep breath and slowly let it out. I thought about the evening spent with Mark and Seb and how not even once did I wish we'd been in a casino instead of Seb's living room.

"Yeah, I think so," I said. He nodded, and I left his room, going to mine.

I took a long shower, then climbed in bed and slept deeply.

Fifteen

I AWOKE TO CHILD'S LAUGHTER AND A SPLASH. SIMPLE sounds, but not ones I heard often.

It was ten in the morning, and, given that I was up at seven most mornings for breakfast, it felt like I'd slept half the day away.

Peeking out the sliding doors, I saw Ben, Jack, and Casey in the pool area. Casey, with floaties around his upper arms, was in the shallow end of the pool, with Jack sitting on one of the steps leading into the pool, board shorts and a tee shirt on. Ben sat at one of the tables on that end of the pool, a smile on his face as he watched his grandson in the water.

"Throw me, Daddy. Like you did that one time," Casey said, excitement in his voice.

"I can't, buddy. Remember I told you I wouldn't be able to play like we usually do in the pool?"

Casey nodded his little head and a stoicism came across his face. "Because you got hurt."

"That's right. I'm still not all better, but next time you visit, I'll be able to throw you around. This time, you're going to have to just do your own thing."

"And Grandpa can't even come in the pool?"

Ben's face lit up to hear Casey call him Grandpa. "I'd just slow you down, Casey," Ben said. "With this old hip. You're a much faster swimmer than I ever was."

Casey smiled at Ben, and I thought that maybe he was missing a front tooth, though I couldn't be sure from where I was.

"Watch me, Daddy," Casey said, then half jumped, half dove to a spot in the pool about two feet away.

"I'm watching, buddy," Jack said. I tried to see his expression, knowing it would match the joy in Ben's, but Jack was turned away from me.

A part of me wanted to find the earplugs I often used and crawl back into bed. Another part of me wanted to call Seb and Mark and see if they wanted to meet for lunch and hang out. A really big part of me wanted to get in my car and head to the Red Rock and put some money down on any game that was playing today.

But the tiny part of me that thought I could maybe someday lead a normal life went to my dresser and rooted around until I found an old swimsuit and headed for the bathroom.

A few minutes later, I was opening my sliding door, causing Ben and Casey to turn and look at me. Jack kept facing forward, watching his son, who was treading water about four feet away from him.

"How's the water?" I asked, making my way to the Lowenstein boys. It didn't matter that Jack and Casey had Jack's adoptive family's name; it was clear to see that the three of them were a family.

A family I was now trying to join, if only to toss a kid around in a pool.

"Casey, this is Anna Dawson. She's the one I told you about."

My breath hitched as I thought of all the things Jack *could* say about me. None of which would be appropriate for a six-year-old.

"The woman who owns this house and who lives with

Grandpa."

Oh, yeah, that. That was good. That would do.

I patted Ben's shoulder as I threw my towel over a chair at the table. He put his hand on top of mine and squeezed. We were getting back to where we'd been before Jack had been shot, and it felt good. My getting help had been a big part of that.

I moved to the edge of the pool and Jack looked up at me, then quirked a brow as he stared at my body. Looking down, I realized I'd grabbed one of his shirts to use as a cover-up.

"Nothing Freudian about it. Just the first thing I grabbed that was long enough," I said, and he grunted. But I thought I saw a hint of a smile.

"Thought Lor had moved all of those to my room," he said quietly.

"Guess not," I said, and tried not to read more into my choice than what I'd just offered Jack.

"Good morning, Casey, it's nice to finally meet you," I said to the kid, who had now made his way to the first step and was hopping up on it, then back.

"Hello," he said. "This is your pool?" I nodded. "It's a good pool."

"I'm glad you think so. And I'm glad it's getting some use."

"Daddy can't throw me 'cause he got hurt getting bad guys."

"I know," I said. I looked down at Jack, and he turned from his son to look up at me. "I was there," I added, more to Jack than Casey.

"He was very brave," Casey said, the words sounding like something his mother would have told him.

"He *was* very brave," I agreed, still looking at Jack. His eyes slid over me one more time, taking in his blue chambray shirt, then he sighed deeply and turned to Casey.

"Can you throw me?" Casey asked me, both hope and skepticism in his voice.

"I'm not sure. I haven't done that in a while, but I can show you how I used to throw my little brother in the air when we were kids. How about that?"

He nodded furiously, hopped off the step, and walked backward deeper into the pool. I pulled Jack's shirt over my head and tossed it on the back of the chair over my towel. I noticed a carafe of coffee on the table, mugs, creamer and sugar, a bottle of Gatorade, and an assortment of sunscreens in various SPFs.

"I see Lor's been busy," I said, not surprised.

Ben nodded, taking a sip from his cup of coffee. "Bagels will be out soon."

Saturday was bagel day, but of course with Lor it was more elaborate than just a brown paper bag and a tub of Philadelphia cream cheese. Sunday was brunch day, a full buffet set up in the dining room. And, of course, Monday through Friday we had breakfast with the Corporation at Arizona Charlie's.

Wading in the pool, I realized Lor must have heated the pool warmer than normal—for Casey's sake, I was sure, but I was also grateful. Although it'd been so long since I'd used the pool, maybe it was always this temp.

A flash went through my mind of Monty talking about replacing compulsive destructive behavior with good behavior, like exercise. I knew I'd never be a runner—hated it. But maybe I could swim more regularly? I had the pool at my disposal. Maybe if I was so exhausted from swimming laps I wouldn't think about how close the nearest casino was?

"Show me what you used to do when you were a kid," Casey said, demanding my attention.

I pulled him deeper into the pool and looked to Jack for permission. He just shrugged and nodded for us to proceed. I cupped my hands together with laced fingers, held them down for Casey to get a foothold, then gave a three-count warning and hoisted him into the air, hurling his little body a few feet away, where he came down with a thudding splash that soaked me.

He came up spluttering, and I almost reached for him, but

the smile across his face stopped me. Indeed, a front tooth was missing, obvious to see as he beamed and shouted, “Again!”

BAGELS WERE DELIVERED with a smile by Lor, whose sappy expression as she watched me play in the water with Casey made me itchy and uncomfortable.

After the breakfast, we played in the water some more, sunscreen reapplied when needed, juice and coffee breaks when needed. I tried not to think about what I needed…to feel the Hummer.

Lorelei was bringing out lunch when Raymond came out of his room carrying my phone. “This has been going off for the past twenty minutes. I heard it while I was in the hallway; thought you’d want it.”

“Thanks,” I said, taking it and looking at the three missed calls from a number I had in my contacts but had never called.

Jordan from group. Huh.

Monty had asked if we were cool with giving our numbers out so he could do a group text if needed, since the rental place he had was so iffy. We’d all complied, and he sent one text to us all so we had each other’s numbers. If I had expected a call from anyone in the group—which I hadn’t—it would have been Seb or Mark. After that *moment* in the parking lot last night, I wouldn’t have been surprised if Mark had called today. But Jordan?

“Sorry, I need to make a call,” I said, wrapping myself in my towel, grabbing my cover-up—okay, Jack’s shirt—and heading into my room, careful to shut the slider tightly behind me.

“Jordan?” I said when he answered my call. “What’s up? Are you okay?”

“Umm…not really. What are you doing right now?”

I looked out to my group on the patio. Jimmy had just

come from the kitchen entrance, helping Lorelei carry a large platter of what looked like sandwich ingredients. Raymond and Ben were arranging things on the table to make room for the meal Jimmy and Lor were bringing out. Raymond even pulled over one of the other small tables to make a larger one. Jack was toweling off Casey, but looking into my room. I didn't think he could see in with the reflection, but I turned my back to the outdoor area anyway. "Nothing that can't wait," I said to Jordan. "Why?"

"I was wondering if you could maybe come and get me?"

"Get you? Like pick you up somewhere?"

"Yeah. Could you? I'm on the Strip. In the Venetian."

Cabs abounded on the Strip. Not to mention Uber and Lyft. Not to mention the Camaro that seemed to be Jordan's usual mode of transportation. But he knew of all those options and had still called me.

"Yeah, I can be there in an hour. Where will you be?"

There was a pause, and his voice was soft and haunted when he said, "In the poker room."

Shit.

"Can you wait somewhere else? Can you get up and leave the table and meet me in the food court?"

Another pause. His breath came out shaky. "I don't think I can."

Double shit.

"Okay. Hang on, Jordan. I'll be there as soon as I can."

"Thanks, Anna."

"Sure. Jordan?"

"Yeah?"

"Only bet if you have pocket queens or better. Promise me."

"What?" He spoke like he thought I was crazy, and for someone who was probably in a deep poker haze, I was talking nonsense. But maybe I could save him a little bit of money, if I couldn't get him to step away from the table entirely.

"Promise me. You'll fold if you don't have queens or better. No bluffing. No betting on crap hands because you have a feeling you'll pull a hand on the flop. Promise me, Jordan." I tried to sound stern, but it was hard while I was also striding to the bathroom and pulling my suit off. I'd just have to go to the Strip with chlorinated hair and skin.

Hell, I'd been there looking much worse, I was sure.

"Queens or better," he said quietly, and I knew he was near the table and didn't want to be overheard declaring his betting strategy. He couldn't have made the call from the table itself, but he hadn't strayed far, at least not far enough that he felt able to keep on walking.

"Yes. That's it, Jordan. Queens or better. I'll get there as soon as I can."

"Thanks, Anna," he said, and the call ended.

I quickly dressed, grabbed my wallet and keys, and was just about to leave my room when I remembered the pool party going on beyond my glass doors.

I opened the doors and walked out. Jack's eyes were on me first. Detective that he was, his eyes took in my state of dress, the phone in one hand, and the keys dangling from my other. His jaw set and his brow furrowed, but he didn't say anything, just handed a napkin to his son and motioned that Casey had something on his face.

"Hey, Jo, come and make yourself a sandwich," Lorelei said.

"I can't," I said. "Hey, Jimmy, good to see you." A nod due to his full mouth. "I need to go see someone. I'm not sure when I'll be back."

"Now?" Lor asked.

"Yeah, sorry. It just came up." I looked at Jack. "And it's important."

A tiny, barely noticeable nod from him. Not that I had to explain myself to Jack Schiller, but I didn't want him to think a morning of playing with his kid had me running for the hills.

It kind of did, but not entirely.

"Who's going to throw me?" Casey said, looking up at me with an expression not unlike his father's.

"I'm sorry, Casey. I'd like to stay, but a friend needs some help, so I've got to go."

"Okay," he said. He pursed his lips and moved from side to side, like he was trying to figure out a problem.

"I'll swim with you," Raymond said. "After you've eaten."

"And taken a little rest," Jack added. Casey was all smiles again and digging into his sandwich, mayo getting on his face exactly where he'd just wiped it off.

I mouthed "thank you" to Raymond, who nodded in return.

"Hurry back, Hannah darling," Ben said, and I said that I would try.

I was walking away from the group, going to use the kitchen entrance to get to the front of the house, when Jack called my name.

He walked over to me, moving well if a little stiffly. Sitting on the sidelines while his kid played in the water must have been hard for him, but all he needed was to pull something, and he'd set back his recovery.

"Everything okay?" he said quietly when he reached me.

"Yeah, I think so. Just somebody from group who needs a ride. Maybe somebody to talk to."

"And you're strong enough to handle that? Being the one to come to the rescue?" He voiced the thoughts I'd been having since I hung up with Jordan. What was walking into a poker room going to do to me? Would I pull Jordan out of his seat at the table to only take it myself?

"I don't know," I said. "But I think I've got it."

"You want me to go with you?"

God, that would be so nice, to have Jack at my side through this. But I shook my head. "Nah. I don't think that would be appreciated. Me showing up with a cop for backup."

"Is a cop needed?"

"No, he's just in a poker room on the Strip and can't walk away. I've got it."

He leaned forward, almost like he was going to touch my hand, but stopped himself. "Be careful. And call me if you get sucked in to something you don't want."

"Thanks," I said. I had no intention of calling Jack for that kind of help. Besides, apparently I now had a whole group of people I could call if I was ever in Jordan's spot. "Hopefully I'll be home for dinner."

"Movie night after. *Dory* or something like that," he said. "Lor's got a bunch of options queued up."

The thought of my state-of-the-art book room being used to screen the latest Pixar or Disney movie (or both!) made me smile.

"See ya," I said, and left. I could feel Jack's eyes on me as I left through the kitchen door.

Sixteen

I COULD HAVE GONE DOWN THE FIRST ESCALATOR after the parking garage at the Venetian, but I liked walking through the shops at the Grand Canal, sometimes even catching a gondolier serenading his fare. The second escalator came down overlooking the poker room, and as I rode down I could make out Jordan at one of the tables at the back. He was throwing his cards in, mucking his hand, and I took the last few steps down on my own, hustling across the poker room to get to him before a new hand was dealt.

I knew too well what damage could be done on just one last hand.

"Hey, there you are," I said to him as I approached the table. Normally I would have waited until the hand was finished so as not to disturb those still in it, but this time I didn't. "I'm all done shopping, and need to get home." Let the table think he had a naggy friend (older sister? girlfriend?). I didn't care.

"Um, yeah, okay," he said, his eyes barely registering me before he turned back to the table. "Just one more hand."

The dealer was pushing the pot toward the player who had just won the hand, then collecting the cards. Soon he'd be dealing again. I had no idea how long Jordan had been sitting at the table, how many hands of poker he'd played. Given his stubble and the faint smell coming from him, I'd guess a while.

So really, what did one more hand matter? And yet I knew that I couldn't let him be dealt in again. Not on my watch.

"I really have to go. Now. Grab your chips and let's go."

"But I—"

I put a hip into his shoulder, not caring anymore if he saved face with his fellow players. A quick glance told me that all but one were tourists anyway.

Yes, I could tell that quickly and accurately.

"Now," I said firmly, practically shoving him out of his chair. I knew not to grab his chips—I'd get pushback from the dealer on that one—but I nodded to his small stack and put a hand firmly on Jordan's shoulder. "I. Need. To. Get. Home."

Something crossed his face, and the same flash of sanity that had him calling me an hour ago returned briefly enough for him to nod, take his chips, grab his backpack from under the table, and follow me to the cashier's cage.

"Give me your chips," I said.

"What?"

"Do it."

He did, and I cashed them in for him. Four hundred and seventy dollars. I didn't bother asking him what he started with. I knew it had been more.

You don't make a rescue call if you're winning.

Putting the money in my pocket, I gave him a warning glare and led the way to the parking deck, taking the escalator that got us off the casino floor the most quickly.

"Huh," he said as we walked past the shops. "I've never been up here. It's nice."

"Yeah, I think so too. I know it's cheesy and everything, but I like the canal and the painted-on sky."

He looked up and around, like a little kid tourist who was soaking it all in. I imagined Jordan had been to the Venetian poker room an awful lot, and yet had never ventured very far beyond the tables.

I knew the feeling.

"When was the last time you ate?" I asked him.

A dazed look on his face as he said, "What day is it?"

"Come on," I said, and detoured through to the food court. "This place does a good, fast chicken wrap."

I ordered for us both, getting vacant nods of approval from Jordan as I did. I paid for us both from my wallet, keeping his money separate—but still keeping it on me.

We grabbed a table, and he sucked down his Mountain Dew so quickly I got another two of them for him while I waited for our wraps and fries. Setting down the two trays, he devoured the hot French fries, and I went back and got another couple orders of them as well. It probably wasn't a great idea to let the kid consume so much sugar and fat when he was obviously in bad shape, but I figured anything in his stomach at this point could only be a good thing. To make myself feel a little better, I also got a huge salad with grilled chicken for him.

He went to town, eating it all. I found I was hungry, too, and ate my fries and wrap, large as it was, easily.

Maybe it had been all that throwing around of Casey in the pool that had me so hungry. Maybe it was watching Jordan wolf down his food. Either way, the lunch was good and there wasn't a spare fry or speck of chicken left on either of our plates when we were done.

"Okay," I said, "home? Where's that?"

"North side. Almost to Nellis."

I nodded. That wasn't anywhere near Summerlin and my home, but then, I hadn't expected Jordan would be living out where I did. It had taken me many years and many wins to own that home.

When I was Jordan's age I was sharing an apartment with three people, all sketchy as hell, and playing for hours—days—at a time, making a win and trying to build it into something bigger. And then losing. Always the losing.

When I was Jordan's age, I was still a year away from meeting Ben and the Corporation. My salvation.

"Is your car here?"

He gave a slurp of his Mountain Dew that reminded me of Herb getting every last drop of his smoothie during group. "Don't have a car."

"The Camaro that drops you off and picks you up from group?" I asked. It was uncharted waters for me. I wanted to help Jordan if I could, but I wasn't Monty, somebody trained to do this kind of thing. It really was a case of the blind leading the blind. The degenerate gambler leading the degenerate gambler.

"Roommate. He gives me rides sometimes. He works second shift so he can give me rides for group. He's just getting up then."

"And is he working now?" It was Saturday afternoon. Most casino workers, if they were in positions that received tips, wanted to work on the weekends. But there were a lot of different types of positions that worked second shifts.

"Yes, but I'm not sure what shift. I'm not sure if he's home or not."

"Just the one roommate?"

He nodded, putting down the drained cup onto the tray with all his other empties.

"How much does he know about your gambling? And that you're trying to stop?"

"Pretty much everything. Or at least that I play cards too much and I'm trying therapy to stop. I'm guessing after today he might not think driving my ass to group is worth it."

"You called me. How many times have you ever called someone to help you stop before?"

"Never," he admitted, then got my point and sighed.

"So, yeah, it's made a difference, if only one that seems kind of small right now," I said.

"Yeah, okay." He rose and slung his backpack over his

shoulder, then gathered up his tray, balancing the pile of debris.

"Hey, Jordan," I said firmly, causing him to stop with the tray and look down to where I was sitting. "You called me to help you stop. That's different. *You're* different."

His chest moved heavily, his breathing seemed deeper, and I thought for a second he was going to cry. I wouldn't have blamed him.

"Yeah," he said softly. "I think I am."

Seventeen

"DO YOU HAVE ANY FOOD AT YOUR PLACE?" I ASKED Jordan as we drove off the Strip and headed north to his apartment.

He blinked a couple of times, then looked over at me. "I have no idea."

Yeah, that was me before Ben. I always made sure there was food in the house after I moved in with him, sometimes because he handed me a grocery list when I'd come home from a marathon card game. Lor took care of all of that now. I couldn't remember the last time I was in a grocery store.

I pulled into the next Albertsons I came across and made Jordan come in with me. I wasn't going to leave him alone in the car with his phone, just in case he started playing cards online or something.

We took our time wheeling the cart through the aisles. I'd suggest something and Jordan would either yay or nay it, and I'd throw it in the cart or put it back on the shelf. I tried to steer him toward fruits, veggies, and protein, but also stuff that he could just grab and eat. If he was like me when I was in a card-playing haze, I'd skip a meal—or two—rather than take the time to actually cook anything.

He lived in a shithole apartment in a crappy neighborhood. We carried the groceries up to the second floor, where he shared a two-bedroom place with the aforementioned roommate of the second shift. It took a couple of trips to get all the food in, then Jordan led me through the dark, dirty place. It was a typical guys-in-their-early-twenties apartment: neon beer sign on the wall, scarred wooden coffee table with a couple of bongs on it, lumpy couch that looked like it'd been picked up from somebody's curb, and a beautiful TV.

"Could you get some sleep, do you think?" I asked. "I can take care of these." I motioned to the bags of groceries we'd set on the wobbly kitchen table, having to push away discarded odds sheets. My fingers itched to pick them up and look at them, but I knew they would have been old ones anyway. Still, I wanted to feel them in my hands. Instead, I plunked down the grocery bags on top of them.

"Yeah, maybe. I could probably zonk out for a few hours."

"How long were you playing?"

That dazed look came over his face again. "Um...what time did we leave group yesterday?"

"Jesus," I mumbled. Going to him, I placed my hands gently on his shoulders and turned him toward the hallway, where I could see two doors to what would be bedrooms, and an open door at the end of the hall that was a bathroom. Even from here I could tell I'd be holding it until I left, no matter how bad I might have to go later. The whole place smelled like damp socks, partly just a guys' place and probably partly because Jordan was either gone for long periods playing poker or cramped up here playing online for equally long periods.

"Wait," I said before pushing him down the hallway. "Where is your computer? Where you play online?"

"In my room," he said. I went with him down the hallway, and the smell got worse as we entered his room. His setup wasn't anywhere close to Mark's elaborate wall of computers. Nor even as utilitarian as Seb's. But it was a place where Jordan obviously spent a lot of time, if the myriad of Monster cans, fast food wrappers, and overflowing ashtrays were any indication. His bed was unmade and there were sweat stains on the pillowcases.

"Does your roommate have a computer in his room?" Jordan shook his head. "Think he'd mind if you crashed in his bed for now?" A shrug from him. "Give me your phone." A look of panic crossed his face, confirming my suspicion about him playing on his phone if left alone with it. "You need to sleep. I'll stay here until your roommate gets home. I'm not sure what to do about this." I waved at his computer station. "I don't know how to disable anything so you can't play. And even if I did, you could play on your phone, or find a way." He seemed to relax, realizing he'd have a way to play cards after I left. As I watched, the relaxation turned to something else, something darker, and his shoulders slumped, defeat coming over him.

"Exactly," I said. "You can *always* find a way to play poker. So it has to be you that stops. That's the whole philosophy behind GREET. It's on you."

"I'm so tired of this shit," he said with no energy in his voice. He was talking about the binging and the guilt and shame, and, of course, the Hummer. What was Jordan's feeling again? Oh, yeah.

"I know you think you need Oxygen to breathe, but you don't. You can live without it. Remember what Monty said: we can find it in other places."

"Have you?" he asked with hope in his voice. I hadn't placed a bet or played cards since Jack and I were shot. That was well over a month ago. The longest I'd ever gone. And yet…

"No," I said. "Nothing that's come close."

"Fuck."

"Yeah." I held out my hand, and he gave me his phone. We walked out of his room and across the hall to his roommate's room, which was much cleaner and neater than Jordan's. And had no computer of any kind. "But that's not to say that I won't find my Hummer somewhere, somehow, that doesn't involve gambling."

He popped into the bathroom and I heard a medicine cabinet open and shut. When I stuck my head in, he was putting a pill in his mouth and downing it with a glass of water. The glass looked like it had seen better days.

"Are you okay?" I asked.

Wiping a sleeve across his mouth, he passed me in the doorway and headed down the hall to the roommate's room. "Yeah. Ambien. I take it when I need to crash but might be too wired."

"Oh."

"Though I probably don't need it today. I'm wiped." He half fell, half climbed onto the roommate's made bed, pulling a throw over himself.

"What's your roommate's name?"

"Eric," he mumbled, already half-asleep.

I shut the door behind me and made my way back to the kitchen to put away the groceries.

Lor would have been proud of me. Or not recognized me. I spent the next three hours cleaning Jordan's apartment and getting rid of anything in his room that was gambling related—old odds sheets, poker magazines, and the like. I plucked all the sticky notes from the edge of his computer, thinking about Mark and Seb as I did. I even hauled his bedding and towels down to the basement and used all the quarters I had in my car to do his laundry. I opened the windows to try and air the place out, did the dishes, and found the vacuum in the hall closet and ran it, hoping it wouldn't wake Jordan. It didn't.

I knew that sleep of the dead; there wasn't much that could wake him after playing so many hours in a row. Throw in the Ambien and who knew how long he'd sleep.

You wouldn't think just sitting at a table for long periods could be so exhausting, but it was. All that mental energy, I supposed.

I was just finishing up when Eric came home, startled to find me cleaning out the dishwasher. (Yes, I'd even cleaned the bathroom, once I realized I couldn't hold it until I got home.)

I explained the situation to him after I introduced myself, and although Eric seemed surprised to see me, he didn't seem all that surprised to find out Jordan was coming off a poker bender.

"I thought it was working," Eric said, running a hand over his face. He was wearing a uniform from the Excalibur, though I wasn't sure what type. I didn't think it was for a dealer, but it didn't look like a waiter, either. He was around Jordan's age, stocky, with close-cropped black hair. He looked tired, but the I-just-got-off-work tired, not the I-just-played-twenty-four-straight-hours-of-poker tired.

"It might have just been a slip," I said. "I hope he comes back to group on Monday."

"You're in his group, too, right? I've seen you when I've dropped him off. Or am I not supposed to say that?"

"It's fine. Yeah, I'm in his group. That's why he called me. I knew what he was going through."

Another hand through his short hair, which popped back up in place afterward. "I'm sympathetic to him, really. But I don't get it, you know? I mean, I like to play poker from time to time, but I have no problem walking away."

"Yeah, most people can. Walk away, that is."

He nodded, then looked around, noticing the cleaned place for the first time. "You do all this?"

I shrugged. "I was killing time until you got home. I didn't want to leave him alone. Are you in for the night?"

"I can be, if you think I should."

He was a good-looking kid, who wasn't a degenerate

gambler, and it was Saturday night in Vegas, so of course he had plans. But then, so did I. I wasn't going to miss another family dinner with Casey. "I think it'd be better if someone were here when he wakes up."

"Yeah, no problem," Eric said. "Thanks for all this." He waved his arm around the tidy room.

"Sure." I didn't add "anytime."

"I just don't know how long I can keep up with his shit, you know. I really like the guy, and he's a good roommate, but he's, like, two months behind on his share of the rent. I can't cover him much longer."

"How much does he owe you?" I said, trying to remember how much cash I had on me, and how much was in an envelope I often kept in my glove box. An envelope I hadn't taken from in a while.

"Twelve hundred. That's just rent. I haven't said anything about all my shit that he's eaten. Which isn't all that much, really—the guy doesn't eat a whole lot."

No, it was mostly energy drinks and cigarettes for the daily diet of Jordan.

"Hang on, I'll be right back." I went out to my Porsche and pulled out the envelope. With it and what I had in my pockets, it was around two thousand dollars. I went upstairs and gave it all to Eric. "That covers his rent, and what he owes you for groceries, plus a little extra. You do drive him to and from therapy, after all, and it's not real close to here, so let's say it's gas money."

"I wasn't fishing for this," Eric said as I held the money out to him. "I was just bitching about him, you know. I didn't mean you had to—"

"I know you weren't. But I've got it to spare right now. Don't tell Jordan; just take it off his tab of what he owes you. And thank you for getting him to group."

Eric eyed the money but finally took it. I went back to Jordan's room and put his four hundred dollars from the Venetian under the mouse of his computer. I scrawled a note on one of the odds sheets I'd left out of the trash for that very reason.

Hang tight on Sunday. Call if you want to talk. See you on Monday at group.

You can live without Oxygen until Monday.

Eighteen

THROUGHOUT DINNER I THOUGHT ABOUT JORDAN living in that apartment, in the same room, with that computer—the method of his destruction. Though, as today had shown, he had a whole city at his disposal as methods of his destruction.

"You okay?" Raymond said quietly to me as he passed me the mashed potatoes. "Kind of quiet tonight."

"Just worried for a friend," I said. "But I'm good, thanks."

He studied me before nodding, then returned his attention to his plate. I looked up and across the table and saw Jack was watching me as he cut up Casey's meat.

Lor had outdone herself with a tremendous prime rib dinner, complete with creamed spinach the way Ben loved. It reminded me of a prime rib place that used to be in the Excalibur that Ben and I would go to when I won big. They'd walk around with this cart and cut off your slice of prime rib right at the table, adding a ladle of mashed potatoes and one of creamed spinach, both from tureens on the cart. It was delicious, but they'd converted it to something else years ago and we hadn't been back. Thinking of it reminded me of Eric's uniform from the Excalibur, which brought my mind back to Jordan.

Had I done the right thing giving Eric his rent money? Was I enabling Jordan? There was no way I would have given him money outright, but maybe this way he wouldn't feel any pressure about rent or anything that might lead him to feel he needed to win at cards to keep a roof over his head.

I'd had that feeling, that pressure of needing a win to make sure I had a dry place to sleep. And that had been in an apartment even shittier than Jordan's.

Could I have done more? Brought Lor over there to put on the same kind of controls on his machine that she'd done to mine so he couldn't play online poker? Nah. He was a kid in his twenties; he was going to figure out a workaround from anything Lor had up her sleeve.

Again I felt lucky that I had never gotten into online poker—it seemed to be such a downfall for Mark, Seb, and Jordan. Probably Herb, too, but I didn't think he'd mentioned it in group at all.

I could have packed up Jordan and brought him back here for a while. Or at least until this current fever burned out. We were full up tonight with Jack, Casey, and Raymond each taking bedrooms. But Casey would only be here another two nights, and could sleep in Jack's room with him.

The bigger question was: how many strays would Lor let me bring home before balking?

And I really didn't know anything about Jordan. He seemed like an all right kid, but if he stayed here, who knew if he wouldn't take off in the dead of night with the good silver and in my Porsche. (I wasn't even sure we had good silver—Lor had been instructed not to buy anything of value that I could easily hock.)

Ultimately, though, I knew the idea of bringing Jordan back here with me wasn't good for one really good reason. I could barely help myself—I was in no position to take on helping someone else.

INSTEAD OF CARDS LIKE WE USED to play before I quit, we

all went to the book room after dinner and watched a double feature of *Finding Nemo* and *Finding Dory*, which Casey loved and I dozed through.

Raymond was working a game for Carla, so left after dinner in one of his dark suits, looking stern and enforcer-like.

I went to my room after the movie and was tempted to text Jordan to see if he was all right, but didn't, hoping he was still sleeping. I hadn't gotten Eric's number or I would have checked in with him.

I turned on my television and cleaned up in my bathroom, then changed into a tee shirt and cutoff sweats that I slept in. I flipped through the channels, nothing catching my eye. When I came to something that was silent, I could hear Jack's voice coming from down the hall, so I muted the TV.

He was reading a story to Casey, and I got under my covers and turned off the television, content to hear Jack's voice as I drifted off to sleep.

SUNDAY MORNING WAS A REPLAY of Saturday, with a pool party where I tossed Casey around in the pool until Raymond woke up and tapped in so I could help Lor bring brunch out to the patio. I couldn't remember our outdoor furniture ever getting this much action in forty-eight hours.

"We should do this more often," I said as I fixed a plate for Ben and brought it over to him, then adjusted the umbrella to shade him. "It's lovely out here."

He chuckled and patted my hand. "It is, isn't it? We're always stuck inside watching games. Yes, we should do this more often."

"It's just as close to the kitchen as the dining room is," Lor said. "It'd be no extra trouble to take more of our meals out here."

After fixing a plate for myself, I sat beside Lor at the table with Ben and Jack. Casey was still in the pool with Raymond, and Jack seemed content to let them play until they were ready to eat.

"He's got Rachael's smile," Ben said as he watched Casey laughing with Raymond. "Such a beautiful smile." He sounded sad and wistful, and I knew he was thinking about the love of his life. The woman married to his best friend. Jack's mother. Dead for over thirty years.

I rubbed his back. "It's a great smile," I said. "But he's got your eyes. So does Jack."

Ben looked up at me and smiled. "Does he? My eyes?"

I nodded. "Yes. Jack is obvious, but I see it in Casey, too." I looked at Jack. "Don't you?"

Jack nodded, looking at me, then to his father. "God help the kid," he joked, and his father joined him in laughter.

My heart clenched hearing the men I loved laughing with each other.

Just your regular—albeit unconventional—family having Sunday brunch around the pool. Nobody in debt to loan sharks. Nobody a suspect in a murder case.

And nobody sitting in the book room doggedly looking at scores with a pile of bet slips in their sweaty hands.

It was Americana at its best, and a lovely feeling of normalcy ran through my veins.

It wasn't a Hummer, but it was still nice.

Nineteen

"SO TODAY I WANT TO TALK ABOUT YOUR CHILDHOODS," Monty said on Monday. He was answered by a bunch of groans.

The rest of Sunday had been nice, sticking around the house, having a big family dinner with Gus and Jimmy joining us.

Happily, Lisa and Rick picked up Casey while Ben and I were at breakfast Monday morning, so I totally skated on having to meet her.

When we got home, Jack was in his room with his door shut, so I just did some home business stuff with Lor in the office until it was time to come to group.

Something, surprisingly, that I was looking forward to.

Until Monty started off with his childhood announcement.

"Christ, that was too damn long ago for me to remember," Herb said. "And what the hell does it matter now?" Everybody nodded with that, even Jordan, who wasn't that many years removed from his childhood.

He had given me an "I'm good" nod when he came into the building. And he looked good. Rested. Alert. A world better than when I'd left him Saturday. I was hoping that was because he'd gotten a lot of sleep, and not because he'd gotten a lot of Oxygen.

"Hear me out," Monty said. "The idea behind GREET is

that your gambling is based in emotion. The emotion you get from gambling. The shame and regret you feel after gambling. The euphoria you feel when you win; the despair when you lose. There is a school of thought that the emotions we, let's say *chase*, are ones that are based in our childhoods. If you can isolate them, and re-create them in other ways—non-gambling ways—the need, the compulsion, to gamble diminishes."

I'd talked about this with Monty before, when we were working together one on one. The theory made sense, but when I delved into my childhood with him, I didn't come up with anything that I was either trying to escape or recapture.

I have two brothers and a sister, all raised in the same home with the same parents. All of us are different, but I was the only one of us with something as heavy as compulsive gambling.

That I knew of.

"Sounds like psychobabble bullshit to me," Herb said. He had been particularly testy today, all but growling at me when I said hello, and pretty much balking at anything Monty brought up. It made me wonder if something was going on with him. Other than him being in therapy for gambling.

"Humor me," Monty said. "Why don't you go first, Herb. Where were you brought up?"

At the end of our hour, Herb was still talking and I was beginning to think there might be something to Monty's theory. It was obvious Herb had some baggage over his father leaving the family when Herb was six. I thought about Casey and wondered if he'd find his way to a therapist's couch someday over Jack and Lisa splitting.

From what Jack had told me, the last year of their marriage wasn't a pretty one, with Jack's drinking and Lisa taking up with his partner Rick. I wasn't sure how much of that had spilled onto Casey, though he seemed pretty well adjusted.

"And can you equate the feelings you had being left as the man in the house at such a young age, with those you feel when you're gambling, Herb?" Monty asked when Herb paused.

"I...I don't know...maybe." He weaved a hand through his thinning, bi-colored overgrown head of hair and his shoulders slumped. "The pressure, I guess, feels kind of similar."

"Yes, that was a lot of pressure you put on yourself. Kind of like the pressure you're under when you lose a bet."

"But I didn't like that feeling, so why would I be trying to re-create it?"

Monty leaned forward, elbows on his thighs. "There could be many reasons. You're trying to re-create it to have a different ending this time. On some level there may be guilt so you feel you *deserve* that kind of pressure. Or perhaps you're not trying to re-create it as much as outrun it."

"Jesus Christ," Herb said, his shoulders slumping even further.

It wasn't quite a Freudian "Eureka!" moment, but I could tell that it had hit a nerve with Herb. In a good way. Kind of.

"Before the Wednesday session, I'd like you all to journal about your childhoods, and I'd like to you to pick out five memories that still stand out to you. They could be something as monumental as your father leaving, or something as simple as a favorite birthday present you received. But I want you to pay attention to the feelings that you had at the time, and, just as importantly, what you're feeling as you write about it."

There was nodding and a couple of "okays" within the group, and then Monty dismissed us.

Herb was outside and lighting a cigarette before the rest of us could even fold up our chairs and move them to the side of the room.

"Drink?" Mark asked Seb and me as we walked out of the shop together. We both nodded and I subtly motioned to Herb. Mark shrugged and looked to Seb, who did a "whatever" thing with his face.

"Hey, Herb," I said, and he turned to me as he took a deep

drag from his cigarette. "I'm not sure if you drink or not, but we're going to go get one if you'd like to join us."

"Yes," he said before I could even get the invitation out. "Hell yes, I could use a drink right now."

"Great. Jordan, can you join us? I'd give you a ride home after." He had joined us out on the sidewalk, and I noticed Eric hadn't yet arrived in his Camaro for pick-up duty.

"Um…yeah, okay," he said, pulling out his phone. "Let me just text Eric that I've got a ride."

We agreed on a place to meet and all drove off, Jordan riding with me. As I was pulling away from the curb, I saw Lorelei pulling in. She got out of her BMW and pulled a stack of things from the passenger side, then went in to meet Monty.

Maybe I should have stayed, been a part of whatever they were discussing, using my money as an investment. But I didn't want to.

Oddly, I wanted to spend more time with my new buddies.

WE DRANK (LIGHTLY) and ate (heavily) for two hours then called it a night. I was all for continuing, but nobody mentioned it, so I let it go. I wondered if the reason Mark and Seb didn't want to keep the party going was because they wanted to get home to their online poker. Or maybe Mark didn't want to be alone with me again after that *moment* in front of Seb's on Friday.

As we were all leaving the lounge, Jordan trailing behind me, Herb walked next to me and tugged at my elbow, pulling me to the side. "Hey, Anna, you available tomorrow?"

My days, now that I wasn't playing cards or betting, were extremely open. Breakfast every morning with the Corporation, and group on Monday, Wednesday, and Friday, but other than that, the days—and nights—sprawled ahead of me. Monty had suggested I look to try and fill that time with volunteer work, a part-time job, exercise classes—anything that wouldn't just have me sitting around being tempted.

"I'm free. What do you have in mind?" I answered Herb.

"I want to get some new clothes, kind of change my look. Surprise my wife. But I'm shit at that kind of thing. I thought maybe you could help me."

I pointed down to my regular uniform of running shoes, cargo pants, Henley, and jean jacket. "I'm not sure I'm the person to help you with that, Herb. Maybe one of the guys?" I started to motion to Mark—who always looked his preppy best—but Herb pulled down my arm.

"Never mind. I can just do it myself." He looked away, and I realized he was embarrassed to even be asking me for help, let alone a fellow male.

"Listen, I'm no fashion maven, but I know a guy who is. Let me give him a call and get a few recommendations for you. Then I can meet you tomorrow and give you my opinion on stuff if you want it. Would that work?"

He nodded. "Nothing too pricey, though, right?"

"Right. Got it." That would definitely rule out Lorenzo, Vince Santini's—and recently Raymond's—tailor. I was thinking I'd talk to Gus at breakfast tomorrow and get some pointers on where to take Herb. And I was thinking about more than clothes.

"Would you be open to going to a barber with me?" I asked him.

He ran his hand through his hair just like he'd done earlier at group when talking about his father leaving. And he appeared just as confused now as then. "A barber? Really?"

I put my hand gently on his arm and looked at him hard until I had his attention. "Really, Herb."

He sighed and nodded. "Whatever you think. I put myself in your hands. Just know I only have about three hundred total to spend on this whole thing."

I was guessing that wouldn't even cover Gus's barber, let

alone clothes. "We'll make that work," I said, not wanting to scare him off. I guessed if I could spring for Jordan's groceries and rent, it was only fair that I spring for a new Herb.

"I'm in Summerlin," I said. "What area do you live in?"

"Spring Valley." Good, so he wasn't far from me.

"Why don't I meet you at one at the Lazy Dog in Downtown Summerlin—do you know it?"

"I know Downtown Summerlin, but not that place. I'll find it, though."

"Great," I said. "We'll have some lunch and plan our attack."

He nodded, we said our goodbyes, and he left. Jordan joined me, and I drove him home. I asked if he wanted me to stay until Eric got off work, or until Jordan went to bed, but he said no, he'd be fine.

I was tempted to go feel his computer, to see if it had been left on while he was at group, just waiting for him to return and be dealt in.

But I wasn't there to play police. I was just there to offer a ride and company. One was done, and the other not needed, so I left.

Twenty

EVERYBODY WAS PLAYING CARDS AT THE DINING ROOM table when I got home, and the guilty looks on their faces made me crack up.

"It's okay, you guys. You can play cards around me. I'm not going to lose it and run back to the casino."

Lor rose from the table, placing her cards down hard, like she'd been caught in bed with my husband. "Of course you wouldn't. But it's still insensitive of us to play cards in front of you."

"Don't stop on my account. I'm going to call it an early night anyway. Monty gave us homework today, and I want to get on that."

"Brown-noser," Jack teased.

"Teacher's pet," Raymond added.

"Good for you, Hannah darling," said Ben.

"See, she's good. Let's get back to cards," Jimmy said.

I waved to them all and headed to my office, where I grabbed one of the journals Jack had given me. I hadn't done much with it since that first time when JoJo's voice came out on the page, which had freaked me out.

I took the one I'd started in to my bedroom, then peeled out of my clothes and threw on some running shorts and tee. I went to the kitchen and got a bottle of sparkling water, then took it and my journal out to the pool area. The night was just starting to cool off, the sun gone, but it was still warm enough to be in shorts and a tee. I sprawled on one of the chaise lounges, the deep cushion enveloping me, and I wrote.

And wrote. And wrote.

"ANNA," I HEARD JACK whisper, and it sounded so good, so familiar. I rolled over, wanting to cuddle into him in bed, feel his heat next to me. But instead of his body being next to mine, it was air, and I started to fall before strong hands held me by the shoulders.

"Anna? Wake up," he said. I knew it was him, but he wasn't next to me. "Hey," he said softly, as he gently shook my shoulder.

I woke up fully, seeing his face above mine and realizing I'd fallen asleep on the chaise lounge.

"What time is it?" I asked, looking around. The kitchen was dark, as were the bedrooms along both wings of the house.

"Almost three in the morning. Are you okay?"

I nodded. "I was writing in my journal out here and I guess I fell asleep."

"I debated letting you sleep, but didn't want you to wake up stiff and cold," he said.

I had my bearings now, and sat up on the chaise, my legs swinging to the patio. Jack still had his hands on my shoulders and our faces were mere inches apart. I looked up into his brown eyes. Eyes I'd just commented on the day before as the eyes of his father, and of his son. We stayed where we were, neither of us moving. I sensed he wouldn't have turned away if I reached out for him, if I raised my head just a little bit and pressed my lips to his.

But I was tired of reaching for Jack. After our last break, I knew it had to be him who reached for me. And either he couldn't or didn't want to, or maybe both.

Not wanting to put myself through that, I bowed my head and moved to gather my pen, water, and journal, forcing him to release me.

"Thanks for waking me," I said.

Stepping away from me, he only nodded. He stood there until I got to my sliding door and entered my bedroom. Keeping the light off, I could see Jack outside still watching my room, watching me. Then he turned, but instead of walking back to the sliders to his room, he went the other way to the kitchen door, opening it and shutting it.

As I brushed my teeth and got ready for bed, it occurred to me that Jack hadn't come out to the patio through his bedroom door, that it was still locked. And my bedroom slider had been unlocked even though I'd gone out via the kitchen.

Jack had gone out to the patio through my bedroom sliders. He'd been in my room at three a.m. and noticed I wasn't there, and had looked for me.

That thought kept me awake until after five.

WHILE AT THE SOURDOUGH for breakfast, Gus did me a solid and called his barber, who agreed to squeeze Herb in later that afternoon.

"My guy's not cheap," Gus said.

"It's my treat for him," I said.

"Hannah darling, don't let these people take advantage of you," Ben said on our drive home.

Touched that he was looking out for me, I replied, "I won't. And I don't think that's what this is. He just asked me to go along for my opinion. I'm the one who suggested doing something with his hair." I patted Ben's hand on his lap.

"You have to be careful with these people," he added. "They

might be at a place where they would do anything for the money to bet with."

I chuckled. "Ben, *I'm* one of those people."

I expected him to be shocked, or deny it, or make excuses for me. But he didn't. "I know, dear," he said.

"DO YOU TRUST ME?" I said to Herb later after lunch, at Gus's barber. You could hardly call it a barbershop, though. Turned out Gus had his hair done by the premier stylist at the spa at the Red Rock casino. I shouldn't have been surprised.

"I guess, but this place is pricey," Herb whispered to me.

"Don't worry about it," I said. "It's my anniversary gift to you. To your wife, actually."

He grunted at that, and I stepped back and let the stylist take over.

Over lunch, Herb had told me that today was his and his wife's fortieth anniversary. From what he said, the first twenty-five had been good with he and Elaine raising two kids, putting them through college, and basically living the middle-class American dream. And then Herb had been bitten by the gambling bug, and the last fifteen years of their lives together had been a struggle, with Elaine threatening to leave when Herb would get in debt. He'd get himself out (I could easily imagine the ways he'd done this, having done some nasty things myself), and things would go back to normal, and then he'd start gambling again, always leading to lies, shame, and debt.

They were supposed to be retired, living off their investments, pensions, and social security. But the investments were gone, as was their house, and Elaine was in her late sixties and still working in the Clark County school system as an aide every day.

Listening to Herb talk, I said a silent prayer of thanks that I had met Ben and the Corporation and then later Lorelei.

Without them, I would surely be in Herb's spot, having lost my home and living in a small apartment, working jobs that my aging body balked at.

Instead I had a beautiful home, nice cars, all not in my name so I *couldn't* have used them to gamble with, and even many investments that apparently did well, though I had no idea how to access them.

I was even soon to be a silent partner in a compulsive gambling treatment center.

None of that would have happened if I hadn't met Ben Lowenstein and Lorelei Samuels.

Herb was a new man after the stylist had finished. And an even newer man after the no-polish manicure and facial I insisted upon.

After that we went to Dillard's and Macy's, and he again balked at me paying, but I insisted. We ended up with five pairs of slacks, several dress shirts, casual shirts, and three pairs of shoes. A couple of belts rounded out our spree.

At our last stop, I had the sales clerk cut off the tags of the last outfit he tried on—nice chinos and a striped cotton button-down—so he could wear them home. The tassels on his leather loafers flopped as he walked, making me smile.

"Now," I said, leading him back through the women's department on our way out. "Let's find something nice for Elaine. A sweater or scarf. Or a piece of jewelry, maybe?"

He used the money he had planned on himself on a pretty locket for his wife. I didn't try to pay for it, and I suspected Herb wouldn't have let me anyway.

Or maybe he would have. He hadn't put up a huge fight about the clothes, and had even brought over a few shirts himself to put in the pile.

Ben's words about being taken advantage of played through my mind, but I let it go. Maybe Herb was playing me a little bit, though I was pretty sure that hadn't been his intention when he'd asked me to accompany him. I chalked it up to the "making amends" column of life. I hadn't done Herb any wrong during my gambling, but there was no way I would be able to make it up to those whom I had. So, Herb's wardrobe and coiffeur were the benefactors. I could live with that.

As we were loading our many bags into his trunk, a look of panic came over Herb. I knew that look, but I couldn't equate it with harmless shopping. It was the "oh, God, I fucked up and gambled when I shouldn't have" look.

"Elaine won't believe me that I didn't spend more than three hundred dollars today. That's what we agreed on. Oh, shit."

"Just tell her the truth. That it was my present to you…to you both."

He was shaking his head, his now all one shade of white hair shining in the late afternoon sun. Taking two steps from the still-open trunk, he looked at the bags like they were a trunk full of writhing snakes just waiting to strike out at him.

I'd looked at a pile of bet slips in just the same way.

"She won't believe me," he said, his voice full of resignation. He'd been down this road before—telling his wife things he knew she wouldn't believe. Because they were lies.

"Would it help if I called her? Talked to her?" I offered. I'd done stupider things than call a woman and tell her I'd bought her husband a bunch of clothes.

"She'll think I put you up to it," he said. But apparently it gave him a different idea. "Would you…would you come home with me? Tell her in person? I think she'd believe you in person. Plus then she could see you were…" He waved his hand in my general direction, and I tried not to be offended.

"Not a threat to her?" I asked.

"That you're young enough to be my daughter," he said, making me feel better.

I looked at my watch; it was nearing five. Lor usually served dinner around six if we were eating in, family-style, which we were tonight.

"She's home from work at five thirty. You could just say hello, explain about all this"—he pointed at the shopping bags—"and then be on your way. I hate to ask for anything else after you've done so much today."

"That works," I said. "Why don't I pick up something for dinner on the way to your place so she doesn't have to cook on your anniversary? Or were you planning on going out?"

"Well, I thought to maybe take her out, but after all this..." Again a wave at the bags, but there was an uptick in his voice, a hopefulness that maybe, *somehow*, he could still take his wife out for their fortieth anniversary.

"I'll treat for your dinner out," I said, and he smiled and sighed.

I knew then Ben had been right. Degenerate gamblers, man, you had to always be on your toes around them.

Myself included.

We waited in Herb's apartment for Elaine to come home. He'd put the shopping bags in their bedroom and invited me to sit in their tiny living room. It was a cramped apartment filled with heavy furniture and knickknacks that had come from a larger home and not given up during whatever downsizing Herb and Elaine had gone through during his gambling years.

It was incredibly clean, though, even as crowded as it was, and I thought about how I wouldn't be needed to do a deep-dive cleaning like I'd done at Jordan's.

Shortly after five thirty, Elaine came home. When she first saw me there was a momentary flash of "Oh God, what has he done now?" in her eyes, and I felt a pang of sympathy for her. Okay, more than a pang. A big freakin' helping of sympathy.

Elaine was a lovely woman, dressed smartly in pressed slacks and a silk blouse, her hair colored and "set," as my grandmother used to say. She was not expensively dressed, but much more kempt and orderly than Herb always was, at least when I saw him on GREET days.

Tears came to her eyes when Herb came out of the bedroom, his hair neatly trimmed and all one shade, wearing his new clothes. I was witnessing Elaine once again seeing the man she'd married forty years ago, and any ill feeling I might have had toward Herb for pushing the bank fell away.

I explained to Elaine that Herb's new look was an anniversary present from me, and I gave her a hundred dollars for them to have dinner that night. She looked tired after a full day of work at her age, and seemed grateful at the thought of not having to cook.

I bade my farewells, getting a long hug from Elaine, and headed home.

On the drive, I mused at how I'd now been to the apartments of everyone from group, save Monty—and he didn't really count, not being one of *us*.

It would only be fair to have them to my place at some point, I guessed, but the idea didn't sit well with me.

For one thing, though their places ranged from shitty (Jordan), to quite nice (Mark), none rivaled the sheer expanse of my home. Would it be rubbing their noses in what gambling had paid for?

Just a few more winning hands, and this, too, could be yours!

Plus, my entourage at home was there most of the time with Jack still recuperating and Raymond working nights for Carla, and only sporadically. How would the two groups interact?

Would Jack pick up on the fact that Mark and I had… whatever we had done. Flirted? Made eye contact? Almost kissed?

And would that be so bad if he did? If he knew that someone other than him found me attractive, even knowing I was a compulsive gambler?

I shook the thoughts from my head, not wanting to deal with them at the moment, and drove home.

Later, though, I wrote seven pages in my journal.

Twenty-One

AT GROUP THE NEXT DAY, IT WAS OBVIOUS THAT LOR and Monty had made great strides in the space since Monday. If these were just changes for the short term, I could only imagine the space they would get for a permanent spot.

Gone were any lingering smells of the previous takeout place, and much more comfortable chairs had replaced the folding ones we'd been using. And on the counter sat a Keurig, many coffee pods, a sleeve of Styrofoam cups, and all the accouterments of a well-stocked coffee bar. They'd even had a refrigerator added to the kitchen, which, when I could see behind Jordan, who had the door open, was filled with bottles of water, creamers, and various soft drinks. Even a few energy drinks, one of which Jordan pulled out.

Seb walked in with his usual carrying tray of smoothies, and he stopped in his tracks when spotting the coffee bar, which was already surrounded by Herb and Mark.

Not wanting him to feel bad, I scrambled over to him and took one of the smoothies from the tray, thanking him and taking a large draw from the straw. He gave me a smile and an eye roll, acknowledging that I was giving him a pity "Mmm" as I swallowed the frosty stuff. Slowly. I was learning not to give myself brain freeze every Monday, Wednesday, and Friday.

"Much better than coffee," I said, and he laughed. I liked

the sound of it. Low and throaty, not too dissimilar from Jack's. In fact, there were quite a few things about Seb that reminded me of Jack. A younger Jack. Without a taste for bourbon.

There was that pesky compulsive gambling problem, though.

"Herb," Seb said as he approached the counter and placed his tray down, "looking good."

Herb glanced at me, then thanked Seb for the compliment. "Anniversary yesterday. The wife was happy."

"I'll bet she was," Mark said with a tiny bit of eighth-grade innuendo. The men all laughed, and I made a show of fake disgust. The truth was that I spent the majority of my time around groups of men, whether it be the Corporation, or at poker tables, or in sports book rooms. The lewdness varied from group to group, but there was no denying that I was inured to guy talk.

Jordan took one of Seb's smoothies, bringing it and the energy drink with him to try out the new chairs. He smiled and nodded when he sat in the cushier replacement for the cold, hard metal. "We're movin' on up," he said, and a couple of us laughed. Seb set the tray of smoothies next to the coffee stuff, took one out, and he and I walked to the circle and sat down, joining Jordan.

Monty came out from the back room and looked satisfied when he saw Mark and Herb getting coffee, and Jordan with his energy dink.

"You've been busy," Mark said to Monty.

"I've had help," Monty said.

"If it was from the redhead, then you're a lucky man," Herb said. There wasn't lasciviousness in his voice, rather pure appreciation. Since I appreciated Lor's other assets, I understood.

"So, let's start up where we left off on Monday, shall we?" Monty said as Mark and Herb moved to join us. "We were talking about childhoods. Herb shared quite a bit with us about this. Who would like to start us off this time?"

Herb's father leaving and what that did to him as a kid was a tough act to follow. Especially if you had a Norman Rockwell upbringing in America's heartland. Nothing but cheddar and Packers for me to talk about. But seeing as everyone else was staying silent—

"I'll go," Jordan said, surprising everyone. "Mine's fresher in my mind than all of you, anyway," he joked, and we all laughed.

Something had changed in Jordan since his poker bender last Friday and Saturday. Maybe it was as simple as some good sleep. Maybe it was a personal breakthrough. Whatever it was, he was off and running, speaking more in the next fifty minutes than he had in the previous weeks combined. Sure, it was his story he was telling, but the words spilled out of him like water rushing through a crack in a dam.

It wasn't dairy farms and green pastures, but Jordan's upbringing was basically routine. Parents divorced but civil, Jordan was the youngest of three, upper middle class, had attended college at San Jose State, got his degree in computer science, played in a regular poker game, got into online poker. Made enough playing that so he didn't have to find a real job after graduation. Moved to Vegas to be closer to the action.

And two years later he sat with us, deeply in credit card debt from the online playing. No skills, no job, and unable to stay away from his computer or a card table for more than twenty-four hours.

"Except for now. I haven't played since Saturday." He caught my eye when he said this and gave me a slight nod, which I returned. When I looked away, I saw Seb watching me.

"That's good, Jordan," Monty said. "And thanks for sharing. I'd like to talk more about some of those feelings you had when you and your father…" Monty went on, but I lost track of what he was saying because I was trying to decipher the look Seb was giving me. Was it something to do with the nod Jordan had made in my direction? Or something else?

"Much like Jordan would benefit from a more structured existence, like a steady job, I would like to suggest something to the group," Monty said, bringing my attention from Seb back to what was being said.

"I'd like to propose adding a Tuesday and Thursday session to the group." There were glances all around, and simultaneous nods and agreements. We all knew it would be helpful to have more of these group sessions, but I also thought we looked forward to hanging out afterward.

There was something about being with people who got you on the most embarrassing level, and yet weren't a part of your everyday life. You could be "you" in the realest sense, but you didn't have to live there. A couple more hours a week sounded good to all of us.

"But before you agree, here's the thing. The added days wouldn't be group session like this; they would be yoga sessions."

Silence. Everybody looked at me, like maybe I'd put Monty up to this…feminine idea. I gave an "it wasn't me" shrug, and we all turned our attention back to Monty.

"It's a big part of GREET—yoga, meditation, things that can give you a chance to refocus your emotions. We're working on discovering how your emotions, from perhaps a very early age, have become entangled with gambling for each of you. Discovery is a huge part of this, but refocusing those emotions in a non-destructive way is the key to having a healthy future."

I knew he meant healthy in the mental well-being kind of way, but given how lots of degenerate gamblers ended up—with broken knee caps, no pinkies, or a mangled left foot—"healthy" took on a double meaning for all of us.

"Are you serious?" Herb said. "Like on the floor?"

"On mats, yes," Monty said. "Which would be provided. All you'd need to do is show up tomorrow, but wear loose, comfortable clothing."

Herb had finally upped his game fashion-wise and was now going to have to take a step back.

"You really think this is a good idea?" Mark said. "Wouldn't, like, a group jog or something work just as well?"

Monty shook his head. "It's not about the exercise, though that is encouraged in GREET as well. Yoga is about mindfulness, and that is key. Knowing how you're feeling, and how to channel those emotions."

The room was silent. GREET and its theories had been explained to each of us when we'd started working with Monty individually, and then again throughout these sessions. The idea of retraining your emotions was all well and good on paper. And sitting in a circle talking about how fucked up your family was also seemed to be "normal" in the way of recovery.

But rolling around on the floor with your legs over your ears? (Which I could only assume was what the guys were internally calling yoga.) All to get a better handle on our emotions so that they wouldn't lead us down the dark path of card games?

It wasn't that it was too far-fetched that had us hesitating; it was because I thought we all sensed that we were on the precipice of *really* getting better.

And that raised the question—did we really want to stop gambling?

"OF COURSE I REALLY WANT to stop gambling. Why else would I be here?" Herb groused, and took a sip of beer.

We'd all gone to a Chili's after group. Even Herb and Jordan. I liked it when we were all together, though the times when it had just been Seb, Mark, and me were nice too.

Basically, I liked hanging out with people where I wasn't the only one with secrets and some monumental fuck-ups in my past.

Though I did miss my posse, even changed as it was. When I texted Lor that I was having dinner with the gang, she replied that she was having Raymond pick up something for him, Ben, and Jack because she was meeting with Monty and a contractor.

"No, it's a legitimate question," Seb said from beside me. We were at one of those large round pub tables, and at first we'd gone to seats that would have put us in the exact same positions we always assumed for group. With some chuckling, we shuffled around, but now it seemed odd, somehow, to look to my left and see Seb. And, of course, there was no Monty, no head of our circle.

Was it any wonder we seemed to be floundering?

"Oh, bullshit," Herb said to Seb. "Of course we want to stop. Why else bother?"

Mark set down his gin and tonic, shaking his head. "No. Not really. I don't want to stop. I want to stop the cycle of big losses, of what it does to me. But actually not play poker ever again? Whether it be online or not? No. I don't really want to stop."

Herb started to grumble again, but Mark continued. "I can't imagine next fall coming, and not being in a book room every Saturday and Sunday morning for football."

"You can still watch the games," I lamely said. Seb, Mark, and Herb all stared at me, and then we all burst out laughing. A sound so unified that a passing waitress turned to look at us, smiling as if in on the joke.

But she wouldn't get it. Wouldn't understand why just watching a football game when you didn't have any money on it was odd.

Jordan hadn't laughed, and it was a reminder that the kid had so far only become hooked on poker, not sports betting.

Maybe there was hope for him yet. Living in Vegas wouldn't help. Yes, you could sports-bet anywhere via a bookie or online sites, but there was nothing like being in a packed book room watching a game when you had money on it. Each completed pass, each first down, was met with cheers and jeers from fellow bettors. It was Oxygen, Sin, and Caviar all rolled into one.

The Hummer at its purest.

"Oh God, what will happen next fall?" Seb said, putting his head in his hand. "I hadn't thought about that."

"One day at a time," I said.

He jerked his head up. "I thought we weren't twelve-stepping it with GREET."

"Oh, is that a twelve-step thing? I thought it was just common sense," I said.

The tension went out of his body and he flashed me a chagrinned smile, which I returned with a mock toast of my beer glass before taking a sip.

"You're right, though," Jordan said. "I think about all the time I spend playing poker. What the hell else will I do with that time?"

"Yoga, apparently," Mark said. We all looked at each other and burst out laughing again.

Even Jordan this time.

Twenty-Two

Raymond was working a game for Carla that night, so he was gone when I got home. I made a mental note to check in with him soon and make sure he was doing okay. I was pretty sure that he'd given up all thoughts of taking on running games himself, but I wanted to be sure.

The talk at dinner of having spare time that was once used gambling had me edgy about how Raymond would spend the summer before starting classes at UNLV in the fall. Even once he started school, he didn't have that many credits to get in before graduating. And he was used to holding down a full class schedule *and* playing Division I college basketball. I'd definitely check in with Raymond soon and make sure he had enough to do.

Which, as it often did lately, led me back to what I'd do with all my time now that it wasn't spent at card tables, in book rooms, or making trips as JoJo.

"Penny for your thoughts." Ben's voice pulled me from said thoughts. He was sitting at the dining room table, no lights on, just the glow from the foyer shining in on him.

I made my way in to join him at the table. "No cards tonight? No Yankees game?" He shook his head. "Raymond get you and Jack fed okay?"

"Yes," Ben said, "he went and got us Chinese takeout and

joined us for dinner before he had to leave. It was very good." In a conspiratorial whisper, he added, "But don't tell Lorelei."

I smiled and nodded. "So what are you doing sitting by yourself in the dark? I'm guessing your thoughts would be worth more than a penny."

A small, soft smile came across his wrinkled face. "Oh, Hannah dear, I'm not sure they would be. Just musings of an old man and a life that has passed before me in record time."

I reached over and patted his hand. "A good life, though, right?"

I knew Ben had lost the only woman he'd loved, and hadn't known he had a son until this year. But a life could be fulfilling in other ways.

Couldn't it?

God, I hoped so.

"Is this a private party?" Jack asked from the foyer, and both Ben and I waved him in. He sat across from me, kitty-corner from his father.

"Thinking deep thoughts in the dark?"

"I just got home," I said. Jack looked like he wanted to say something, but didn't. I absolutely did not have to tell him where I was—or with whom. Absolutely not.

"The group went out for a drink after session. It turned into dinner."

Jack nodded. "I didn't ask," he said.

I sighed. "I know."

"And do you like the group you're working with?" Ben asked. "They seem to be helping you?"

I thought about pulling Jordan away from the tables and taking Herb shopping. So far they seemed to be just costing me money. "I guess," I said. "I'm not really sure how it's supposed to go, you know?"

Both men nodded. "But do you…do you still *want* to bet?" Ben asked.

The conversation reminded me in ways of the one I'd just had with the guys at Chili's. Could I be as honest with Jack and Ben as I'd been with my other cronies?

Could I not be and hope to have the relationship with both of them that I wanted? Whatever that was.

"Yeah, I still do. All the time. I don't miss cards as much as betting, though I miss them both."

"Do you think that will ever go away?" Ben asked.

I shrugged. "Who knows. What we're working on now is trying to find other things that give us the same emotional payoff that gambling does." I told them about the theory behind GREET, and some of the things we talked about in group, without breaking anyone's trust, and even about the yoga we'd begin tomorrow, which made Ben chuckle. Jack didn't chuckle, only studied me while I spoke. After I was done, he slowly nodded and rose from the table. The movement was smooth, with little hitch, and I didn't even detect the slightest of winces from him. Jack was getting better. Soon he'd be back at work, back at his own apartment.

Yeah, I'd been working hard at getting "in touch with" my emotions, but right now I couldn't say how the idea of Jack being away from this house made me feel.

YOGA WAS HILARIOUS.

One might think that I, being the only woman in the group, would have an advantage over the others when it came to performance. One would be wrong.

At least it wasn't me who farted that one time.

I was pretty sure it wasn't me.

But I kind of liked it. And I guessed the other guys did, too, because they all came back for it the following Tuesday. And Thursday.

That might have been because of Jessica, the yoga instructor Monty had hired to lead us all. She was everything Lorelei wasn't—willowy, no curves—but a knockout just the same.

We seemed to be doing good work on our regular session days. There were no cries of "Eureka! *That's* why I gamble. Knowing that, I'm now cured!" but there were certainly moments that seemed obvious to the person speaking that they were onto something.

Seb and Mark even took to going for a run after yoga. They invited me, but I declined. And it was only partly because I feared passing out in front of them and them having to carry me back to our cars.

Mostly, I liked going home after yoga, taking my journal out to the pool, and writing.

Two new journals, matching the ones Jack had given me, showed up on my desk at about the time I had filled up the second one. I didn't fear Jack was looking to see if I needed a new one or not, but he somehow knew when I did, and provided them.

Lor said he'd gotten clearance to drive, so he must have gotten them himself this time. She also said that he had a physical to be reinstated at work soon. Desk duty at first, but I knew he was itching to get back to detective work.

I hadn't had a single dead body in my orbit in over two months—he must have been bored out of his mind.

Our lives settled into the hot summer, with activity outside in the early mornings and late evenings, everybody in the air conditioning in the afternoons. Lor laid out the business plan she and Monty prepared for his GREET treatment center, my stake in it, and other details. It made good sense to me, and though I wasn't necessarily looking to make a profit off others' gambling problems, I was glad that some of my winnings could be put to this good use.

The takeout place was more and more transformed each day,

with a bin of yoga mats in one corner, a stereo system in place for the new-agey stuff Monty played while we did our thing, and, best of all, new carpeting throughout the whole place.

Although some of my money had gone for all the improvements, Lor still hadn't produced final contracts for me to sign. She said there were still some due diligence t's to cross and i's to dot. I wondered if they had to do with the background check she was having done on Monty. I certainly didn't want to invest money in something—or someone—unsound, but I really felt that Monty was onto something with GREET, so I hoped that nothing came up about him that gave Lorelei pause.

Twenty-Three

ON A FRIDAY AFTER GROUP, WE STARTED TO TALK ABOUT where we were going for dinner, but both Herb and Jordan said they couldn't make it. Herb said he was taking Elaine out for dinner, and did seem to have a spark in his step. Jordan had seemed distracted during group, not talking much, and only said he couldn't make it, then stepped into Eric's Camaro when it pulled up to the curb. I leaned over and waved to Eric, but he either didn't see me, or didn't recognize me, because he didn't respond in any way, just waited for Jordan to get in, then roared away.

"Looks like it's just the original three," Mark said when it was just him, Seb, and me on the sidewalk. Monty had gone to the back of the building and was already shutting the lights out in the front area.

I hadn't talked much during group that day, and Monty shutting out the lights, darkening the place where I was starting to breathe again, stirred something in me. A sense of panic overcame me for absolutely no reason that I could think of.

"Distill? That okay? Anna?"

"Huh?"

"We were thinking Distill. By the Costco at Canyon Pointe. It's in your neck of the woods, right?"

"Yes. Not far from me at all. I'll meet you guys there."

They both arrived before me and had taken one of the cozy seating areas that seemed more like a small living room than a bar. It seemed we'd arrived in time for happy hour (a nice perk of getting done with group around four), and we set about ordering a couple rounds of drinks and appetizers, which were also on special.

The first beer went down way too easily, so I ordered a vodka tonic for my second. Not a drink I liked much, so I knew I would sip it. Something about the whole day felt a little off kilter to me, and I was thinking it'd be a good idea to have a semi-clear head. I tried to do some of the things we'd learned to do, such as check in with my emotions, letting them "speak" to me. (Yeah, they had been hard concepts not to laugh at initially, but they seemed to work, so the laughs lessened.)

Nothing during my check-in rang any bells as to why I felt off, so I tuned back in to what Mark and Seb were talking about. Since they'd started running together after yoga, it seemed like they'd found a lot of common ground. Things other than gambling, apparently.

They were looking at me, waiting for a response. I shrugged. "Sorry, guys. Wool gathering. No clue what we're even talking about."

Mark laughed, standing from his slouchy leather chair. "No worries. It wasn't that important. Another round?" Seb and I both nodded, and Mark made the circular motion to someone at the bar behind me, then excused himself to use the restroom.

Seb and I were sitting together on a loveseat across from Mark's chair. The loveseat was cushy and comfy, and I'd slouched deeply while nursing my vodka.

"You okay?" Seb asked, turning toward me. He put his arm along the back of the loveseat, past my head, and crooked a knee up, so it was almost touching my thigh.

"Yeah," I said. "Why?"

"I don't know. You seem a little…distracted."

"I am, but I don't know why. Just feeling kind of weird today, for no reason."

He looked at me, studying, his hand edging closer to the top of my head that was slouched into the back of the loveseat. His thumb reached out and gently touched my hair. "Want to talk about it? What you're feeling?"

"That's just it—I don't know what I'm feeling."

"Should we run through the emotional check-in?" he asked.

I was happy to know that I wasn't the only one who had been listening during group.

"I've kind of been doing that in my head," I said. "No luck."

His fingers joined his thumb, and it felt nice on my scalp, like a mini-massage. In fact, being close to Seb, his hand on my head, his body leaning so closely to mine, suddenly felt very nice.

A little too nice, perhaps.

"If you don't want to get in touch with your emotions, maybe I can distract you in other ways," he said, his voice deeper and yet softer.

I looked up at him, gauging whether he was going to start grinning, as if he was joking. There was a sparkle in his eye, and a small smile on his face, but he definitely wasn't joking.

I thought back to the night Mark walked me to my car and we almost kissed. I knew if I leaned just the slightest bit in Seb's direction, he would meet me halfway. More than halfway, I was betting. (If I still bet, that was.)

And much like I would have liked to kiss Mark that night, I really wanted to kiss Seb now. To just sink into mindless sensation that wasn't gambling related.

But kissing Seb would be gambling of a different kind. A bet that I wasn't willing to make.

"Tempting," I whispered. "But I'm good, thanks."

His nod of understanding was tiny, but he was close enough to me that I saw it. "Offer stands," he said softly.

I swallowed hard and nodded. He moved away, but kept his knee up on the loveseat and his arm along the back.

"What'd I miss?" Mark said, rejoining our table.

"Alas, nothing, I'm afraid," Seb said. I chuckled, and Mark looked back and forth between us as he sat and drained his glass. Good timing, because the bartender came with our new round and the waitress was right behind him with our load of appetizers.

Food and booze had been great, if fattening, substitutes for gambling thus far. And sadly, it would have to be a substitute for other, more physical pleasures as well.

Twenty-Four

I LEFT SHORTLY AFTER WE WERE DONE EATING. MARK and Seb both tried to talk me into staying, saying they were going to make an evening of it. But I needed to get home. My emotional state was such that I didn't trust myself to be around my new posse. I just wasn't sure what wagon I might fall off if I spent the night in their company—gambling or sex. And if it was sex, which one would I sleep with?

I drove home carefully, aware that I probably shouldn't be driving. Thankfully, it was only a five-minute drive to my house from Distill. When I pulled into the driveway, there was a car out front that I recognized as belonging to Frank Botz, Jack's former partner.

Former because Jack was hurt, but also because Jack had been on leave before he was shot, and Botz had been partnered with Peter Faxon, a well-dressed, pompous ass who was partially responsible for Jack being shot.

Though I guess you could say I was partially responsible, too.

I had stumbled upon a guy that we thought might be involved in a murder and followed him when I probably should have just let the police handle it. When I caught up to the guy, he found me, causing a standoff with Jack, him, and me. It looked like it would end peacefully until Faxon stumbled on something, creating a crash and freaking out the suspect, causing him to shoot. Faxon and I had both messed up, and Jack barely made it into surgery.

It would be nice to see Frank, and though I sometimes got the feeling that he thought I wasn't good for Jack, he liked me well enough. Or maybe he just felt that Jack and I were bad for each other.

He wouldn't have been wrong on either account.

They were in the living room, and the smile I had for Frank quickly died when I saw Faxon was also there. And then it really died when I saw a tumbler of bourbon in Jack's hand.

He wasn't drinking alone—the other two men had drinks as well—but a rush of rage shot up my spine. One I couldn't define or pin to any one thing that was before me, but I knew that I needed to say a quick hello and then depart—preferably with my journal—before the rage turned into something I'd regret.

Either by saying something to the cops or Jack, or—and this was more likely—turn it on myself.

"Gentlemen," I said, walking into the room. I waved them down as Faxon and Frank started to rise. Faxon stayed seated, but Frank rose and gave me a light kiss on the cheek as I greeted him. He then sat back down in the chair, one that was next to where Faxon sat. The likely place for me to sit would be next to Jack on the couch, but I wasn't sure that was a good idea. A quick getaway was still the best possible outcome, not sitting next to my not-boyfriend, watching as he had what I assumed was his first drink nearly two months.

It must have been all those emotional check-ins I'd been working on, because I realized relatively easily (something that surely wouldn't have happened before GREET) that the rage I thought I was feeling was actually jealousy.

Oh, not of Jack having buddies that came calling to see to his welfare. And not because the lot of them looked like they were having fun without me. No, I was jealous because Jack was drinking, and I was not gambling.

"Can I get you a drink?" Jack asked me. His brow was up, and I wasn't entirely sure if it was because he knew I'd already had quite enough to drink, or because he was waiting for me to question the fact that *he* was drinking.

Not that I'd do that in a million years. For one, he and I had agreed from the night we met that we wouldn't try to fix each other. I dealt with my gambling (or didn't, as the case may be), and the drinking issues were his. For another, we both lived in very large, very glass houses, and I would not throw stones.

I wished the best for Jack, of course, whether we were together or not. But I could only help myself, and that was shaky most of the time. I certainly couldn't help a man stop drinking who didn't want to.

"I'm good, thanks," I said to Jack, who stayed seated. He hadn't really made a move to get up and get a drink for me. "I don't want to interrupt cop shop talk. I'll just—"

"You're not interrupting anything, Anna," Frank said. He motioned to the empty side of the couch. "Join us. Really, we're just shooting the shit. Just came by to see how Jack's doing."

"He's doing well. Or so Lorelei tells me," I said. Yeah, it was a subtle dig that I got my information about Jack via Lor. He gave me a "touché" nod then his gaze slid to the empty seat on the couch next to him, challenge in his eyes.

"Right as rain," he said as I took the seat beside him, careful not to sink into his side, to not touch him at all. I could smell the bourbon from his glass, and it conjured up memories of times when I was not careful at all about touching Jack. When I touched him all I wanted.

And I'd wanted to a lot.

But tonight, while he sat feeding his demon, feeling *his* Hummer, and I sat with my only buzz being from alcohol—not from what truly fed my soul—I didn't want to touch Jack Schiller.

Except, perhaps, to punch him in the face.

"How've you been, Frank?" I asked, not wanting to talk about Jack's health. If he really was right as rain, he'd be back to work soon, out of the house. In days past, that thought had made me sad, and slightly panicky. Tonight, it was something I was cool with. "Catch any juicy murderers lately?"

Frank smiled and started to speak, but Faxon cut him off. "Why? Have you been busy again?"

"Shut up, Peter," Frank said, winning my thanks, which I tried to convey with a look to him before turning my attention to Faxon.

"Have *you* been busy, Faxon? Got any other cops shot lately?"

"What the fuck are you talking about?" he said to me, then looked at Jack. "You don't seriously think—"

"No," Jack said firmly, then he looked at me with "not another word out of you" glare. "Nobody thinks anything. Anna's just had a few, I'm guessing."

"I have," I said, then bobbed my chin toward his near-empty glass. "And not being a professional, it tends to affect me more."

Another brow raise from Jack. His brown eyes bored into me, but I couldn't read him. I never could.

That was never more evident when he chuckled and turned back to Frank and Faxon. "No, Anna hasn't been involved in any murder cases lately, and she won't be. She's stopped gambling, and with that goes away hanging with that element."

"I'd say hanging with a homicide detective was as much the *element* as anything," I said.

"But then, you're not hanging with a homicide detective much anymore either, are you?" he said.

I wanted to knock that glass of bourbon out of his hands. Hear it smash against the marble floor, see the smoky liquid seep toward the rich, creamy area rug. But I didn't do any of that. Or, more accurately, before I could do any of that, Frank said,

"You've stopped gambling, Anna? Good for you."

"Yeah, well," I said, "we'll see how it goes."

"One day at a time, right?" Frank said, and I only nodded.

I shouldn't have cared that Jack mentioned to his partner that I'd stopped gambling—it wasn't exactly a secret. Hell, when some of the big tournaments came up and I didn't play in them, the whole poker world would know I'd quit.

But it felt wrong to have said something when Faxon—whom I didn't like, who didn't like me, and whom even Jack didn't like—was here, too. I felt like I'd been thrown under the bus, but I wasn't sure where the bus was headed and who was driving.

But I sure knew who'd done the throwing.

"Listen, I'm really going to leave you guys to it. Let you get back to your chat," I said, rising from the couch. This time Jack did get up, as did Frank. Faxon remained seated, enjoying whatever emotion was obviously evident on my face.

Damn emotions. Why couldn't they all just stay in the background, waiting for me to place a bet or play a game of high-stakes poker?

Jack reached for me, but I turned quickly enough for it to look like he missed me, not that I was ducking him. "Good to see you Frank," I called, waving a hand over my shoulder. I walked quickly from the living room before turning around and this time actually slapping Jack's drink from his hand. Starting toward my room, I detoured and went to the center of the house and the office.

Feeling it was going to be a journal overspill kind of night, I was grabbing the newest unused journal from the top of my desk when Jack followed me in. Not for the first time, I wished that I'd put a little bell on him, he moved so quietly.

"What was that about?" he asked.

"What was what about?" I answered.

His eyes went to my hand reaching toward the new journal,

but that wasn't what Jack thought I was reaching for. Next to the journal sat my cigar box where I kept my stash of betting money. I'd throw my winnings in there and draw out when I was going gambling. Most of my winnings I handed over to Lor for the household, keeping a small percentage to fund my next foray. (Binge? Foray? What's the difference?)

Not having gambled recently, I had no idea how much cash was currently in the cigar box, or if Lor had cleaned it out completely, though I suspected she wouldn't have done that—nobody went in that box but me.

But Jack knew what it was, and thought I was reaching for it now.

My hand sprang back as if his look had burned me. And that natural response pissed me off even more.

"Don't, Anna," he said. His voice was soft, with more pleading than any kind of censure.

I wanted to tell him I was reaching for the new journal. That I was tired, raw, and a little drunk, and all I wanted to do was retreat to the pool area, sink into a chaise, and write out all my frustrations.

But that wasn't really all I wanted to do.

I wanted to feel a Hummer. The equivalent of what that heavy crystal glass must have felt like in Jack's hand.

And so I said nothing. Which, of course, Jack took as defiance.

"You're doing so well. I'm in awe, really. I mean, if you can do this…not gamble." He paused, and I looked up at him from the desk, the journal, and cigar box. Three feet and a desk width away, and yet so, so far away. "It could be good again, baby," he said so softly I wasn't sure if it was to me or himself.

It was the "baby" that made me bristle. He'd called me baby many times, and I'd always liked it in context. But now it just seemed all wrong.

And manipulative. Very manipulative. Something I'd seen

Jack do before, but never with me. Always on a case.

"Are you, what? Waiting to see if and when I fall off the wagon, Jack? Am I *auditioning* for our relationship? Am I on the clock?"

It took him a second too long before he shook his head. "No," he said.

"Bullshit," I said. "You're just waiting to see if I slip up, aren't you? How much time were you going to give me? Or is the better question how much rope were you going to give me?"

"You're being paranoid."

That pushed the needle up, dangerously close to the red zone. And not only because he might be right.

"Yeah, maybe," I said, "but that doesn't mean they're not out to get you."

He set his glass down on the desk and took a step toward my side. The thud of the crystal on the oak was solid and reverberated down my spine.

"Anna," he said.

I put up my hand, and, surprisingly, he stopped moving in my direction. "You were right to end things with us, Jack. And I don't want the promise of you being held out as a carrot. You breaking up with me is not why I stopped gambling. And the idea of getting back together, believe me, is not the incentive I use to stay out of the book rooms."

"I know," he said, and I believed he really did. He was no dummy when it came to addictions and compulsions.

The urge to run overcame me, and I knew I had to get out of the house, get away from Jack before I said or did something I'd really regret later. Like tell him he wasn't welcome in the house where his father lived.

Or, I don't know, sleep with him, maybe.

"I need to go," I said.

"You just got home. And you're drunk,"

"Not quite," I said, "but the night is still young." And it

was. Faxon and Frank must have stopped over on their way home from work. It was still early enough that Lor and Ben and probably Raymond must be out for dinner, seeing as none of them had made an appearance since I'd been home.

Early enough that the West Coast games hadn't yet started.

And with that thought—and wanting to get the hell away from drinking Jack Schiller—I reached for the cigar box, opened it, and grabbed at one of the three wads of cash that were in it.

I took the rubber band off the roll, folded the substantial pile of bills in half, and jammed it in my pants pocket. I didn't see all the denominations, but the ones on top were hundreds, so it was a good bet (ha!) that they all were. Probably around ten grand, but I didn't let my mind grasp that number.

"Anna, don't. Forget about everything I just said. Remember all the hard work you've done over the past month."

I snorted at that, moving past him. He tried to reach for my arm, but I flung it away, coming into contact with his glass of bourbon on the desk. Down it fell, crashing against the hardwood floor, bourbon splashing the pant of my leg, glass spraying across the room.

I kept going, my Nikes crunching through the broken crystal.

"Anna, wait," Jack said behind me. I didn't run, but walked quickly to the front of the house, knowing it would be hard for Jack to catch me with his injuries.

"Who are you meeting?" he called after me, his voice echoing down the hallway. "Who the hell are you going to see?"

I rounded the corner and saw both Frank and Faxon standing in the living room, their eyes wide. Faxon even had his mouth open in disbelief.

They were cops. Surely they'd been called in for domestic disputes before. Mentally laughing at my own joke, I had on a goofy smile as I passed the living room, giving them another goodbye wave over my shoulder.

"Let me call Monty," Jack shouted, his voice getting closer in the hallway. "Don't go see anybody else."

If you didn't know the situation—and I was guessing Frank and Faxon didn't completely—Jack's words would sound like those of a jealous lover, afraid I was walking into the arms of another man.

It wasn't a new lover I was fleeing the building for, but the look of shock on Faxon's face almost had me believing it was.

"Too late," I yelled out to Jack. Faxon's look changed to amusement and smugness. It was the last thing that registered before I slammed the door behind me and walked out into the warm Vegas night.

Twenty-Five

I WALKED BACK INTO DISTILL AND MY BOYS—ALL OF them this time—sent up a hurrah that had me feeling a little better after my rift with Jack. I'd group-texted Seb and Mark after I left the house, asking if they were still out. They'd replied that not only were they still at Distill, but Herb and Jordan had joined the group after all.

When I left my house, I walked out to the gatehouse, requesting an Uber. I'd barely paid attention when Lor had put the app on my phone and given me a crash course on how to use it. It wasn't often I gave up control of my Porsche. I'd been in too many tight jams not to want my own wheels at my disposal.

But I probably shouldn't have driven home from Distill the first time, and once I knew Seb and Mark were still partying, I knew I'd be joining in, and I wouldn't want to leave my car in a bar parking lot overnight and take a cab home.

Thus I stood with Eddie in the gatehouse as I waited for my ride. I'd started walking to the gate right away, not willing to wait for the Uber in front of my house, lest Jack follow me out. Or worse, in case he didn't.

Or worse yet, having to face Frank and Faxon after what they'd witnessed.

"Look what the cat dragged in," Herb said, moving over to make room for me on the same loveseat I'd shared with Seb earlier. Seb had moved to a chair that had been pulled over to the little circle after I left. Mark was still in his same seat, and Jordan in the other.

"Dragged *back* in," I said, plopping down next to Herb.

"I heard," he said. "Just couldn't stay away, eh?"

"What are you doing here? I thought you and Elaine were having date night?"

Herb's smile faded and a waft of shame overcame him before he put up a mask of indifference and shrugged. "Change of plans."

Ah. So Herb had done something to piss off Elaine. A part of me wanted to press him, see if he'd gambled. And, I hated to admit it, not for altruistic reasons of wanting to console or counsel Herb, but because I wanted to know if yet another person in my circle was getting their Hummer on while I was settling for booze as a poor substitute.

"Welcome back," the waitress said when she approached our group. "Same as before?"

"I'll switch back to beer," I said. I'd just sip for a while, and maybe this night wouldn't turn into the complete shit show that I—and the wad of cash in my pocket—sensed it could become.

I asked her to have the bartender make me a Radler, thinking the added citrus might slow down whatever excesses awaited me.

And I knew they were out there, and by heading out of my home, getting that Uber, I was setting it all in motion.

But it doesn't have to be. You can stop it before it goes too far.

Was that JoJo's voice? The voice of reason?

"What'd I miss?" I said, hoping the conversation was something trivial that I could maintain with one ear while I tried to get control over myself.

It helped being with these guys. I wasn't sure if they were slipping up at home—or elsewhere—and gambling, but none of us wanted to be the first one to gamble in front of the others. I'd bet good money on that.

If I was still betting.

"Oh, you know, keeping it light," Herb said. "Just throwing out our biggest fuck-ups."

"Unicorns and rainbows shit," Jordan added. I smiled at his joke, but he didn't meet my glance. After Herb's telling answer, I didn't bother asking Jordan why he joined us.

The fact that we wanted to be with each other rather than with friends or family (or ex-boyfriends who were living at their house) basically told me all I needed to know. It was safer not to gamble with each other than anyone else.

"We've had some doozies," Mark said. "Care to share with the class?"

The waitress handed me my beer, and I took a long drink then set the glass down on the low table in front of our group. It was next to Herb's glass of wine. Also on the table were Seb's and Mark's drink glasses, and what looked to be like a soft drink in a glass in front of Jordan. Next to that was a can of energy drink that I was guessing he brought in himself. There were clean small plates and a couple of dirty ones. A plate of sliders sat in the center of the table, as did a platter of nachos, both of them half finished.

They'd been busy in the short time I'd been gone.

I realized the group was staring at me, and I remembered Mark had asked me about my stories.

"What kind do you want?" I said. "Bad beats in cards? A missed field goal that cost me thousands? Spending way too much money on a team I despise?" I could easily have told a dozen stories in each category.

"I YouTubed that bad beat you had from Negreanu a couple of years ago. That must have stung," Jordan said, surprising me. He'd never mentioned knowing much about my professional poker exploits.

"That one cost about a million dollars in prize money," I said. "So yeah, it stung."

Seb gave me a small smile. Herb shook his head and Mark watched me, I guessed waiting for more.

"No fair. I missed all of your stories, but you all get to hear mine?" I said in a light tone. I motioned to Jordan. "Besides, apparently you—and the whole world—can see my biggest disgraces on YouTube."

"I'm going to get these out of here so I don't eat anymore. Unless you all…" Seb said, motioning to the food. I'd never known him to watch what he ate, and he certainly didn't need to. He picked up the platter of nachos and nodded at me to grab the sliders. "Give me a hand," he said, rising with the nachos and some stacked plates.

I was about to teasingly call him out on asking the only woman at the table to help him with the dishes, but something in his eyes made me just pick up the nachos and a couple of other plates and follow Seb away from our little alcove and to the bar.

"I'm so sorry," the waitress said, rushing over to us. "I thought you guys were still working on that. I would have—"

"No problem. We were. I just needed to stretch my legs," Seb said, setting down his load onto the bar. I did as well. Our waitress hovered to see if we needed anything, then realized—about the same time I did—that Seb wanted to talk to me alone, and hurried off.

"About earlier," I started, but stopped when Seb gave a tiny shake of his head.

"It's not that."

I looked back to our cluster of chairs and loveseat, Herb's back to us. Jordan and Mark leaned toward each other, the coffee table between them. Herb must have been speaking, because the other two were looking at him.

"Unless that's why you came back?" Seb said, a tiny bit of hope in his voice.

Crap. I'd actually forgotten about Seb's flirtation earlier in the night until he'd signaled for me to follow him to the bar. I didn't want to play games with the guy.

And yet a part of me didn't want to totally discourage him, either.

If he was a safety net, or a consolation prize of some sort, I could do a lot worse than Seb.

"No," I said, trying to be gentle. "Not entirely," I added, though I probably shouldn't have.

My mind was playing out scenarios of how the night could end. Two likely contenders were me blowing all that cash in my pocket, or ending up in bed with Seb.

Both would give me instant gratification. Both would have me feeling like shit in the morning. One would cost me a lot of money.

The other would cost me a friend.

He studied me, waiting for more. When I retreated into myself, he shook his head as if to get off the train of thought we both were on.

"Well, I just wanted to say that things are kind of shaky tonight."

"For Herb?" I asked.

"It started when he came in. Turned the whole vibe. And it only got darker when Jordan came in. Then the conversation turned to messing up, and… I don't know. It feels a lot more… fragile, I guess, without Monty as a guide."

Yeah, he had a point. It was good to talk about this kind of stuff with others that could understand it so well. But before when we'd gone out we'd kept it light, or an extension of what we'd just been talking about in group.

I didn't know if any of us were qualified to steer an evening that had the potential to go off the rails back onto the right track.

Could any of us be the engineer if the choo-choo was jumping the rails?

THE CONVERSATION KEPT GOING, and the drinks kept flowing. Everybody told some stories, but Seb and I tried to keep them light, and it seemed the others followed our lead.

"But there are fuck-ups," Mark said an hour later, "and then there's the stuff that, you know, drove us to finally get help."

I *knew* that none of us should go there without Monty in the room. Rock-bottom stories should not be told with drinks and appetizers.

"Maybe we should turn this boat around," I said.

Mark either didn't hear me, or ignored me. "I mean, I know *I've* done not only messed-up shit, but stuff that could land me in prison. I'm guessing every compulsive gambler gets to that point eventually. Whatever it takes to get that next stake."

Substitute "stake" with "taste" and it was like he was talking about a drug addict. And he was exactly right.

Still, there was no way I could share JoJo stories, even as much as I liked and trusted this group of guys. Even if they could be used as a cautionary tale for someone like Jordan.

JoJo could never see the light of day.

I guessed that everybody else felt the same way about whatever secrets they held, because everybody looked from Mark to each other, waiting.

"I mean, for me—" Mark started, but was cut off by Seb.

"God, I want to make a bet right now."

The tension that Mark's topic raised deflated with Seb stating what everyone else was feeling. I could actually feel Herb relax next to me and see Jordan's shoulders drop.

"Well, sure," Mark said. "After all the talk about bad beats and different bets we've made, I'm sure we all do. But back to the things we've done in the past. I once—"

"The Cavaliers are playing on the West Coast tonight. Game five…" Herb said, trailing off at the end, as if perhaps it was just the beginning of a bigger thought.

And of course it was. For all of us.

No one wanted to be the first, but if we were all in it together? I glanced at my phone sitting on the table next to my drink. "Fifteen minutes until the game starts."

"I've deleted my betting app," Seb said, fumbling for his phone.

A look of consternation played across Mark's handsome face, but I wasn't sure if it was because we didn't want to share our stories of past felonies committed, or if because he knew what I now did.

We were going to bet tonight.

"We can walk to the Red Rock in four minutes," I said. Before my sentence was finished, Jordan had risen, Seb was pulling out his wallet and throwing cash on the table, and Herb was throwing back the rest of his wine.

I did the same with my beer, one hand on the glass and my other going into my pocket to touch the folded bills.

Soon. Soon you can come out and play.

Twenty-Six

WE MUST HAVE BEEN A SIGHT, RUNNING THROUGH the parking lot of Distill, then Olive Garden, out to Charleston, where we could barely wait for the traffic light to change before darting across eight lanes of traffic. The driveway into the Red Rock casino had never seemed so long as it did with the clock ticking down to tipoff.

Out of breath, Jordan in the lead, Herb bringing up the rear, we all dashed into the book room and gazed up at that board, a couple of us grabbing betting sheets to take a proper look at the different prop bets available. It being a playoff game, there were a quite a few, with things like how many fouls LeBron would get, if a technical would be called, and other inconsequential-to-the-outcome wagers.

They all looked like sure things to me, even when I changed my mind on some of them the closer I looked. The Hummer rushed through my body, and the buzz from the alcohol dimmed in comparison to what it *truly* felt like to be alive.

Thoughts of emotional check-ins, how to re-channel my feelings, or even sublimation with some Ben and Jerry's or Fat Burger, which were both just yards away in the food court, fled from my mind, leaving me with just the heat and glow of betting.

God, it felt good.

I grabbed one of the little pencils from the box—pencils I

only saw gamblers and golfers use—and took a seat in the front row, using the desk arm to begin circling all the lovely, wondrous bets I was going to place.

A glass of beer was set down in the cup holder at the top of the desk table, and I looked up to see Mark with a few other drinks, passing them out to everyone.

"Thanks," I said, not daring to take the time and sip my beer, lest I miss the betting cutoff when the game started. I was shocked Mark had taken the time to go to the bar for a round. "Better hurry," I said, "just a couple of minutes until tipoff."

"I'm good," he said, then gave a glass of red wine to Herb, who was sitting to my right, also furiously circling his bet sheet. I wasn't sure if Mark meant he'd already placed a bet (he could have; I hadn't paid attention to anybody else since I fell under the spell of the betting board), felt he had time yet, or if he wasn't making any at all. I wanted to ponder that—why he would come with us if he wasn't going to bet, and yet not try to talk us out of it—but the wad of cash in my pocket felt heavy and hurtful, and the only sense of relief I could see was to offer it up to the lovely man behind the counter.

The lovely man was Craig, a worker I'd chatted with many times over the years. "Haven't seen you for a bit, Anna," he said when I approached the counter, counting my money and slapping the odds sheet on the glossy countertop.

"Haven't done much betting lately, Craig," I said. He only nodded, and I bit my tongue before regaling poor Craig with my tale of wagons and falling off them.

I made my bets, keeping none of the money, spending every last dollar, even though it made one of the bets an uneven amount. Nine thousand and eight hundred dollars I spent on a game I didn't even care about.

But it didn't matter. Holding those little slips of paper was what mattered. Whereas the cash had burned and weighed me down, the bet slips I now tucked in my pocket glowed with a peaceful heat that surged through my body.

The Hummer at its finest.

"Ah, fucking Sin, am I right?" Herb said when I sat back down beside him.

"You're right," I said.

Seb and Jordan were at the counter with clerks other than Craig, and Mark was sitting on the opposite side of Herb. Once finished, Seb and Jordan made their way to us and sat next to each other on my left. The five of us completed the entire first row of chairs in the book room. All with bet slips in front of us and drinks in our cup holders, thanks to Mark.

"You know, there's a smoothie place in the food court. It could be just like we're at group," Seb said, making me laugh. He chuckled, too, and that made me laugh harder. Or maybe it was just the Hummer coursing through me that made me think he was so hilarious. I looked at him and he watched me, a twinkle of humor in his eye. A sexiness that I'd certainly noticed before, but had tried to ignore.

Maybe it was time to stop ignoring it all.

He nodded toward my beer. "Drink up. Game's about to start."

I pulled my beer from the cup holder and toasted Seb. "Here's to a good game. And may we all be winners tonight."

AT HALFTIME I WASN'T feeling very well. I thought it might be the booze, but it wasn't a drunk kind of wooziness. It might have been the food from earlier, but it didn't feel like that either. It was like a kind of brain fog, as if I were watching myself in the front row, but from a seat in the back row of the book room.

I went to the ladies' room, took care of business, then splashed cold water on my face to try and snap out of it.

Was it guilt? Was what I'd just done—what we'd *all* just

done—making me physically ill? Two months of hard work, therapy, and even frickin' *yoga* down the drain in a matter of minutes.

I should feel worse, but the cheers from the book room as some player made a huge three-pointer had me pushing all guilt deep, deep down and out of the way.

If I was going to slip up, shouldn't I at least enjoy it for more than the first half?

My phone buzzed in my pocket and I checked it, seeing a text from Jack.

Just need to know that you're okay.

Shit. There went the Hummer. Shame rose to the forefront.

Okay. With friends, I sent back.

Nothing else from him, but the spell had been broken.

I made my way back to my seat, trying not to stumble over my own feet, curious now if I really was getting sick or if my *sickness* had just enveloped me.

"You okay?" Seb asked as I slowly lowered myself to my chair. I nodded and took a long drink of beer, trying to make my mouth less dry.

I slunk back in the chair, stretching my legs out in front of me, and checked the score. I liked touching my bet slips during a game, but I never really had to *look* at them. I always remembered exactly what I'd bet—the point spreads, over/under, everything.

But as I stared up at the game on the large screen, I couldn't quite remember if I'd bet for or against the Cavaliers.

That was when I knew something was definitely wrong, and not just guilt and shame making their appearance.

And that was the last thought I remembered.

Twenty-Seven

THE NEXT MORNING, I HUDDLED ON THE COUCH WHILE Frank sat on the coffee table in front of me.

A dead man was in the bedroom. A man I'd spent the night with.

"Okay, let's try this again. Anna?" Frank said.

"Yes?" I answered. A uniformed officer walked quickly past us from the bedroom and out the front door of the apartment. My mind tried to focus on Frank's words.

"Can you start at the beginning for me? Who is the man in the bed?"

"He's...he's someone from my compulsive gamblers support group."

"And you spent the night with him?" No censure from Frank, no judgment. Just the facts, ma'am. He was wearing a *Finding Nemo* tie, and I was reminded of Casey's visit.

I nodded, but as I did, I took a physical inventory of myself. "But..."

"But what?"

I knew Faxon was somewhere behind us, either in this room or the bedroom. I leaned closer to Frank. "I don't think we had sex."

He nodded, watching me. "Have you had sex with him before?"

"No. Not ever."

"Are you sure?"

I looked at Frank like he was crazy, but maybe I was the crazy one. I guessed if I couldn't say for sure that I had or hadn't had sex the night before, then it was a legitimate question.

"I'm sure. Frank, I think I was drugged or something. I started feeling weird last night at the casino, and I don't remember anything after that." Right, the casino. I'd forgotten that until now. Bits and pieces were coming back to me. Distill. The Red Rock. Nothing after that, though. I wasn't sure how I'd ended up here. And given what I *could* remember, his was not the bed I thought I'd end up in that night.

Frank wrote something down in his notebook, stood, and stretched his back. Taking a seat next to me on the couch, he turned toward me and placed a warm, meaty hand on my back. "We'll get you to the hospital soon. Just a few more questions first, if you're up to it."

I nodded but then shook my head. "I don't need to go to the hospital. I'm just groggy, but okay."

"We'll want to do a tox screening to see what you ingested. And we should probably…"

I looked at him. "What?"

"We'll want to do a rape kit as well."

"I don't think that's necessary. Like I said—"

He put his other hand on my knee, steadying it, though I hadn't even realized it was shaking. "It's just a precaution. If you can't remember what happened, maybe there's some kind of physical evidence that will tell us. Kind of like the toxicity tests."

A little different than drawing blood, but I just nodded. It was in my best interest to know what had happened, but I was trusting that my body knew what had or hadn't gone on.

"Anna, once you woke up, saw the man, what did you do then? Take your time. Don't leave anything out."

I told him. About waking up naked, first putting the shirt

on. Going to the bathroom, sitting back on the bed, then finally crawling over to the other side and discovering the body. The body. It sounded so distant, detached, for someone I'd spent so much time with.

"And when you were in the bathroom, did you wash your hands? After you were done?"

It seemed odd that he was asking after my personal hygiene when a man lay dead in the next room, but I only nodded.

"With soap? How high? Just the hands or your wrists and arms, too?"

"Ummm." I looked down at my hands, trying to remember how I did something that was as natural as breathing. How did you describe your normal way of washing your hands?

"Pretend you're washing them now, without water," he said when he saw I was just staring at my hands. I pantomimed the action, and he nodded.

He motioned to an officer who was standing behind me. I could hear the scratching of a pencil against paper from the officer, but I didn't look to see what he was writing.

Of course I knew how bad this looked—me waking up naked with a dead man. But whatever was in my system, plus the shock, had my mind so muddled that I couldn't quite go into self-defense mode as I knew I probably should.

Still, some pieces were beginning to fall into place.

"Oh, residue," I said, and Frank's eyes came back to mine. "You need to test for gunshot residue and you're afraid I washed it off."

Yeah, I probably should have kept that thought to myself. But Frank just nodded and squeezed my knee. I did seem to remember from some old cop show that it was more complicated than just washing with soap and water to remove gunshot residue. I kept my mouth shut on that.

"Standard procedure. Nothing more."

"Right," I said. Suddenly the weight of his hand wasn't

enough to keep my leg from going into full-blown shakes, and my hands followed suit. "Umm…" I held my hand up for Frank to see. "I think…"

Frank was already standing. "Shock is setting in. Plus whatever you took last night."

I wanted to point out that I didn't voluntarily *take* anything, but thought that was a minor point to bring up right now. "We're going to get you to the hospital now. We'll finish up all the questions after we get you checked out." Frank was on his feet, motioning for the officer to come around the front of the couch. "This is Officer Kessler. He'll be riding in the ambulance with you."

"I don't need an ambulance," I said, but Frank just waved my objection away.

He gave some instructions to Officer Kessler, who nodded and seemed to relish the idea of being in charge of me—the likely suspect at this time.

I almost didn't have the heart to tell him there was no way that I would have done it.

"Okay, Anna, one more thing and then we'll get you to the hospital."

"Yes?"

Frank put his hands on my shoulders, steadying me. "Who is the man in the bed? What is his name?"

Oh. Right. I hadn't said, had I? Although the cops probably had that information by now, being that we were in his apartment and everything. In fact, they probably knew more than I did about the poor man in the bedroom with a bullet where his heart used to be.

"We didn't do last names. In therapy. We only had each other's first names."

"And that was?" Frank asked, his warm hands still on my shoulders, giving a tiny squeeze of encouragement.

"Mark," I said. "His name is…*was* Mark."

Twenty-Eight

MARK WAS DEAD. SHOT IN HIS OWN BED, IN HIS OWN stylish apartment, while I slept naked not three feet away.

At some point that fact slowly crept into my being, and that was when the shaking really leapt out of control.

The nurse assigned to me was great, giving me blankets to try and warm myself. Promising it would all soon get better.

They did the residue test, swabbing my hands. They took the shirt I'd been wearing the night before, giving me a scrubs top to wear. I didn't bother mentioning I would probably have been naked if I'd shot Mark, as I wasn't likely to take my clothes off after doing it and then going to sleep.

They took a ton of blood for the toxicity tests. Then the nurse did a rape kit, and I was even more convinced that I had not had sex the night before, which she tended to agree with, given no evidence to the contrary.

It was embarrassing and intrusive—all of it was—and my heart went out to the thousands of women who had to go through the procedure with different results.

When all the various testing the police could possibly need was finished, the doctor prescribed an IV with something in it, and the shakes and coldness that had taken over my body subsided somewhat.

I asked the doctor if there was something in the IV to make

me sleep as I became drowsy quickly. He said no, but I could barely stay awake for his answer before I drifted off.

WHEN I AWOKE, I could tell by the shadows on the wall that it was late afternoon. I was still in the emergency area, but in a more secluded partition, with curtains drawn on the two sides that weren't the outside wall.

Jack Schiller sat in a hard chair by my bed, his head bowed, hands cradled. If I didn't know better, I'd swear he was praying for my speedy recovery.

More like praying to go back in time and never have met me.

Yeah, who was I kidding. Jack wasn't the praying type.

"Hey," I said, and his head snapped up.

"How do you feel?" he asked. He hadn't moved toward me, his hands still in prayer position, but his gaze roamed over my face, down my body, and back up.

I took mental stock. Except for the scrubs shirt, I was still wearing my clothes from the night before, which I'd put on at Mark's this morning when I woke up. I felt grimy and lethargic. But no shakes, and my mind had cleared considerably.

"I still can't remember what happened," I said. "But I'm okay."

He nodded then sat back, pushing his legs out and grasping the chair arms with his hands. "Tell me what you do remember."

I told him everything I could, some more pieces coming together, but still nothing after making my bets at the Red Rock and sitting back down with the guys.

"Let's go farther back," he said. "Tell me about Mark. From the first day of group."

I did, not leaving anything out, even that moment we'd shared at my car the night we left Seb's apartment. Jack took it all in, watching me as I spoke, interrupting only to ask clarifying questions.

No emotion. No jealousy. Total cop mode.

But there was something in his eyes, just a spark, a tiny glint that made me know it wasn't just another homicide case to Jack.

And it wasn't just another dead body to me, either.

As I told Jack about Mark, it finally sank in that he was gone. As if uncovering his dead body hadn't been my first clue. "In some ways I knew him really well, you know?" I said, and Jack nodded. "In therapy, you kind of jump to the messy stuff. And we spent a lot of time together. Usually with Seb," I added, but didn't really need to. Still no judgment from Jack. Not that he had a right to any, but still. "But in some ways…I didn't know him at all."

I certainly didn't have any idea who would want him dead. And why'd they need to do it while I was passed out next to him.

Surely if I was to be framed for murdering Mark, there'd be a better way to do it than to drug me with something that most likely was being identified in a lab somewhere in the hospital right now.

"But I started feeling woozy at the Red Rock," I said, finishing my own thought, if not what I'd been talking about.

"Yeah?" Jack asked.

"So whatever had been slipped to me was either there, or at Distill just before."

Jack nodded. "Or, conceivably, at your house. We'll know once they determine what was in your system, then they can figure out how fast-acting it was."

"I didn't eat or drink anything at my place," I said, but he was already nodding, knowing my actions during that brief stay. "So it must have been one of the guys from group."

"Or Mark himself. If his plan was to get you into bed."

But Seb had been the one making a play last night, not Mark. I told that to Jack, and he filed it away with a small nod.

"Could have been anyone who came into contact with your drink," he added. "Waitstaff. Passersby. But yeah, looks like one of your crew wanted you out of the picture for the evening."

"So they could kill Mark? But why?"

A shrug from Jack, and he sat further back in his chair. He watched me until I got it. The two motives Jack once said were the root of most homicides.

Revenge or money.

But how could either of those apply to Mark and the therapy group?

I MUST HAVE DOZED AGAIN, because there were full-on shadows when I woke up. Jack was still in his chair, and I thought about how stiff he was going to be. He was still recuperating himself—he shouldn't have been sitting on a hard chair staring at me for most of the day. Let alone having all the thoughts that must have been running through his head as he watched me recover from being involved in yet another murder.

And it had been going so well. Hadn't it?

Had Mark been killed because we'd fallen off the wagon last night? Did our tumble precipitate what had happened later? Were the winning bet slips in my pocket as much of a murder weapon as the gun that had killed Mark?

"When can I get out of here?" I asked, startling Jack. He hadn't been sleeping, but I guessed he hadn't noticed that I'd woken up.

"Anytime," he said. "You got the all-clear an hour ago. Your system is pretty much cleaned out and back up to snuff." He nodded at the IV that was still dripping slowly into my system. "All they have to do is take that out, and you're all set." He leaned over and pushed a call button on the side of my bed.

"And I can just leave? I'm not under arrest, right?"

"Not under arrest. A cop is here with you—he's outside—and we're going to go answer questions if you're up to it. But no, not under arrest. Did you think you would be?"

I shrugged, feeling the sting of the IV needle in the back of my hand. "Who knows. So you're going to go with me for the questioning?"

He nodded. "They probably won't let me in the room. But yeah. We can call a lawyer, too, if you want."

I didn't want. I knew Jack would tell me to get one if he thought I should have one. He was a cop, yes, and a good one. But even though we weren't together, I knew he'd never let me walk into something I shouldn't.

He had my back.

"In fact," he said, "maybe we just head them off. Play offense instead of defense."

"Surely they're not letting you on this case," I said.

He snorted. A good, robust snort that had me smiling. Yeah, even in a hospital bed, with a friend of mine cold in the morgue, the sound of Jack's snort made me smile.

"On the case? No." He chuckled, and I was smiling as I nudged his knee with my foot.

"What?" I asked.

He looked at me with those deep brown eyes. A crinkle of amusement coming from them had me smiling. "On the case? Johanna, I'm a goddamned suspect."

Twenty-Nine

"ARE WE SUPPOSED TO BE HERE?" I ASKED JACK AS WE made our way down the hallway to Mark's apartment. He'd shown his badge to the cops outside and they'd let him pass, though they'd given me a stink eye and then one had grabbed his walkie-talkie. This was Jack playing offense.

"Yeah, sure," he said. "It's fine."

"What the fuck do you think you're doing coming here?" Peter Faxon said to us as he stepped out of Mark's doorway as we approached.

"Figured now that Anna's feeling better she should take a look around. Maybe something will jog her memory."

"And you just thought you'd be the one to bring her here? Trample all over a crime scene?"

Jack's brow furrowed. "I don't *trample*, Faxon. And I'm sure forensics has come and gone by now anyway."

"Hey, Jack, probably not a good move. We had planned to meet you at the station," Frank said, joining Faxon at the doorway. He looked like I felt—as if he'd been drugged the night before and woken up with a dead body beside him. A dead *friend* beside him.

Which now occurred to me. "Is he… Is Mark gone?"

Frank nodded while Faxon shot daggers at me. "Yeah. Coroner took the body a couple of hours ago. We're just about to wrap up." He took a quick glance at Faxon, then sighed and said, "Why don't you come in, Anna? Jack's right. Maybe something will come to you now."

Nothing did.

I walked around the apartment—with Faxon right on my ass—but couldn't remember coming back here with Mark last night. The bed was stripped and there was a bloodstain where Mark had been. I was glad Faxon was behind me, or I might have crumpled. No way was I going to let that guy see me lose it.

"Bed doesn't bring back memories?" Faxon said. I didn't take his bait and only shook my head. Mark's nightstand was cleared off; I was guessing they'd already taken his phone like they'd taken mine.

In the kitchen were two empty beer bottles in the sink, no glasses. I tried to remember if I'd used a glass when I'd been here before with Seb, but I couldn't. No remnants of food that we'd eaten.

In the living room, Mark's online poker setup was as I remembered it. A sea of black monitors with two expensive office chairs. "Were the chairs like this when you got here?" I asked Faxon and Frank as I walked closer to the computer monitors.

"Yes. Is that odd?" Frank asked.

I shrugged. "The other time I was here, one of the chairs was over here"—I pointed to the corner—"out of the way. Only one chair was pulled to the computers."

"So, maybe you sat here with him last night? What's with all the computers, anyway? Porn?" Faxon asked.

I shot him a glare over my shoulder. Amateur. "Online poker. Mark was a compulsive gambler. Online playing was his main vice."

"Do you think you played with him here last night?" Frank asked.

I knew Jack was behind us, hovering in the main part of the living room. I also knew he was listening to every word.

"No, I wouldn't have played online poker with him. I don't play online," I said. "I mean, I could have sat here while he played, I guess…"

"But you don't think so," Frank said.

I shook my head. "I don't think so. But who knows." I could almost feel the weight of the bet slips in my pocket. "I wasn't exactly in my normal state of mind."

"Yeah, let's go back over last night again," Frank said, pulling one of the two chairs out for me, and taking the other.

"Why don't we do that down at the station?" Faxon said.

"She's here now. The room is fresh in her mind," Frank said, taking out his phone and turning on the voice memo app.

"She's not answering anything more," Jack said, pushing past Faxon and coming to stand behind my chair, placing a hand on my shoulder.

"Come on, Jack. You're the one who brought her here. You'd know how this would play out," Frank said.

"It's okay," I said. "I told them what I knew this morning. Nothing else has changed. I can go over it again."

"And it's okay if I record it?" Frank said, but his question was more for Jack, I could tell.

He growled a little behind me, but I only nodded and once again told them everything I could remember from the night before.

"Okay, why don't you go home and we'll stop by your place tomorrow," Frank said a couple of hours later.

Not only had I repeated what I'd remembered, but I'd told them all about the other members of the group. I wished I could have texted and warned them all that the cops would be knocking on their door and asking questions, but the cops had my phone with their numbers in it. The only member of the group whose last name I knew was Monty.

Then it occurred to me that the others in the group could be in danger. "Will you let me know that they're all okay?" I asked. "No matter how late it is?"

Frank, Faxon, and Jack exchanged glances, and my dread ratcheted up a few notches. "Do you think Mark's death was related to the group somehow?"

More glances. Finally, a shrug from Frank. "Too soon to say anything right now. We've got a compulsive gambler with a bullet through his heart. Quick answer is a gambling debt paid and you were just caught in the wrong place at the wrong time."

"But that doesn't explain why Anna would be drugged," Jack said.

"If she *was* drugged," Faxon said. I wanted to spin the desk chair around and clip him in the shin, but Jack's hands tightened on the back, holding me in place.

"Blood tests will let us know that," Frank said, rising from his seat. Looking down at me, he added, "We'll be sure to let you know if any of your friends are not accounted for."

"Thank you," I said.

Jack stepped back and I rose from the chair, taking in the room one last time as I did. Something was off, and I didn't think it was just the chair placement.

"What is it?" both Jack and Frank asked me.

I shook my head. "It looks different somehow. But I'm not sure why." I counted the monitors. Same as before. Shiny and black, unadorned and expensive. The desk was clear like it had been before, with only a pencil on it. My eyes settled on a cup at one end, with a Monster can next to it. "Those weren't there before," I said, pointing to the trash. "There was nothing on the desk when I was here the other time."

"So you had beverages last night?" Frank said, moving toward the cans.

"Or he had them anytime in the weeks since you were here before?" Faxon said.

"Right. Of course."

Frank took his pen, stuck it in the Monster can, and lifted it. "Some left." The other container was a smoothie foam cup.

From one of the thousand smoothie places in Vegas. Just like the ones we usually had at group.

"I've never seen Mark drink a Monster," I said. I told them about our frequent smoothies during group.

"Forensics would have dusted them already. We'll make sure the contents are tested," Faxon said, waving toward an officer.

I nodded and walked out of the little gambling alcove, taking a look back as I did. Something still wasn't quite right, but my muddled mind wasn't clicking on it.

"We'll be in touch," Frank said as he led Jack and me to the doorway. "Get some sleep if you can."

"Thanks, Frank," Jack said, and the two men exchanged a handshake.

Faxon was at the door, too, and he looked Jack and me up and down, taking in Jack's hand, which had landed on my shoulder. "Different tune than you two were singing last night," Faxon said.

"Shut up, Faxon," Jack said. He turned me, and I walked down the hallway, my feet heavy, my body still feeling the aftereffects of whatever I'd been given last night.

God, no wonder JoJo's schemes usually went off so well. I couldn't imagine playing a basketball game today at college's highest level with how shitty I felt.

At least when JoJo slipped a guy something, she made sure he was safely tucked into his locked motel room.

Not lying next to somebody with a hole in their heart.

Still, as Jack drove us home in the Lexus SUV usually reserved for taking Ben out, I said a silent "sorry" to all the players I left feeling like I did today.

Again, without the dead body.

"That was probably our only shot at the crime scene," Jack said as he drove. "No way will they let me back in there."

"You're not really a suspect, are you?" I asked, studying his profile.

He sighed. "I'm guessing not. Still, they heard you and me

arguing last night, me yelling about who you were meeting—it didn't sound good, given today's context."

"Which is the wrong context."

"*We* know that."

"Still. Frank would know you're not a real suspect. They're not going to waste time on that."

"Lots of cops commit crimes," he said.

"Yeah, but you don't."

"How do you know?" He looked over at me and raised an eyebrow. "Seriously? How do you know I didn't follow you last night? Do a find your phone thing? Watch you leave the Red Rock with Mark. Follow you to his place. Wait until after you'd gone to bed and—"

"Oh, stop it. This is just wasting time."

He chuckled. "How can you be sure, Anna? A good detective suspects everyone."

"I'm sure."

"How?"

I turned toward him, hitching my knee up on the seat. "I know you didn't do it the same way you know I didn't kill Paulie. Or Vince."

"Or Danny," he added. "Or Lion LaGasse."

"Okay, okay. I get the point. You've had my back. I've got yours now. Can we skip to the part where we figure out what the hell is going on?"

He laughed, and for just a second I forgot about poor Mark, and my aching head, and whether there was a good reason that Mark was lying in a morgue and I wasn't. And I just relaxed at the sound of Jack's laugh and sank into the soft leather seat of the car.

"Yeah, we can skip to that part," he said.

"You mean you're going to let me help?"

He shrugged. "Well, it's not like they're going to keep me in the loop on this. I'm guessing they'll bump my physical, too, so they don't have to deal with me in any capacity on the force."

"So...you're stuck with me?"

"Or *you're* stuck with *me*," he said.

My headache started to ease.

Thirty

FOR THE SECOND MORNING IN A ROW, I WOKE UP NEXT to a man.

This time my clothes were on (sweats and a tee) and the man was alive (though sleeping like the dead). So, a better outcome than the previous morning.

I watched Jack doze, not sure when he'd crawled in with me. Lying above the covers, he was wearing track pants and a long-sleeved UNLV tee, his hair tousled and still a tiny bit damp where he'd been sleeping on it.

Lor and Ben had still been up when we got home from Mark's apartment, and we told them all about my previous night. Or, at least, what I remembered of it. Lor had fed us all, and I'd showered, thrown on the clothes I was now wearing, and barely made it to my bed before falling asleep. The effects of the day, the night before, or whatever had been slipped to me, I wasn't sure, finally took a huge toll.

Raymond had been out working a game for Carla, so I hadn't seen him yet, but I had no doubt Lor or Ben would fill him in this morning. Probably already had, since a quick glance beyond Jack at my clock said it was almost ten in the morning.

Thank goodness Sunday mornings we stayed in for brunch, or I would have missed breakfast with the boys.

And then I remembered my other set of boys was now one

man down, Mark, and a huge sadness came over me.

Sadness, and yet something else, too. Suspicion. Fear. And a nagging sense that perhaps he was the one who had drugged me, had some nefarious plan in mind when he did, but had been interrupted in those plans by someone. Someone with a silencer.

Had Mark's killer done me a solid?

Was his death gambling related and I'd just been in the wrong place at the wrong time?

"Come up with anything?" Jack said, startling me from my thoughts.

"Huh?"

We were on our sides, facing each other, and he reached out and touched my horseshoe pendant, which had slid down to my shoulder. He glided it across my skin back to the center of my clavicle and held it there in place, warming me. "You were obviously thinking about the murder. Come up with anything?"

"How do you know I wasn't thinking about how to kick you out of my bed?"

The corner of his mouth quirked up in a half-smile. "Were you?"

He always said I had a tell that only he could read. It must have been all over my face, because he barked out a laugh even though I hadn't even twitched.

"No, I don't have anything on Mark's murder," I said. "Just wondering if maybe it had been done to protect me?"

"Yeah, I wondered that, too. If one of the others had suspected Mark had drugged you and was up to no good, and followed you to his house."

"But why kill him? Punch him out. Break it up and get me out of there. A bullet through the heart seems a little extreme."

"And premeditated. Frank said at the apartment that no neighbors reported hearing a gunshot, and preliminary ballistics indicates a suppressor was used. Your average gun owner typically doesn't have one at the ready. Though they are legal to have in Nevada."

"Feels professional, you know?"

He nodded, his finger sliding the silver pendant in and out of the little notch in my collarbone.

"So then, what was Mark into, and who did he piss off?"

I tried to remember the times Mark shared in group, and while he, Seb, and I had been out. I relayed it to Jack, figuring Mark's death superseded the "anonymous" part of group therapy.

But there wasn't much to go on. In fact, most of the time Mark was prompting others to open up, sharing some of his own stuff, but seemingly more interested in what other people were saying.

"Is that normal?" Jack asked. "Isn't it all about talking through your own stuff? Wouldn't Monty have been the prompter for others?"

I shrugged and rolled to my back, causing Jack's hand to trail across my body. When we lost contact, he pulled his hand back and tucked it under his pillow.

"I guess. I mean, I found what the others were going through interesting. I asked questions, too."

"But you're curious by nature," he said, surprising me.

"Am I?" He nodded. I turned my head away from him and stared up at the ceiling. I guessed he was right, but I was dealing with my own gambling shit so often that I mostly thought of myself as completely self-absorbed, like I imagined most addicts or compulsive people tended to be.

But maybe Jack was right. I had found group therapy fascinating, and more because I liked hearing what other people were going through than because I had my own breakthroughs.

Was that empathy or Schadenfreude?

"Hannah darling, are you awake?" Ben called from the hallway.

"Yes, Ben," I answered. "You can come in. We're decent."

"I wouldn't go that far," Jack whispered, then swatted my hip as he rolled backward off the bed. He met Ben at the door, and father and son walked over to the sitting area and took the two chairs while I sat up in bed, tucking the covers around me even though I was completely covered.

Ben had a goofy smile upon seeing Jack in my room. I suspected he guessed/hoped Jack was in here and wanted to see for himself.

The fact that Ben might be shipping for Jack and me was a testament to how far we'd come since the day Jack was shot.

Even after I'd told him and Lor about my slip-up on Friday night, he'd only patted my hand and kissed me on the top of the head as he'd gone to bed.

"You okay?" Raymond said from the door. He'd probably heard Ben's walker in our hallway and known I was up. From the concerned look on his face, it was clear Lor or Ben had already filled him in.

"I'm good," I said. "Still don't remember what happened, but physically I'm fine."

"You were probably unconscious for most of it," Jack said. Raymond came in my room and sat on the foot of my bed, then leaned back and let his legs dangle off the side, forming an L with me, my feet by his shoulder.

"Once I was in bed, yeah, but how did I get from the Red Rock to Mark's apartment in the first place?" I sighed. The doctor had said some things might come back, but there was a good chance I'd lost the night permanently.

Maybe that was a good thing, seeing as how it ended.

"In one way, it's a good thing. You're probably not in danger from the killer thinking you'd be a witness. That's why you're alive now," Jack said.

I hadn't thought about that. Had a date-rape scheme inadvertently saved my life?

"Here's where you all are," Lor said, entering the now-filled bedroom. "Brunch is ready. Jimmy and Gus just got here and are dying to hear what happened."

Raymond rose from the bed, and Jack and Ben both lifted themselves from their chairs with subtle groans.

"Let's eat," Jack said.

I was surprised to realize that I was absolutely starving.

Thirty-One

MARK'S DEATH WAS IN THE PAPER. RAKOWSKI WAS HIS last name, which didn't seem to fit, but what did I know about last names?

In true Lorelei fashion, hours after telling her about the police taking my phone, she handed me a new one with my contacts (the ones she knew, anyway) and apps intact. Which was a good thing, because it blew up all day with texts and calls from Seb, Jordan, and Herb, all wondering if I was okay, if I'd been there, what I knew—all the questions I didn't have answers for.

Each one of them had been questioned by the cops, and they'd all told them the same thing: Mark had made a play for me at the Red Rock during the Cavaliers game and I'd decided to go home with him. They'd all watched us leave together before the game finished.

That was when I knew for sure I'd been drugged. No way would I have left a game I had that much money on if I'd been of sound mind.

Not that I was ever completely of sound mind when in a gambling frenzy.

Monty wondered if we should cancel group on Monday, but I suggested we still meet. A suggestion that everyone agreed with.

Jack went with me.

I introduced him to the group honestly, as someone I used to be involved with and a homicide detective who was currently on medical leave, but was helping me try to piece together what had happened.

Seb eyed him suspiciously, and Herb and Jordan were not much more welcoming, but once I told the group the last things I remembered, they jumped in to bring me up to speed.

"I went to use the bathroom, and when I came back, Mark was in my seat, next to you," Herb said, Seb and Jordan nodding. "I didn't really pay attention to what he was saying because… you know, the game." His voice was filled with shame. The same shame I vaguely remembered feeling that night before I blacked out.

Shame that seeped through when I thought about the winning bet slips that were now sitting in the cigar box on my desk. I hadn't wanted to go back to the Red Rock to cash them in, thinking maybe I'd still need to offer them up to the cops or something. I was somewhat surprised that I hadn't been searched at Mark's place and they'd been taken right then. Although Officer Fisher had patted me down, probably looking for the gun that killed Mark.

"Did you hear what Mark said to me? Or me to him?" I asked Seb.

He shook his head. "Not really. I heard tone, more than words. It was flirting, that's for sure. And it was mostly on his part. I never heard you answer much. Then I went to the bar."

"You stayed at the bar? With money on a game?" Jack asked. I would have asked the same thing, but I knew that Seb wouldn't have wanted to stay and listen to Mark and me flirting, though he probably wouldn't say that. Besides…

"From the bar you can still see the big screen. I was watching the game the whole time."

I nodded. Seb looked from Jack to me and added, "And I

met a woman at the bar, so I stuck around."

I guessed I should have felt a stab of something—embarrassment, jealousy, at the very least curiosity—but I didn't. I nodded again at Seb and said, "And you didn't come back to our seats in the book?"

"No. I could see you all, though. It wasn't too long after that when you left with Mark."

"Was she walking okay?" Jack asked. "Did it seem like Mark was guiding her, leading her?"

Seb looked down at the floor, thinking. Even though Jack was here and we were spending our meeting time rehashing Friday night, we'd all sat in our usual seats, Jack taking the one where Mark typically sat. That seemed wrong somehow, but it would have been silly to add a seventh chair and then have one sit empty.

"I don't recall anything feeling off as they walked out. He certainly wasn't carrying her out. But I wasn't watching their every move, either. By that time, I was hitting it off with the woman I'd met."

"And that's who you left with, that woman?" Jack said it less as a question and more of a foregone conclusion. It made me wonder if Jack had spoken to Frank since we'd left Mark's apartment Saturday afternoon.

He better not be holding out on me.

"Yeah. We ended up going back to my place. She was gone when I woke up."

"And you left with her when?" Jack asked.

"Eleven. The game had just ended," Seb said.

"That's when I left, too," Herb said. "Elaine said I got home at eleven thirty. The news was just ending. That's what she told the police when they came by yesterday."

"I left the same time Herb did," Jordan said. "Eric picked me up out front. Herb saw as he was walking across the lot back to Distill."

Herb nodded at Jordan, and the kid continued, "The cops questioned Eric and me yesterday, but we were home all night after he picked me up."

I didn't ask if our gambling rampage had translated to an online poker binge for Jordan, who hadn't seemed all that interested in betting on the basketball game.

We all looked to Monty, who hadn't been with us, but who had surely also been questioned. "Yeah, they came to me yesterday, too," he said. "I was at home all night Friday after I got home from here. I texted Lorelei a couple of times about the business stuff, but I was alone all night."

So, no alibi, but then, he hadn't been with us, so there was no way he would have known I'd gone home with Mark. Unless…

"They can see what tower you pinged when you texted Lorelei," Seb said. "To see if you were really in your apartment, or nearby."

Jack looked carefully at Seb. It wasn't a stretch; the cell tower was something I'd thought of right away, too. But was it a case of guilty minds thinking alike?

So it seemed like our little group was set with alibis—if Monty's texts were to be considered—for Friday night while I was lying next to a dead man.

Not that I'd really suspected anyone in the group of pulling the trigger. But would one of them have done it if they thought they were protecting me?

"What do you think?" Jack asked on the ride home after group.

It seemed odd to not go out for a drink afterward. But it would have been even weirder to go out without Mark.

"I'm not sure," I said. "Seems like everyone is accounted for. Nobody seemed crazy shocked that Mark had been killed, but they'd had a couple of days for it to sink in, so I suppose…"

"You don't seem crazy shocked either," he said.

I sighed, shifting the Porsche down for a yellow light. "I'm not sure anything shocks me anymore, you know?" From the corner of my eye I saw Jack nod then look out his window. "If you're at the point that you're working with Monty, chances are you've done some things in your life that might catch up with you."

Another nod. I started to shift to first when the light changed to green, but Jack put his hand over mine.

"Beyond the stuff we said to each other Friday night. About me waiting to see if your therapy stuck or whatever…"

"Yeah?" A car behind me honked, wanting me to go on the green, but I stayed where I was, Jack's hand still on mine on the gear shift.

"Without it being about us, or sounding condescending, I am so fucking relieved that the things in your life have not caught up to you the way Mark's did."

My throat tingled, but I wasn't sure if it was from fear, dread, or relief.

I knew I had a past out there that could show up on my doorstep at any time. Some of those people were already dead, but there were others that I'd wronged.

"Me too," I whispered.

He released my hand and I sped through the light, taking us home.

Thirty-Two

WE WENT INTO MY OFFICE WHEN WE GOT HOME. I could smell something amazing coming from the kitchen, and was grateful I'd be home for dinner this evening, as opposed to all the other times after group when I'd hung with Mark and Seb.

Ben was probably napping and Raymond wasn't in any of the common areas, if he was even home. Jack followed me to the office and sat on Lor's side of the desk while I went to my side, pulling out a blank yellow legal pad. Grabbing a pen, I held it poised over the paper and stared at Jack.

"Yes?" he said.

"I don't know how this works. I feel like we should be taking notes or something. Don't you always have one of those tiny pads on you?"

"I'm not on active duty," he said, a little smile playing on his face.

"You're amused by me."

"A little."

I scoffed and made a show of writing something down, but it was only the date and the list of everyone who was at group. Not exactly breaking news.

Putting a dash next to their names, I wrote down the whereabouts that they'd given to the police and repeated to Jack and me. All nice and neat in little columns, and yet it didn't feel right to me. Something was off with each of them.

"You know they were all lying, right?" Jack said.

I nodded. "How did you know?"

He didn't seem surprised that I'd come to the same conclusion. "How do you know when a poker player is bluffing?" he asked.

It wasn't a rhetorical question, so I tried to put into words something that was as innate to me as breathing.

"Body language for one. Inflection in their voices. Too much talking. Not enough talking. Staring me down. Not looking at me at all."

"Yeah, all of that," Jack said, and I wasn't sure if he was talking about poker or the past hour with my group.

"In the end, it comes down to instinct," I said. "Reading people…I don't know, it just comes naturally to me now."

"And to every good detective," Jack said.

"But sometimes I get no read at all. And sometimes I'm completely wrong."

"So is every good detective. Sometimes."

"I could never read you," I admitted. I thought he'd smile, or gloat, or at the very least quirk a damn eyebrow at me, but he didn't.

"You read me better than anyone ever has," he said quietly.

It might have been a compliment, but—disproving his exact words—I wasn't sure what Jack meant by it.

I held his gaze a moment longer than was comfortable—especially in this new, unknown space we found ourselves in. Looking back down at my paper, I wrote *Lying. Why?* in the margin across all five of the men's names.

"People lie because they don't want you to know what they really did," he said. "Even if it wasn't what you're suspecting them of."

"Like if each of the guys went off and gambled more or something?"

"Right, like that. Or people lie because they *did* do what you suspected them of."

"Okay. So, how do you cops do this? Means, motive, and opportunity, right?"

He shrugged. "Those are your basics, yeah. Sometimes the evidence points that all out right away and you're just connecting the lines between the three. Sometimes it's really obvious who did it, but there's no evidence so there are no lines to connect to who you know is the guilty party."

I watched him carefully as I asked, "After meeting them all, do you think one of them was involved?"

"Yes," he said without hesitation.

Shit. So did I.

"Which one?" I asked.

"That I don't know."

Shit. Neither did I.

"Okay. So what *do* we know as far as means, motive, and opportunity?"

"It's never as easy as Colonel Mustard in the billiard room with a lead pipe."

"I know. How do you usually start?"

He sighed, ran a hand across his face, and pulled his chair in tighter to the desk, a move I imagined he did all the time when at the office working on a real case.

Of course, Mark being dead *was* a real case; Jack just found himself partnered with me instead of Frank Botz.

I may have lacked Frank's experience—and collection of cartoon neckwear—but I made up for that with personal interest and determination.

Somebody had killed Mark either to protect me (thanks!) or to frame me (screw you!) or despite me being right next to him (again, screw you!) and I wanted to know why.

And who.

"How'd it go at group?" Lorelei asked, moving into the

office. Jack started to rise from her chair, but she waved him down and sat in one of the chairs along the side of the room, facing the desk. "Was it awful?"

"Not great," I said. "Seems like everyone was accounted for during Mark's murder."

"Except Monty," Jack said.

"Right."

An odd look came over Lorelei's face. "What?" both Jack and I said.

"Nothing. I mean, nothing that makes me think... Did you see the folder I left for you?" she asked, pointing to the side of my desk. Sitting next to my cigar box was a manila folder with a sticky note. *Monty Information. Read ASAP.*

I slid it over and placed it on top of my legal pad. "No, I didn't see it." I traced the sticky note with my hand, feeling the edges pull away from the folder as I did. Something started tingling at the back of my skull, but I couldn't place the feeling. Not a Hummer, but...something.

"Is that information about Monty?" Jack asked. "Where'd you get that?"

"The report came in from the due diligence we did on investing Jo's money in Monty's treatment center."

Jack looked confused, and I couldn't remember how much he knew about the work Lor and Monty had done, or my possible investment in his center.

"And did the person you hired find out something about him?"

"Yes," she said. "But I didn't put that in there. I just put his final report about financials. He advises against investing."

"Investing in the treatment center at all, or against investing with Monty?"

"With Monty."

Jack sat up in his seat. "Okay. If you have information—"

"Here's the thing," Lor said. "He's really helping Jo." She

looked from Jack back to me. "Right?"

I nodded. "Yes."

"Except for gambling Friday night and waking up with a dead body," Jack added.

"Except for that," I said, and he groaned. "You yourself said I was doing well, that you'd seen changes in me."

He reluctantly nodded, then looked at Lor to continue.

"So, I'm hesitant to show you anything that might color your opinion of him as your therapist," she said. "Especially now."

"Why especially now?" I asked.

"Because of the slip you had. You'll really want to dive back into therapy, and with someone who has been helping you." Both of them were staring at me. "Right?" Lor asked.

"Yes. Right," I said. Doing a quick emotional check-in, I realized that I meant it.

"So, I didn't put that info in there. Who cares about Monty's past if he's helping you now, right?"

"Right," I said again, but I wasn't quite so convinced. Yes, reformed addicts made the best counselors for the very reason that they'd been through everything themselves. But…

"Let's do this," Jack said. "You read the financial report. I'll look over the stuff the other guy found out about Monty. If I think it's something that might pertain to Rakowski's murder, we'll talk about it. Maybe have to hand it over to Frank. If it's just stuff that won't affect the case, but might affect your opinion of Monty as a therapist, I'll sit on it."

I thought about that. Could I live with not knowing what it was, now that I knew there was an "it"?

But every one of us in that room had an "it" in our past, or we wouldn't be in that room at all. I didn't want people knowing about JoJo, so why did I need to know about Monty's former life?

"Okay," I said. "If I need to know, let me know." Jack

nodded at that, and I turned to Lor. "If not, I'll just look over the financial stuff and we can make a decision."

"It's your decision," she said. "Your money."

"Based on what you know about him," I said, then tapped the folder, my finger hitting the edge of the sticky note, "and what it says in here, if it were *your* money, would you still invest it in Monty?"

"Yes," she said without hesitation. "Based on the difference I have seen in you? Yes."

"Even given Friday night?"

She hesitated this time, but finally gave a decisive nod.

"Okay. I'll take a look." She nodded again and left the room. "Dinner's in a hour," she said from down the hallway.

I took a deep breath and, as Jack watched me, slid the file folder more in front of me, the edge of the sticky note catching on my legal pad.

Oh, holy shit, how could I have missed it?

"The stickies," I said.

"What?" Jack asked.

"The sticky notes on Mark's computers. The ones that had the stats of all the people he plays against."

Jack looked down at the desk as his mind played back to Mark's apartment yesterday. "There were no sticky notes on his computers."

"Exactly," I said. "But there *were*."

Thirty-Three

I COULD TELL JACK STRUGGLED WITH CALLING FRANK about the sticky note information. The cop in him wanted to investigate it himself; the *competitive* cop in him wanted to break the case first. But ultimately, the *experienced* cop in him knew we had to bring in Frank.

Still, we waited until the next morning, enjoying the chili Lor made all of us, and then he and I went back to my office while Raymond and Ben watched the Yankees, who were playing on the West Coast.

He said there was no harm in waiting until morning, that he was just letting his former partner have a night off. But I thought he was hoping to have something more to go on than just my memories of Mark's stat-keeping operation.

"But that really points us to the online poker aspect," he said as we sat at the desk across from each other.

Lor and I had sat like this millions of times discussing household items, and even trying to solve other mysteries. But there was an ease to how Jack and I worked, playing things off each other, encouraging lines of thought, shooting down others. It felt good, natural.

"So, if it was all about online poker, then me being there was just a coincidence after all?"

"Or you were used as a diversion. He saw you were with

Mark when he came home and knew it'd be easier to get to Mark with someone else in the apartment? Mark wouldn't necessarily be spooked by a sound in the bedroom."

"But I started feeling the effects of the drug in the Red Rock."

Yeah, there was that, which we always came back to, no matter what scenario we spun.

"Maybe they're not connected," Jack said. "You being drugged and Mark being killed."

"That's quite a coincidence," I said. He got it. He was the one who said that there were too many coincidences in my life, that the way I lived brought some of it on. Okay, most of it. Yeah, probably all of it.

"Yeah, I know," he said, then scrubbed his hand across his face.

I was exhausted, and I hadn't been recuperating from a near fatal gunshot wound. I could only imagine what the past two days had done to Jack.

"Let's pick it up again tomorrow," I said, and he quickly nodded, confirming my suspicions about how wiped out he must be.

"I'll call Frank while you're at breakfast with the boys," he said.

"Don't go over anything until I get back."

"We won't," he said, rising from his seat. At the doorway he turned. "You coming?"

"In a minute. I want to read over the financials on the treatment center for Lor, so she can move on it."

"Or kill it?"

I nodded. "Right."

He stood looking at me. "Okay. Night."

"Night," I said, but he still didn't move.

It would have been easy to just get up from the desk, put off the report until tomorrow, move past Jack, while taking his hand

and leading him to my wing of the house.

But I didn't.

Instead I opened up the folder and began to read Lor's report.

I wasn't exactly sure when Jack left the office doorway. I never heard him move.

"ONLINE POKER," Jimmy said at breakfast the next morning. "Nothing but bullshit."

"It's a big business," I said. I'd brought the three remaining members of the Corporation up to speed on what was happening with my other group of boys. Their disgust was evident when I revealed I thought online poker was a key part of the case.

Old school, my boys.

In their day, it was shovels in trunks and bodies in the desert for gambling-related crimes. Not IP addresses and screen names.

The end result was looking to be the same, though—a dead body.

"I'm so glad you never got involved with that nonsense, Hannah darling," Ben said, patting my hand.

"Me too," I admitted. Thinking of Mark's body lying next to me while I slept off some kind of drug, I added, "Really glad."

FRANK AND FAXON arrived just behind Ben and me coming home from breakfast, and I mentally preened that Jack had indeed waited to make sure I'd be home.

He was seeing me as an equal on this. Giving me a professional courtesy. That was almost as much of a turn-on as those beautiful brown eyes of his.

Once all four of us were seated at the dining room table

with coffees in front of us, I was about to launch into the story of the sticky notes when I felt Jack's foot press against my leg.

Probably not a come-on. I kept quiet.

"We've got something that might be useful," Jack said.

"What's that?" Faxon said with a bit of derision. He hated being here, I could tell. Jack and I were the last two people he wanted to play quid pro quo with.

"Not yet," Jack said. That was all he said. And if the way he sat back in his seat and placed his hands on the table were any indication, that was all he was *going* to say.

Faxon got frustrated, scoffing, "This is bullshit," not quite under his breath and starting to push back his chair.

"Mark Rakowski was not his real name," Frank said, causing me to sit up and Faxon to stay in his seat and turn a disbelieving eye toward his partner.

Frank ignored Faxon and went on, "His real name was Mark Fitzpatrick." He waited for any reaction from Jack or me, but there wasn't any. I never knew Mark's last name at all, not to mention a fake one. "He was an FBI agent. Cybercrimes division. Working on a RICO case involving online poker."

Okay, that got a reaction from me, but being a professional poker player, I kept it all inside.

"I see that comes as a surprise to you," Frank said to me.

Okay, maybe I didn't keep it all inside. I also lost at poker from time to time.

"That is a surprise, yes," I said. My mind went back yet again to all the things Mark had said during group and with Seb and me. And it *really* went back to the time he and I almost kissed in Seb's parking lot.

Was I the one he was investigating? Or just a possible perk of the case?

"You said he was investigating online poker?" I said, my heart beating a little faster as I thought about other things Mark could have been investigating.

My mind raced furiously, trying to remember if Raymond Joseph's name had ever come up during any conversation. Or college basketball?

Or point-shaving schemes done to pay off gambling debts?

"Yes. Online poker. Specifically, one site and the suspicion that it was rigged, not only by the site itself, but also by players."

"That brought him to Las Vegas? But you can play those things anywhere," I said.

"This particular site has ties to the Las Vegas area. As do the IP addresses of the players that were suspected of collusion to defraud. Though they took great pains to hide their whereabouts with redirects and whatever all that tech stuff entails."

Collusion to defraud. Gaming the system, in gambler's terms.

Relief that Mark hadn't been investigating JoJo was pushed aside by the realization that he was in group for part of his case.

"So he thought one of the guys in the group was…the colluder?" I asked.

Frank and Faxon exchanged looks, then Frank sighed while Faxon took a drink from his coffee mug. Today Frank had on a Homer Simpson tie, one I hadn't seen before.

"We haven't gotten good cooperation from the FBI as of yet, but that is the premise we're operating under," Frank said.

Faxon rolled his eyes. "They're being complete dicks about it," he added.

Jack shrugged, and the three of them shared long-suffering "whatta ya gonna do about it" looks.

"So Mark was investigating this poker site, found the identity of a player or players who seemed suspicious, and got into a therapy group with them?" I asked.

"You guys open up a lot at those things, right? Tell each other gambling secrets and stuff?" Frank asked.

"Would that even be legal? Wouldn't that be entrapment or something? Inadmissible?"

Jack leaned back in his seat. "He could have just been getting information on how it worked. Gotten to know the players. I think the sticky notes prove that."

"But Seb had notes like that, too," I said. "And so did Jordan—some, anyway. And not as many as Mark. It sounded like all the online players do that, keep stats on players they frequently face online."

They asked about the different poker setups of the apartments I'd been to of the guys in group. I told them what I'd observed—that both Seb and Jordan had setups, obviously had (or still) played a lot of online poker, and were stat keepers of other players. Also that I hadn't seen a computer at Herb's place, but hadn't gone beyond the small living room and kitchen area, so wasn't sure.

I told them about conversations we had, in and out of group, about online playing, but admitted there weren't many, and those we did have, I tended to tune out, as I had never been an online player.

We then went over the alibis each of the guys had given Jack and me the day before at group. Frank and Faxon confirmed that surveillance footage from the Red Rock parking lot showed that Eric indeed picked up Jordan as Herb was also leaving. The various cameras tracked Herb's progress across the huge lot and across Charleston, where he would go to Distill to retrieve his car.

What they couldn't find any trace of was the woman Seb supposedly went home with. Herb and Jordan confirmed seeing Seb at the bar with a woman, but left before they did. No cameras tracked them leaving, but Seb had said they'd left out the door to the back lots by the theaters and there were no cameras there.

"So either Seb was lying about leaving with that woman or… What?" I asked.

"We didn't find any footage of him leaving alone through any other door either, so we tend to believe he exited the building where he claimed to. It's just whether he was alone or not. We have not been able to locate the woman," Frank said.

Jack was watching me. "What are you thinking?"

I was thinking about how fascinated Seb was with the stickies at Mark's place. And how Mark had asked Seb if he was one of the players Mark was tracking. If he was involved in some online scam, did Seb know right then that Mark was a danger to him?

Did a plan hatch that very night?

"I think I need to talk to Seb."

Faxon was shaking his head already, and Jack looked a little pissed off. But Frank proved to be the calm, cool cop of the group when he said, "Would you be willing to wear a wire when you do that?"

Thirty-Four

I PARKED MY PORSCHE NEXT TO SEB'S CAR IN THE parking lot of the municipal park on Desert Inn, not too far from my subdivision. It was halfway between my home and Seb's, and our agreed-upon meeting place.

I saw him sitting on top of a picnic table not far from the parking lot, his feet placed firmly on the bench seat of the table.

I took my keys from the ignition, tapped my horseshoe pendant three times for luck, and whispered while trying not to move my lips in case Seb could see, "Okay, it's showtime." I knew Jack was listening; that was part of the deal he'd made with Frank and Faxon—that he be allowed in what I guessed was a police van parked nearby.

Taking only my phone and keys, I left my car and walked down the pathway toward the cluster of picnic tables. It was a Tuesday afternoon in late June and school was out, so there were bunches of kids playing, but none of them were at the tables. Instead they were running on the soccer fields and playing on the swing sets. There were a few adults on the sidelines of both the fields and the playground equipment, half watching their charges, half eyeing their phones.

"Sorry I'm late," I said to Seb as I neared the table. In fact, it had been Jack's idea that I show up a few minutes late so Seb could see me pull in alone. Why give him any reason to question why I texted him to meet me and talk?

As if our friend's death wouldn't be reason enough.

Though we had decided to continue with group, Monty had put the kibosh to our Tuesday/Thursday yoga sessions. It would have been right now, actually, and a sadness crept over me, thinking that Seb and I should be making jokes with Mark while trying to hold warrior pose.

"No worries," Seb said. "I just got here myself." From behind him he pulled out two smoothies, handing one to me. "Watch out for brain freeze," he said with a small smile.

"I'm getting better at it," I said, then I took a small drag from the straw and joined him on the top of the table. "Thanks for coming."

"Of course," he replied. "Not like I have somewhere to be."

"I have to say, I actually miss yoga," I said.

He chuckled. "Me too. Shocked as hell, but I do."

"But after Friday night, maybe it's time to reevaluate if any of it's working."

He nodded, took a sip of his smoothie, then sighed, the sound long and taking down his shoulders. "I've been thinking the same thing. But I think it was working. Or at least helping. I hadn't played poker in weeks. Hadn't placed a bet for longer than that."

"Me neither," I said. "But it was quite a slip-up."

"I'll say."

I knew how much money I'd bet on the Cavaliers, but I was so caught up in my Hummer haze, I hadn't paid attention to how much the others had bet, or on whom or what. For all I knew, I might have been the only one betting big money. And the only winner. It wasn't really good gambling etiquette to ask others how much and whom they bet on. And I was nothing if not someone who followed good gambling etiquette.

I'd learned from the best.

"So, besides slipping up, did you take a beating?" I asked.

Not great etiquette either, even though it was a vague enough question and quite a bit of time after the game, but I started thinking that perhaps Seb slipping up on Friday was the impetus for Mark's murder somehow. Maybe the stickies and online poker were just a by-product?

"No, it wasn't that. I actually won a little that night. It was just...another kind of slip-up?"

I looked at him, drawing a blank.

"The woman I hooked up with," he said.

"Oh," I said, still not really getting it. Was the woman a pro? Married? Was Seb secretly married or in a relationship?

"Besides GREET, I've also been doing SLAA."

"What's slah?"

"S-L-A-A. Sex and Love Addicts Anonymous."

"Oh," I said, failing to hide my surprise. I knew I would need my poker face for this meeting, but I hadn't seen that one coming.

I leaned back, needing to take a broader look at him, as if seeing a bigger vision would allow me to see something so deeply personal. Poker player me knew better, but it was still an instinct move.

"It doesn't show or anything," he said, laughing.

I shook my head, embarrassed. "Yeah, I know. Sorry. I'm just surprised."

"I don't look the part? You of all people should know—"

"It's not that. I do know that you can't judge an addiction by its cover. I'm surprised that you hadn't mentioned it before, that's all." He shrugged, and I nudged his foot with mine. "I mean, we all talked about our shit. Why didn't that come up?"

Another shrug, another nudge from me, and then he opened up. "I don't know. It just seemed like it was easier to compartmentalize it all. Talk gambling with you and Mark. And at group. Do the SLAA thing at meetings with them."

"You're spending a lot of time in meetings, then."

A small nod, then he took a slurp from his near-empty cup. It reminded me about mine, and I took a small sip. He'd gotten me a chia banana boost with peanut butter—the kind I'd come to always choose when he'd bring a variety. I was oddly touched that he'd remembered my smoothie.

"Yeah, that's why I'm just doing odd driving jobs right now. It allows me to have a flexible schedule for meetings. I do SLAA in the mornings."

So, it wasn't that he couldn't hold a job because of gambling. Or maybe it was both.

"Anyway, that hookup Friday was the first time I'd had random sex in a while."

"Oh," I said, finally getting it. It was a double slip for him on Friday night.

Triple if you counted murder.

But the conviction that I'd had this morning when telling Frank and Faxon about Seb being so interested in Mark's online setup, and the stickies containing stats, started to ebb. Maybe Seb had been edgy yesterday at the meeting because of the height of the wagon from which he'd fallen.

I felt shitty, and I'd only gambled.

"The thing with SLAA is you're trying to walk the fine line of finding a healthy, non-obsessive relationship—if that's what you want. And to not have random hookups, thinking that you'll find love that way."

"I see," I said, though I didn't really. I was still trying to wrap my brain around Hummers and JoJos and how emotions played into it all, and trying to control your emotions, and yoga, for God's sake. Throw in love and sex and I'd be a basket case.

Though living with Jack while we were broken up was no picnic either.

"Yeah, so. I was feeling pretty crappy…after. With her."

"I can imagine," I said, meaning it. I knew how much shame and regret I'd felt when I woke up on Saturday morning.

And that was before I saw the bullet hole in Mark's chest.

"I didn't even get her name. Didn't want to. And we went to my place, not hers."

I was hoping he wasn't telling me this as a prelude to other things they did that night. I didn't want to hear it. Well, not *all* of it.

"Uh-huh," I said. He was looking at me as if what he said meant something. But I wasn't sure what.

A sigh from him. He tossed his empty cup into the trash can a few feet away.

"The thing is, because I don't know her name, where she lives, or didn't take her number, she can't corroborate that I spent the night with her."

"Ohhhh," I said. "Got it."

He nodded, and I realized we were finally getting to what I'd called him here for—to talk about Mark's murder. And he'd been the one to lead us there. Either I was subversively brilliant at this wire-wearing, question-leading stuff, or I sucked.

I'd like to think brilliant, but I was pretty sure it was the latter.

"Yeah, so my revenge fuck might end up costing me big time."

"Who was it a revenge fuck against?" I asked. As I said it, I started feeling like I knew the answer. His sad look and inability to meet my eyes told me I was right. "Oh, Seb," I said. I wanted to touch his arm, but didn't. "I don't know what to say."

He shook his head and turned it toward the soccer fields where the kids were running and laughing. "It doesn't matter."

"It matters to me," I said.

He turned back, his gaze intense and full of emotion. "Why did you go home with Mark? Just tell me that. I hate that I'm asking, but I have to know. Why him and not me? I know it wasn't because he has money—you've got more than him and me put together."

"I don't know why I went home with him," I said.

He scoffed. "Come on, Anna. I'm being brutally honest with you here. Do the same with me. It would help me to understand."

"No, I mean, I *really* don't know why. I can't remember any of it after sitting back down at the Red Rock."

"Seriously? I assumed that's just what you told the cops."

"It's true. Somebody slipped me something. I have no memories of leaving with Mark. Or you sitting at the bar with a woman. Nothing."

A bark of laughter from him. "Jesus. This is so fucked up."

"Yeah, it is. And let's not forget our friend is dead."

"*I* haven't forgotten." Something in his tone made me stop my next sentence. I'd been about to ask if he knew that Mark was FBI. Jack and Frank had coached me to ask it when it would surprise Seb, when he wouldn't see it coming. That way, they said, his reaction would be pure, that I would be able to tell if Seb was really surprised to learn Mark's real identity.

But I didn't ask it. Some instinct told me not to. That Seb didn't know about Mark, and it might be information better kept quiet. For now.

There was also something in the way he looked at me—a little revulsion, a little fear. It wasn't all just because I went home with Mark and not him.

"You think I killed him," I said. He kept his gaze steady on mine, not looking away, not denying my claim. "I didn't."

"So you *do* remember what happened once you got to Mark's? Just not how you got there?"

"No. I don't remember any of it. From sitting down after placing my bet until I woke up the next morning."

"In Mark's bed."

"With him dead beside me."

"Naked, from what I heard."

"How'd you know that?"

He shrugged. "Cops talk. They interrogated me for hours on Sunday."

I made a mental note to ream out Faxon, as I was sure it was he who gave that little detail to Seb.

Unless Seb himself saw me naked and passed out in Mark's bed.

But I was becoming more and more convinced that it hadn't been Seb in Mark's apartment that night. At least, it wasn't him who pulled the trigger. I still wasn't sure how the missing stickies played into the murder—if they even did. But my gut was screaming that Seb was innocent of Mark's shooting.

Besides, it was pretty obvious that Seb thought I did it.

"I don't remember the night. But I know I didn't kill Mark," I said. "I don't own a gun. I didn't have residue on my person. I…I…" That was about it, really. And two pieces of information that could easily be explained away.

"Okay," Seb said. I wasn't sure if it was an okay of belief or placation, but I nodded and took another sip of my smoothie.

I looked at the cup in my hand. Probably not a smart idea to take a drink from anyone in the group. That thought made me sad—to not be able to trust the guys that I'd been sharing my secrets with. That, almost as much as Mark's death, led me to believe that I'd probably start working one on one with Monty again.

Our group had splintered beyond repair.

"I gotta go," I said, scooting to the edge of the table and dropping my legs over the side. Though I couldn't possibly, I felt like I could hear Frank and Faxon through the wire screaming that I should stay. That I hadn't really gotten any information from Seb. Hadn't asked about the stickies, or mentioned Mark being FBI. Pretty much failed across the board.

But I knew I hadn't. I knew Seb wasn't involved as surely as I knew that LeBron was going to kill it last Friday night.

I was eighty-six thousand dollars richer because of that

instinct.

As I walked away from Seb, I tried not to think about all the bets I lost in my life using that same instinct.

Seb continued to sit on the table, watching me while I got in my Porsche. I took a deep breath and tried to do an emotional check-in.

I was surprised to feel a Hummer.

Thirty-Five

"THAT'S BECAUSE YOU'RE GOOD AT THIS," JACK SAID later when I told him about the feeling I had after meeting with Seb.

"But to have the same feeling I get when I gamble?"

He shrugged. "Explain it to me."

I took a deep breath. Jack and I had talked about our demons before, but I'd never really been able to liken it to anything else—at least not anything I thought he'd relate to. But this?

"When you're working a case, and you *know* your gut is right? Either someone is lying and you know it, or they're telling the truth?" He nodded. "Like, even if you can't prove it, you know they are or aren't the perp?" He smiled at my attempt at cop lingo. "Whatever. You know what I mean, right?"

He nodded. "I do."

"Well, that's how I feel when I make a bet. That I *know* some team is going to cover, even though I have no reason to logically think it."

He watched me as I struggled to put into words what I felt when talking with Seb. "It was like that today. A rush of epic proportions. Part thrill of the chase, part fight or flight, and part sheer gut."

We were back at my house. Frank and Faxon were not quite

as understanding as Jack when I met them back at the agreed-upon coffee shop near the park and told them that I'd called an audible with Seb when I felt that he hadn't been involved. Faxon had mumbled some words about me that almost had Jack going over the table for him, but I grabbed on to his jacket at the last minute. I had to admit, I almost let him go, but didn't want him to reinjure himself. Not over that ass Faxon.

They tried to talk me into having another run at him, and I put them off, saying I'd try again after group session the next day if I felt like I had a chance.

I didn't go over the fact that Seb suspected me. They'd heard the conversation. No need to refresh that thought process.

Frank did tell me when we were putting the wire in place that the residue testing on my hands came back negative. Faxon mentioned that I had washed my hands when I'd gone to the bathroom upon waking up, but Frank gave him a "shut up" look.

Faxon wanted to believe I was involved. Frank wanted to solve the case. Big difference in how the two cops operated.

Now Jack and I sat in the sitting area of his bedroom. When we got home, it was obvious that the activity of the past three days was probably more than Jack should be doing, though he certainly never complained. Still, I led the way to his room, plunked down in one of the chairs, and motioned for him to lie down on the bed. He snorted, ignored my suggestion, and sat in the chair opposite me. He did deign to put his feet up on the ottoman, which I considered a moral victory.

"The thing is," he said, "you can do your research on teams, you can have a hunch on who's going to win, but the point spread the odds makers set basically makes the game an even playing field, right?"

"Yes," I said.

"So, how can you have the feeling that you know someone's going to cover? At that point it's a fifty/fifty proposition."

I shrugged, sinking deeper into the chair, raising my feet to share the ottoman with him. "You just feel it."

"And that's what you call a…what was it?"

"A Hummer."

"Right."

"But not just before a bet. After, too. When you're holding the bet slips." I remembered the rush that enveloped me Friday night at the Red Rock, feeling the weight of the small slips of paper in my fingers, the heft of them in my pants pocket. "And when you're watching the game…it just flows through you." I was pissed at whoever slipped me something Friday night, for obvious reasons, but even more so because they robbed me of the continued Hummer while the game was on.

I didn't linger on the messed-up thought that I was nearly as pissed that I missed a bit of my high as I maybe was waking up with a murdered friend beside me.

"Even if you're losing?"

I nodded. "Sometimes even more."

"But here's the thing," he said. "I'd respect your choice of bets, would know that you did your research, but I wouldn't necessarily put my own money on a bet you made simply because you had a Hummer about it."

"Sure. Of course. Totally understandable."

He took his feet from the ottoman and leaned forward, placing his elbows on his knees, hands dangling between his legs. "But Johanna, I *would* put money on the fact that you're right about Sebastian. On *those* instincts. *That* Hummer."

It was like he told me I was the most beautiful woman he'd ever seen. It felt that good.

Better. Because I knew Jack's priorities.

"So where does that leave us?" I asked.

He sat back in the seat, letting out a long sigh and rubbing a hand across his face. "I won't go back to group with you tomorrow. It might not have been a good move yesterday, but we wanted to let them know somebody had your back. That you weren't just a..."

"Degenerate gambler?"

He waved a hand, whether encompassing or dismissing my words I wasn't sure. "Whatever. That you're not alone."

That felt good, too, but I didn't fool myself into thinking Jack meant more than just the case or not wanting his father's good friend to go to prison for a murder she didn't commit.

Okay, I let myself think that it was a *little* more than just that.

"Should I wear a wire tomorrow? To group?" I didn't like the idea; it felt really wrong to go into what I felt was a sacred place while recording.

"No," he said, and I relaxed. "Just use your instincts, like you did this afternoon."

"Okay."

"But if it feels like you can do it naturally, feed them the information that Mark was FBI. Watch the reactions."

"And if they ask how I know?"

He laid a hand on his chest. "Privileged information. Pillow talk."

I scoffed. I wasn't getting much pillow action with Jack lately. Like, for a while now. Which, coupled with whatever was in my system, might have been the reason I'd said yes when Mark made his pitch. If only I'd been drugged sooner in the evening, I might have said yes to Seb back at Distill.

And maybe Mark would still be alive.

Or maybe not.

We sat in silence, and it was nice. Comfortable. "So," I said after a few minutes, "do *you* get that feeling I described when you're working a case?"

"I have the instincts, yeah."

"But you've honed those over the years."

"So have you," he said. "You just honed yours staring across a poker table instead of an interrogation table."

He wasn't wrong. "What about the rush? The Hummer?" I asked.

It seemed like he wasn't going to answer me, but then he shifted in his seat, like he needed to be more comfortable—or more on edge—to do his answer justice.

"No, not a rush. A...dread. A deep, sinking feeling, a black fog."

He'd told me once that he drank to forget, to feel numb. At the same time, I told him I gambled to feel alive.

"That makes sense, seeing as your cases are all homicides."

"The feelings probably are a little similar—consuming, addictive. But it never feels good to me."

"Even when you solve the case?"

He shook his head. "It feels lighter then. Like the black fog is lifting. But no, it never feels *good*."

Thus the bourbon, I thought, but didn't say.

"Thus the bourbon," he said. "But lately, I've been thinking of a change."

"Getting shot could do that."

"It wasn't that. Or it wasn't *just* that," he said.

"No?"

"No. It was Casey's visit."

"It was a good visit. Or seemed to be." He didn't mention me bailing on the first night of his son's visit, and I certainly wasn't going to remind him.

Not that Jack would forget.

"It just felt really good. Lighter than I'd felt in years, being with him."

"That's nice," I said.

He nodded. "I'm sure a part of it was not drinking since being shot. Whatever withdrawal I went through, I was unconscious for."

"A nice perk."

"Very nice. No hangovers, no physical yearnings. And then

a great time with my kid. And my father."

He didn't add in the rest of our little family, but I could tell by the pointed look he gave me that I was included in his summary.

"And I started thinking… Maybe I don't need to bring murder home every night. Maybe there's something else."

His thoughts mirrored the ones I'd been having lately. If not poker and gambling, then what? I waited for him to expound, to mention any alternative livelihoods he might be thinking of, but he didn't.

"Speaking of bourbon, I kind of feel like I cheated on you Friday night," he said. "When you came in and I was drinking—after you'd been at group therapy—I felt like you caught me in bed with someone."

"Thus the bit of attitude."

"Though it seemed there was plenty of attitude to go around."

I sighed. "Well, if you felt you cheated on me by drinking," I said, "and, of course, we're not *together* to be cheating on each other anyway." I waited for him to make some comment on that, but he just nodded for me to go on. "If that was cheating, I certainly did my own by gambling later that night."

I could have mentioned ending up in bed with Mark, but I decided not to count that. I'd said no to Seb earlier that night. Only when I'd been impaired did I succumb.

Again, not that I really would be cheating on Jack. He was the one who ended things, after all.

"Whatever," he said. "I felt shitty about it after you left."

"You only felt shitty about drinking because I walked in?" No judgment in my voice (like I had any right to judge), only curiosity.

"No," he said. "No."

"I'd like to say let's just write that night off. Clean slate, new days, all of that."

"Except for a murder investigation," he said.

"Except for that."

We smiled at each other, and I felt like a cog had slid into place in a machine that I hadn't realized wasn't quite working.

"Feels kind of good, being on the same side," he said.

I thought about how the Lion LaGasse case—and my involvement with it—had sidelined Jack. And Vince's death before that, and how I'd stepped on Jack and Frank's toes while they worked with Carla. But before that, we had been good partners. In the sense that Jack was the cop and I was sticking my nose in every way I could.

"Kind of like Chicago," I said. "When we went to see Raymond."

"And you *won* him," he said, and I laughed.

"Only because you stacked the deck."

He put his feet back on the ottoman, inches from mine, but not touching. "I did. But who knows, you might have won anyway."

He watched me, and I knew he was thinking the same thing I was—how the night before that had played out in our Chicago hotel room. I had put on one of my JoJo tops under a tee shirt, and when I'd revealed it to Jack, we couldn't make it to the bed fast enough. We'd been apart before that—but made up for lost time that night.

"It was a good trip," he said.

"Yeah," I said, "having Raymond around to help with Ben, and then you, has been great."

He laughed, a loud, gruff sound, and I smiled at him.

"Yeah, *that's* the reason," he said.

We sat quietly. I even closed my eyes for a while, debating if I should lead Jack to bed like I'd led him to his room.

Why not? It didn't have to mean anything. Not that we were back together. Just a night of being close again.

I opened my eyes, and Jack had his closed. As I was about

to nudge his feet, he let out a soft snore. Getting up quietly, I pulled a throw from the back of my chair and draped it over Jack, half of me wishing he'd wake up.

Okay, ninety percent of me.

But he slept on, and I left his room, turning out the light and letting Jack sleep after a big day of sleuthing.

Thirty-Six

"No cop boyfriend today?" Herb said Wednesday afternoon at group.

"He's not my boyfriend," I said. Herb grunted and turned away from me. "Not a cop right now, either," I added. And from what Jack had said the night before, possibly not again. Though I suspected that might have been a momentary feeling for him. I just couldn't see Jack giving it up.

But maybe he had better self-preservation skills than I did.

"Not cool," Jordan said. "Bringing him here on Monday."

Seb, I noticed, said nothing, nor did Monty.

In fact, Monty had been avoiding making eye contact with me before today's meeting, as well as on Monday.

My instincts said something was up, but I was guessing it had more to do with Lor getting all the investment stuff to a breaking point rather than Mark's murder.

It might be an instinct I should ignore—it could be deadly to write Monty off as just being concerned about the treatment center. After all, he was the only one of us who didn't have a solid alibi for when Mark was killed.

Well, and also me. My alibi was that I was lying right next to him.

Probably wouldn't look good on a witness stand.

I still hadn't looked through the final report Lor had

prepared for me. Part of me didn't want to deal with it while Mark's murder was at the forefront of my thoughts.

The other part of me was just procrastinating on making a decision.

I wanted to help Monty out, and I wanted to help others. But I didn't want to be a sucker, either. If I was just going to throw away money on a bad investment, I might as well head to the nearest book room and plunk it all down on the Brewers to win the World Series. It'd likely be the same outcome.

"I would think we'd want to help in any way we could," I said. "For Mark."

"You mean *you'd* like to help. So that you're not charged," Herb said. He was being really pissy today, and I wondered if there wasn't more to his mood.

And then I wondered if Elaine would lie for him, saying that he was home by eleven thirty Friday night and didn't leave again until the next day?

She'd stuck with him as he'd lost their life savings, their home, moving her to that tiny apartment, her having to continue working when she should be retired. What would be the breaking point for Elaine? Being an alibi for a murder?

"Okay, okay, this isn't getting us anywhere," Monty said. Finally, he looked directly at me. He took a deep breath, then addressed the rest of the guys. "Anna asked me if Jack could join us, and I said yes. *I* thought it was a good idea. But we're back to normal today."

All of our eyes went to where Mark typically sat, though Monty had removed that chair and made the circle a little tighter so his absence wouldn't be so obvious. "Okay, not *normal*, obviously," Monty said, noticing our gazes. "But we need to move on. Mourn Mark, of course, but your emotions, and how to harness them, are what's important now. So, how is everyone feeling?"

It was quiet, the mood odd. How could it not be?

"Shaky," Jordan finally said.

"Okay, let's talk about that. Shaky in that you feel you want to gamble?" Monty asked.

"I *always* want to gamble," Jordan said, and we all nodded with him. "But yeah, shaky in that I don't feel strong enough not to right now."

"Because of Mark? Because you've seen what an end result of gambling could be?"

Herb, Seb, and I shared a glance. We'd all been around a lot longer than Jordan, and I was guessing we'd all seen some pretty bad stuff. Hell, I'd experienced the bad stuff myself.

My left foot still ached when it rained from my introduction to gambling debt.

"You're assuming Mark's death was gambling related," Herb said.

"You're right, I am," Monty said. "And it might not be. But as we sit here, do any of you think that it might *not* be gambling related?"

More glances around the tight circle. No hands came up. We knew. Even Jordan, new to this world as he was.

You learned quick in Vegas.

We talked some more about the edge we all kind of felt like we were on, raw and battered from our slip-ups Friday and Mark's death. Some deep breathing exercises were done, as well as our emotional check-ins. All too soon, the meeting was drawing to an end and I still hadn't brought up that Mark was FBI and investigating online poker crimes.

"Okay, so before Friday I'd like you to all journal some thoughts about what Mark's death means to you. Not about Mark personally, but what the death of someone you've spent time with, most likely because of gambling… How does that make you feel? Really expound on what we talked about today. So, we'll see you all—"

"Actually," I interrupted, and all eyes came to me. "I really feel like I should share something with you all."

There were curious and outright horrified looks, and I realized that, to a one, all of the men in my group thought I was about to confess to killing Mark. Or maybe that was what I projected onto them, but there were some perplexed looks pointed at me.

"Because of my involvement, I was privy to some information that maybe would help us all when dealing with our emotions."

I could tell Monty wanted a sidebar with me. Whether to vet what I was about to say or to just shut me down, I wasn't sure.

"We've all assumed that it was Mark's gambling that was the cause of his death, and in a way it was, but not because he had debt or anything."

More looks, these ones with narrowed eyes and tilted heads. They'd been suspicious of me before, and they were even more so now, knowing I'd held out information from them.

"Mark was an FBI agent. He was investigating an online poker corruption ring. Hacking and cheating."

Silence. I looked around quickly, trying to gauge, willing my instincts to kick in. Disbelief from Jordan. Confusion from Herb. Suspicion from Seb. I found that from Seb interesting, but it still didn't override the vibe I'd gotten the day before from him that he wasn't involved.

But maybe it was time to admit that my instincts in murder investigations may be just as faulty as those I used to pick my bets.

As Jack said, a fifty/fifty proposition when you factored in the point spread.

Monty didn't share the looks of the others. He wasn't surprised, not in the least. Had he known? Would he have *had* to know to allow Mark into the group?

Did he form this group at Mark's request, choosing the

participants based on Mark's targets?

Was everyone in here under suspicion for Mark's online case?

I made a mental note to ask Frank if he'd talked to Monty about Mark being a part of the group.

But it seemed like Frank would have mentioned that to me already. So, how did Monty know?

"Bullshit," Herb said.

"It's true," I said. Nobody questioned my source. That fact hit home to me why Jack wanted to come on Monday—to establish my credentials as someone who had an in with the cops.

Pillow talk my ass. He'd thought this move out two days earlier.

And yeah, I guessed part of it was so they'd know someone had my back. At least, I let myself believe that was part of it.

"Christ," Seb said under his breath. All of the men except Monty were looking at the floor, their heads bowed. No empty smoothie cups at our feet today—Seb hadn't made his usual beverage run.

Instead a Monster can was at Jordan's feet, next to his Chuck Taylors crossed at the ankles. Coffee cups from the area Lor and Monty had set up were down at the sides of Seb and Herb.

I was dry. And my throat felt it. But I kept quiet, letting my bombshell sink in, watching for any tells.

They were all jittery, which didn't help. No doubt they were all replaying all their conversations in this very room the same way I had when I'd found out about Mark.

What incriminating evidence had they unwittingly revealed? None that I'd realized, but then, I wasn't looking for possible online poker criminal involvement.

"I need to go," Herb said, scraping his chair back, forgetting his cup as he made his way quickly to the door.

"See you Friday, Herb," Monty called after Herb, who just

waved over his shoulder and exited the building.

I waited in my seat to see if Seb would suggest going somewhere, but he only nodded at me and then followed Herb outside, walking down the sidewalk to his car.

"You okay?" Jordan asked me, and I nodded.

"You going to be?" I asked him. I hadn't forgotten the glazed-over look in his eyes the day I'd come to pull him off the table at the Venetian.

God, that seemed like ages ago.

"Yeah, I think so," he said. He took a deep breath and let it out slowly. "I can live without Oxygen until Friday, right?" He gave me a half-smile as he repeated my words of advice back to me.

"Yes, you can." He nodded and started to leave. "Jordan?" He turned back to me. "If you can't live without it, call me."

He nodded. "Thanks," he said, and left the building with a small wave to Monty.

Monty sat across from me, he and I the only two left.

"I have a question for you," I said.

He nodded, sitting up straighter in his chair. "Shoot," he said.

I wasn't crazy about his choice of verbs, but I wasn't about to let him off the hook.

It was time Monty came clean.

Thirty-Seven

"SO, SPILL," I SAID TO MONTY WHEN WE WERE ALONE.

"About investing in the treatment center, or Mark being a narc?"

Narc? What was this, *21 Jump Street*? And he had an edge to his voice that made me guess Monty hadn't known Mark was an agent before his death. Or at least hadn't willingly let Mark into the group knowing he was investigating someone.

If in fact Mark was. He could have just been trying to glean information on the mind of a compulsive gambler. Frank and Faxon hadn't coughed up any details on Mark's case. Perhaps the FBI hadn't offered many. Or any.

"Let's start with Mark," I said. Monty nodded and took a deep breath then started to speak, but was interrupted by his phone going off. He must have turned it back on when everyone started filing out of the session. That, or he had kept it on during therapy but no one had called. My phone was most likely on, too; I just seldom got calls on it. Mainly because I mostly hung with octogenarians who saw me every morning and didn't feel the need to text me throughout the day with status updates and pictures of their food.

"I have to take this," Monty said when he looked at his phone. He quickly moved to the door and stepped outside as he answered the call.

I gathered up the various empty cups and trashed them, then straightened the coffee bar area, wondering if I should turn the Keurig off or keep it on. I wasn't sure if Monty had more groups put together yet and if arrivals would be imminent or not.

I sat back in my seat, watching Monty's body language as he took the call. Tense. And when he spoke, he was leaning slightly, as if he was beseeching the speaker, almost pleading with them.

Well, shit. Was Monty in trouble? I agreed with Lor's assessment to keep to herself (and Jack) anything about Monty's past that might color how I felt about him as a therapist. But was there something bigger going on with him? And did it have anything to do with Mark?

Finally, he ended the call and came back into the therapy room. (Somewhere along the line I'd stopped thinking of it as a takeout place.)

"I'm sorry. I have to go. Can we talk about this later?"

"Sure. Is everything okay?" He nodded, but looked troubled. "Anything I can help with?"

"No. Thanks, I've got—" He stopped and looked outside toward the parking lot. "Shit. I forgot I lent my car to someone. They're not coming to get me for a couple more hours."

"I can give you a ride."

"Yeah? I just need to get to the Excalibur. Would that be okay?"

I nodded, rising from my seat. Monty was already crossing to the back of the room and hitting the lights. He scooped up his messenger bag from behind the counter as I turned off the Keurig and put the creamer back in the fridge. Seeing all the cans of Monster in there made me think of Jordan, and I smiled.

I'd tried the energy drink route a few times when pulling all-night poker games, but they didn't do it for me. The adrenaline of the game was what kept me going. When that ended, I wanted to be able to crash, not have anything in my system.

He locked up the place behind us and we got in my Porsche and headed toward the Excalibur. Thinking about pulling Jordan off the poker table at the Venetian, I asked, "Are you going to get somebody away from a table?" He nodded but didn't say anything. "I know you can't say who. But can you just tell me if it's Jordan?"

He turned his head quickly to me, puzzlement in his eyes. "No. It's not Jordan. Why would you ask that? We just saw him."

I shrugged and downshifted for the red light. "That doesn't mean he couldn't already be at the Excalibur with poker chips in his hands."

He watched me while I watched the stoplight. "What aren't you telling me?"

I looked over at him. "What aren't you telling *me*?"

He sighed and motioned that the light had turned green. I put it in first and drove on, waiting.

"I didn't know Mark wasn't what he said. Though I guess I should have suspected it."

"Why?"

A long sigh from him, but I kept watching the road and waited for him to continue. "He was the last client to start working with me. The last one I felt would make a good fit with the group I was trying to form."

"So he could have come to you because he was investigating or following one of your previous clients?"

He nodded and put his hand up along the side window, his index finger sliding along the edge where it connected to the door. "In retrospect, yes. That only occurred to me after the detectives told me he was undercover."

"And that fact pissed you off," I said. It wasn't really a question.

"Of course. For me, sure. But I was really pissed off because I put each of you at risk. Letting you think you were in a safe place when really…"

"Yeah," I said. "But we—or at least I—don't even know for sure that he was investigating someone from the group. Do you?"

He looked at me, then back to the road. "No. I guess I just assumed. Why bother being in the group, then?"

I shrugged. I wasn't really sure either. And maybe I just wanted to believe that no one from our group could have been involved in shooting Mark while I was lying unconscious right next to him.

But that had gotten me into trouble before—wanting to believe the best in someone.

Even myself.

"What else made you think you should have known something was off with Mark?" I asked.

"Little things. It felt like the experiences he told me about—when we were working alone—experiences he said he'd had while gambling… They felt off somehow. A little rote. Like he Googled compulsive gambling stories and memorized a few of them."

"I saw the setup at his place," I said. "It might have all been for show, or part of the investigation, but I'd be willing to bet he at least knew online poker. Knew poker."

"Oh, I think he did," Monty said. "Which probably is why he got the case. But I don't think it was a problem for him. I think the compulsive gambling part of it was made up."

A pang of envy rushed through me that someone could gamble, be good at it, and yet not succumb to the pull that it had over me. The Hummer and JoJo.

Then I realized I was envying a dead man and shook that thought away.

We were on Tropicana, nearing the Strip. I would turn into the Excalibur lot before reaching the Strip, dropping Monty at one of the hotel tower doors in the back. I didn't have much more time for this Q&A with Monty. I knew I'd see him again on Friday, but I just had to ask his thoughts on one last thing.

"Listen," he said before I could speak, "I know what information Lorelei found. I wasn't trying to hide it from her or anything. I just really feel it has nothing to do with my plans for the treatment center. But I want you to know that I totally understand if you don't want to invest. It's not a small amount, and I want you to be really sure—"

"It's not about that," I said. I didn't tell him that Lor had not passed on all the information she'd found. My poker instincts told me to hold that card close to the vest.

"*If*—and I still think it's a big if—somebody from our group was involved in Mark's killing—either directly or indirectly—"

"How can you be indirectly involved in someone being shot point blank?" he asked.

Oh, I knew a lot of ways that could happen, having been involved in a few myself.

"Like, he found out Mark was an agent and told someone. Something like that," I said.

He shook his head. Yeah, it was thin. I pulled into the Excalibur lot and around the circle drive to the tower entrance. "But say it was someone in our group, whether they actually pulled the trigger or not," I said. "I'm not asking you to divulge anything privileged. I'm just asking as a gut instinct with people you've been working with. Which one of us would you suspect?"

He got out of the car and leaned down, looking at me.

"That's easy," he said. "You."

Well, that wasn't very helpful. I *knew* I didn't do it. Although, that wasn't true either if you counted all those hours I couldn't remember.

Okay, I was *fairly* sure I hadn't put a bullet into Mark's chest.

And I was leaning toward Seb not being involved, though that was mostly based on gut instinct and the fact that he suspected me, which could just be a shrewd tactic on his part.

I started to pull out of the Excalibur lot when I remembered that they had a Krispy Kreme in the second-level food court. Ben and I would be going to Arizona Charlie's for breakfast the next morning, but surely Lor, Jack, and Raymond would appreciate a dozen original glazed. I parked and went in, careful to keep my head down, not wanting to see Monty with his client—or, more accurately, have Monty see me and think I was following him. Although maybe I should be.

I made my way up the escalator and to the food court. It was near five o'clock, and the area was crowded with tourists getting a quick bite to eat before beginning their night of revelry.

I ordered a dozen original, and while they were boxing them up I added a raspberry, which I asked be kept separate. I also got a coffee and sat at one of the small metal tables to scarf down my donut, hoping that I'd stop with just the one and not return home with a large box with only three donuts in it.

I was finishing up the nirvana that was a raspberry-filled Krispy Kreme when two guys in their twenties came into the food court and ordered from the Popeyes counter. Something about the Excalibur uniforms they were wearing sparked in my head. They were the same as what Jordan's roommate Eric had been wearing the night I pulled Jordan from the poker table at the Venetian.

I remembered thinking that they were different from the uniforms I knew the dealers there wore, and also different from those the staff at the book room wore.

These were golf shirts with the Excalibur logo, and I didn't remember seeing anybody on the floor of the casino wearing them before. They also both wore khakis. More casual than the black slacks most uniforms included.

After cleaning up my sugary mess, I took my box of dozen donuts (okay, eleven would make it home) and made my way out of the food court. At the last minute, I veered over to the table where the two guys sat eating their chicken.

"Hey, do you mind if I ask you where it is that you work

here?" I asked. "What department?"

They looked up at me, then each other. One shrugged at the other, who then answered me. "We're in the IT department. Why?"

"I just recognize the uniform. A friend of mine works there."

"Yeah? Who?"

"Eric," I said. "Actually, he's more a friend of a friend."

They shared a look. "Is he okay?"

"My friend, or Eric?" I asked, confused.

"Eric. Is he okay?"

I tried to remember if I'd seen Jordan get out of or into Eric's Camaro today, but realized I hadn't. But I hadn't *not*, either. "I think so. Why?"

"He hasn't been to work in a few days. Boss won't say if he's called in or what. I just know I'm working his shift tonight because he's not here. Pulling a double."

"Oh," I said. "I can't remember when I saw him last either. Hope he's okay."

"I hope he's in the hospital," the one who was picking up Eric's shift said. "Not to be a dick, but he *better* be sick to be pulling this shit." He sank his teeth into his chicken, grease coating his fingers.

"Well, thanks," I said, gave a nod to them, and left.

On the drive home, I tried to think what—if anything—Eric not showing up for work meant. And the fact that he worked in IT and Mark had been investigating online poker tampering.

Could be nothing, I told myself.

But wait. Hadn't Jordan said he was a computer science major in college?

My Porsche practically flew home, I was so excited to get back and talk with Jack.

The Hummer absolutely soared through my veins.

Thirty-Eight

WHEN I TOLD JACK ABOUT WHAT ERIC'S COWORKERS told me, he was silent. I could tell he was debating letting Frank in on this possible development, or perhaps following it up on his own. On *our* own.

Or maybe he thought it was nothing.

Big deal that Jordan's roommate hadn't shown for work in several days. So he was sick or something. I'd just seen Jordan hours earlier at group, and he seemed fine. Well, as fine as any of us seemed, given Mark's murder and the realization that he was FBI.

And then my crazy brain started wondering if Frank and Faxon had just said that Mark was working on an online poker cheating investigation so as not to tip me off, and maybe he was really investigating JoJo. But no, there were all those computers in his home; there was definitely—

"Hey, stop spinning," Jack said, reading me perfectly. I guessed I did have a tell where he was concerned. "Let me call Frank and just tell him what that guy said to you."

I took a deep breath, bringing my brain back in line. "Okay."

He left me in my office, and I killed time by once again looking through the financial report Lor had left me on the treatment center. My financial guy leaned against it. I wanted to help, but I guessed I really needed to start thinking about a world where I didn't bring in big wins every so often. (Or big losses, either, but usually JoJo took care of those so I didn't drain the household.) If I ever did find something that I thought I could do other than gambling, surely it wouldn't pay like poker did. Should we be in savings mode?

I pushed the report aside, happy to procrastinate on that decision a little longer. I was just about to pull out my journal when Jack came back in.

"They want to come over," he said. "Now."

"Now? Did you tell them about Eric being MIA?"

He nodded, still standing in the doorway, leaning his good shoulder against the jamb. "Frank said they have some things to share. Maybe they do, or maybe they want to question you directly about the Excalibur IT guy rather than just go through me."

"Surely Frank would know that you'd ask me anything pertinent before you called him."

A slight shrug. "Maybe. Or maybe they think I did and I'm holding out on them."

"Well, let's face it, you did think about doing that."

He smiled slowly. "And you said you couldn't read me."

We left my office and went and told Lor that Frank and Faxon were on their way over. She asked if we wanted them to stay for dinner, which both Jack and I answered with a resounding "no." She decided to serve dinner for herself, Raymond, and Ben in the kitchen, freeing up the dining room table for our little confab with the cops.

"I'll put the lasagna and bread back in the oven when we're done. You two just serve yourselves when you're ready. Raymond isn't working tonight, so he can get Ben settled for the night."

After thanking her, and almost staying in the kitchen due to the amazing aroma coming from the oven, we went to the front of the house just as Frank and Faxon arrived.

We got settled in the dining room, not offering them

anything, hoping they wouldn't be staying that long. Maybe we could join Lor, Raymond, and Ben for dinner after all.

"We got some preliminary reports back," Frank said. "Postmortem toxicity reports on Fitzpatrick will take a little longer, usually four to six weeks. But we have a tox screen from your blood. They're not as sophisticated as the full report, but it gives us something to work with."

Faxon laid a manila folder on the table, but made no move to let Jack or me see it. I wouldn't have been surprised to find it empty and just some kind of power play on Faxon's part. The way Jack looked at the folder then smirked confirmed my suspicions. Probably done all the time by cops.

"And?" I said.

"You're actually pretty lucky that you weren't more messed up Saturday morning," Frank said.

"Or worse," Faxon added, with what seemed like a touch of wishful thinking on his part.

"You'd been slipped—"

"Or *took*," Faxon added, earning a dirty look from Jack and a badly hidden eye roll from Frank.

"Rohypnol, commonly known as a roofie," Frank continued.

Oh, I knew what Rohypnol was. Only too well.

"And also a sleep aid of some kind. They couldn't be sure, but they think an Ambien."

That didn't make sense to me. "*Both*?"

Frank nodded while Faxon stared at me. "That doesn't make sense," Jack said. "Why both when one would do the job?"

"Needing to be certain?" Faxon said, but I could tell he was wondering the same thing we were.

"Then why not two of the same thing?" I said. "That would seem more likely. You'd have either roofies or Ambien. But to slip me one of each?"

We sat in silence, looking from one to the other, waiting for one of us to have an inspiration.

"Unless two different people drugged you," Jack said.

"God," I said on a sigh. "This just got even more complicated."

"To be clear, you yourself did not take any kind of sleep aid that night?" Frank asked. "In anticipation of coming home?"

"No," I said. "After I left here—" Frank had the good manners to look away as I remembered that they were here when Jack and I had it out. Faxon had a smirk on his face. "I had no intention of sleeping anytime soon. I never would have taken something."

"It was impossible to tell which was taken first," Frank said. "But they were both in your system for about the same amount of time, so it wasn't a scenario where you were slipped the roofie, went to Fitzpatrick's place, then hours later used something to get to sleep."

"This is really bizarre," I said, trying to wrap my mind around it. And saying a silent prayer of thanks that I came out of it all right. I looked at Jack, who was watching me, but his face held no clues either.

"We thought so, too," Frank said. "And it really is lucky that nothing worse happened to you, like cardiac arrest."

"Or rape," Faxon added.

"I guess waking up next to a dead friend with just some shakes and dizziness was my lucky day," I said.

Faxon glared at me, and I gave him my best "you don't scare me for one second, you little cockroach" poker stare. He looked away first. Asshole.

"Speaking of that," Frank said, "the rape kit shows just what you thought. No signs of sexual intercourse."

I nodded, happy to be right on that account, but still baffled by the thought of—

"Ambien," I said. "The night I was at Jordan's apartment, he took something to help him sleep. He was too keyed up from playing and said sometimes he did that to take the edge off."

"Missing roommate, uses Ambien," Frank said. "Could be coincidences."

Jack looked at me and raised an eyebrow. I smiled then turned to Frank. "They aren't coincidences."

THE LASAGNA WAS STILL warm in the oven because Frank and Faxon left shortly after my Ambien recollection. Jack and I demolished what was left of the dinner and talked over the case while we cleaned up the kitchen.

Just your average couple doing the dishes. Except for the talk of tox screenings, residue tests, and bullet hole trajectories.

I washed and he dried.

At the doorway we stood for a minute, then he headed to his wing and I headed to mine.

About an hour later, he knocked on my door and came into my bedroom. I was sitting in one of the chairs writing in my journal. *Trying* to write in my journal. Because all my thoughts were going back to being drugged twice in one night and how that could shake out.

Deeper than that. I thought back to all the roofies I'd slipped college kids. Not a lot, but enough. Too many, even at one. I had made sure they were safe and comfortable and in locked rooms, and had done my homework on each of them. But what if one of them had been hiding some kind of illness? One they took drugs for? Or had a condition of some sort that the roofie would exacerbate? I had once justified JoJo's actions with the mantra of "victimless crime," but I knew better.

Emotional check-in was cutting close to the bone tonight.

"Frank just called," Jack said, stepping into my room. I waved him to the seat opposite me, closed my journal, and set it on the side table.

"So soon?" I wondered what that could mean. Did they

go to question Jordan and find a pile of roofies and Ambien? Was Eric dead on the floor from an overdose? Damn, I wished I could remember if I'd seen the Camaro at group today.

"No sign of Jordan or this Eric guy at the apartment you told them about. No sign of anything, really. Looks like maybe they split."

"But I just saw Jordan hours ago."

"He didn't say anything about moving or crashing somewhere else?"

I shook my head, playing back today's session. "No. Nothing like that. He seemed normal enough."

"For therapy."

"Right."

He rose from the chair—reluctantly, it seemed—and walked to the doorway, where he turned back toward me. "Frank said they're doing a sweep of the place. Looking for any kind of foul play. If they haven't found either of them by Friday, I'm assuming they'll be staking out your GREET meeting."

That made sense. I felt a twinge of guilt. Had my telling them about Eric not showing up for work and Jordan having Ambien brought a shitstorm down upon our group? We were soldiering on without Mark—could we survive the cops busting down the doors and leading Jordan away for questioning?

"Okay, thanks for everything," I said to Jack.

"Like what? I didn't do anything."

"For being with me when Frank and Faxon were here. For not thinking the Eric thing was a wild goose chase. For taking me seriously, I guess."

He looked at me closely, his brown eyes warming me even from the doorway six feet away. "I've never *not* taken you seriously, Johanna," he said softly. So quietly I almost didn't hear him. But I did.

I stared at him, willing him to make the first move, dying for him to take the one step back into my room. That was all it would take, and I'd be out of this chair and meet him more than halfway.

But I wasn't going to be the one to move first.

He breathed heavily, ran a hand down his face, and looked at me again, this time with regret. "I can't come to you," he said. I was just about to nod when he added, "Yet."

Good thing it was just Jack and not Mr. Chow and a huge pot of chips across from me, because I was sure my face was relaying my every emotion.

Of course, he was right. It was too soon. And I'd just had a major relapse. So had he. To get back together now, even for one night, would probably be a huge mistake.

Still.

He smiled and raised a brow. Rubbing his bad shoulder, he said, "I need to have full range of motion to tangle with you the way I want to."

I barked out a laugh, and he turned and walked out of my door.

"Physical's been rescheduled for next week," he called from the hallway, making me smile even more.

Thirty-Nine

THE NEXT MORNING AT BREAKFAST, I BROUGHT MY BOYS up to speed on all that had gone down the previous day. Jimmy was almost as skeptical as Faxon had been. Gus just nodded and looked thoughtful. Ben beamed at me like I'd caught the killer red-handed, smoking gun dangling from his fingertips. We were a long way from that scenario, but it felt good to bask in Ben's good opinion of me.

We were pretty much back to normal. As long as I didn't mess up again, or put his son's life in danger.

Which was another reason why calling in Frank and Faxon had been a good decision.

Ben and I left Jimmy and Gus to their morning betting, making our way through the casino and out to the parking lot. Moving at a slow pace due to Ben's walker, I put my face up to the morning sun and let the heat envelop me.

We crossed the street to the parking lot and were almost to the Lexus when I heard tires screech behind me.

Turning, I saw Eric's Camaro coming straight toward Ben and me. I quickly moved in front of Ben, and we stood by the Lexus on the passenger side. No car was parked next to us, and Eric pulled the Camaro into that spot, rolling down his window.

I could see that Jordan was in the passenger seat. I could also see that Eric had a gun pointed at me. I stepped more in front of Ben and took a step toward Eric. I'd heard of people being shot even though a body was in front of them.

"Hey, guys," I said, bluffing.

Eric called, raising the gun at me, "Give your keys to the old man, your phone to me, and get in."

Every self-defense thing I'd ever read—and I'd read a bunch, being a single woman who kept crazy hours in a big city and ran in circles with, let's say, undesirables from time to time—said that you didn't get in a car with anyone. That you took your chances where you were. Yelling, screaming, ducking, running, whatever. But if you got in the car, the chances of anyone finding you lessened considerably.

But there was Ben behind me, and the look in Eric's eyes said he meant business. And if the silencer screwed onto his gun was any indication, I may have found Mark's killer.

Actually, he found me.

Not hard to do, considering I came here every morning at the same time.

"Let's just talk about this. Why don't—"

"Give your keys to the old man, your phone to me, and get in the car," Eric repeated, his voice colder than a second ago.

I slowly pulled my keys and phone out of my pockets and put the keys behind me to Ben, not willing to turn my back on Eric and Jordan.

At this point I didn't know who was the mastermind of whatever was going on, or who was the trigger man, though that seemed to be Eric. Maybe it was the same person.

"Hannah, no," Ben said. "Don't go with them."

"It's okay," I said. "Jordan's a friend of mine from group."

"What friends? Friends don't point guns at you."

"You sure you've met all her friends?" Eric said. He wiggled the gun at me in a "hurry up" motion.

"Take the keys, Ben. Go back inside and call your son to come and get you. I'll be fine."

I didn't say the name Jack, as Jordan had met him and knew he was a cop. Not that Ben wouldn't call the cops anyway, and they knew that. But they also figured they had some time before that happened. Ben wasn't going to sprint back into Arizona Charlie's to get to a phone. Not with his hip and walker.

"The phone," Eric said, and I handed it to him. He handed it to Jordan, who quickly took it apart and pulled out what I thought was the SIM card. He opened his door, dropped the card, and crushed it with the heel of his Chuck Taylors. It took a bit of effort with the rubber sole and all, but I heard a crunch. He handed the phone back to Eric. I reached for it, but Eric threw the thing across the parking lot toward the empty section. Likely it would be run over or picked up and Lorelei would set me up with a new phone for the second time in a week.

I *hoped* I'd be around to need a new phone.

"Dick move," I said to Eric, who snorted.

"Get in," he said, indicating I should do so on Jordan's side.

"Keep the gun on me," I said as I moved away from Ben and to the front of the Camaro.

"Nope," he said, moving his focus—and the gun—from me to Ben. "Hurry."

I hustled around the front of the Camaro, and Jordan opened his door for me and leaned forward, pulling his seat with him so I could get in the back. Before I did, I looked across the top of the car and met Ben's eyes.

"Get to a phone. Call your son. I'll be fine."

Anger and fear washed across Ben's wrinkled face. "I love you, Hannah darling," he said, his voice cracking.

My voice was gone, beyond cracking. I could only nod and start getting into the car. But no. If that was the last time I was going to see Ben Lowenstein, a man I thought of as a second father, a man who taught me how to survive in the world of gambling, after how rocky it'd been over the past two months for us, I needed to say the words.

"I love you too, Ben," I said, my voice scratchy but the words clear. I ducked my head and got into the tiny back seat. Jordan closed the door, and I held my breath until Eric pulled his arm back in the window and roared out of the parking lot. I looked out the back to see Ben watching us, then starting to move slowly back toward the casino.

WE WERE NEARING JORDAN'S apartment, and I wondered if maybe I'd given Frank the wrong apartment number last night. If I'd sent them to the wrong place—the one they'd found cleaned out.

But Eric didn't turn in at the apartment complex drive, continuing on for another three blocks then turning into a run-down residential neighborhood. Every third or fourth house had a foreclosure sign across it, some of them with boards across the front doors or garages with the doors open a foot or two—a sign that squatters might be in residence. Squatters were quite common in the poorer neighborhoods in Vegas.

The thought that they didn't blindfold me niggled in the back of my mind. They didn't care that I saw where they took me. So, it was either a place of no consequence to them…or they didn't plan for me to be able to talk.

The driveway that Eric pulled into was attached to a house with cardboard over one of the windows and a completely neglected look about it, but it certainly wasn't the worst house on the block. Eric pulled a fob from the console and opened the garage door, then pulled in. No one would see me getting out of the car.

At least Ben was safe. I couldn't get a handle on why Eric and Jordan wanted me, but I was pretty sure it wasn't to give them poker lessons.

That became abundantly clear when I walked into the house

behind Eric and in front of Jordan. I'd thought Mark's setup was impressive, but it paled in comparison to what Eric and Jordan had going on here.

Computers lined every surface, a huge server in one corner of the living room. The small kitchen's counters were filled with junk food, energy drinks, and takeout containers.

This was where the magic happened. Where online poker games were rigged. By computer science grad Jordan and IT employee Eric.

I walked around the room, Eric watching me wearily, the gun in his hand, though pointed at the floor, thankfully not at me. On several of the monitors, games were going on, and it seemed from a quick glance that even though they weren't at the computer, Jordan—or Eric—was playing.

"I wrote a script to play while I was away," Jordan said with not a little pride in his voice. "I fed it all my tendencies and the stats of all the players we kept a tally on, and it wins almost as much as I do when I play in person."

"And the cheating? The rigging of the games that Mark was investigating? Which one of you figured out how to do that?"

Neither seemed surprised that I knew about it. But then, they'd grabbed me from that parking lot for a reason, so I guessed they knew I was working with Frank and Faxon. Jordan knew firsthand that I was working with Jack, a cop.

"We both did," Jordan said, looking at Eric for agreement. So, Eric was the decision maker. But Jordan wanted his voice heard.

Might be handy to know that later on.

I walked around the room some more. There were sheets of paper with printouts of stats, games, dollars spent, all things I wasn't clear on, but knew led to something that Mark had probably been investigating. Some columns with money made from their cheating—rivaling some of my best nights in poker.

These boys were staying in a shit hole because they didn't

want to be noticed, not because they couldn't afford it.

"I gave you rent money," I said to Eric, nodding at the figure on the bottom of the one sheet of paper.

"Every little bit helps," Eric said, a smirk on his face.

"What? Why would you do that?" Jordan said, but I wasn't sure if he was talking to me or to Eric.

"He told me you were behind in rent. The day I pulled you out of the Venetian. While you were sleeping."

That was obviously news to Jordan, and he gave Eric a disbelieving look. Eric returned a shrug. "What? If she's gullible enough to fall for that…"

"Dude. Not cool," Jordan said.

I almost started laughing. He was chastising Eric like he'd borrowed his favorite sweatshirt, not because he'd scammed me out of money and was now holding a gun on me.

"Whatever," Eric said.

Not wanting to escalate anything at this point, I turned and continued my perusal of their active crime scene.

And there, at the table furthest from the door, was a stack of sticky notes. Not laid out so all could be read, but piled together willy-nilly, like they'd been hastily grabbed from where they'd been placed, and stacked up and jammed in a pocket.

I walked toward them, running a finger along the uneven edge of the stack, then turned back to find Jordan and Eric staring at me, blocking the entrance of the dingy living room.

Both of their gazes went from the stack of stickies that had previously been on Mark's computer to my face. They knew. And they knew I knew. But there was something else in their gazes. They knew I knew, but they didn't know *how* I knew.

They were a stark contrast, Jordan thin and with a nervous, fidgety energy about him, Eric filled out with a calm serenity. I wasn't sure which one was more dangerous, but right now Eric was holding the gun.

But who was ultimately holding the cards?

Forty

"YOU WANT TO TELL ME WHAT YOU KNOW ABOUT THOSE?" Eric said, pointing the gun toward the pile of sticky notes.

Since the gun was pointed at the notes, I moved in the opposite direction to an office chair across from the tables full of computers. "Yeah, I can tell you what I know, but why don't we all sit down? It's been a weird few days, right? Let's just take a breath and talk it out."

In a weird way, the scene before me reminded me of Saul and me months ago. My goal then was to keep Saul talking until the cavalry (which would turn out to be in the form of Jack Schiller) arrived.

The difference here was there was no way for the cavalry to find me. If Frank hadn't found this place when searching for Jordan, then odds were I was on my own this time.

Yes, Ben would eventually get to Jack, who would notify Frank, but there was nothing to trace me to the place. Being in the back seat, it'd been kind of hard to leave breadcrumbs as we'd entered North Las Vegas.

Still, talking was good; it told me their mindsets and gave me time.

Time for *what* was the undecided factor, but like all degenerate gamblers, I felt positive that my next hand would surely be pocket aces, so just keep playing.

Jordan sat in the only chair in the room that wasn't a computer desk chair, a beat-up recliner that looked like it was used for a crashing spot when coding, or hacking, or whatever they were doing to cheat at online poker, became too tiring. He slumped into it, and I could tell that he was tired of it all. Would that mean he wanted Eric to just end it?

I couldn't even pull out the "no harm has been done yet; you can still get out of this" card because Mark—an FBI agent—was dead. No, we were more in the "what's one more body at this point" territory.

"Okay, so the sticky notes," I said when it was obvious Eric wasn't going to join Jordan and me in sitting down. At least the gun was once again pointed at the floor.

"Why were you looking at them like that? What do you know about them?" Eric asked.

I wasn't sure if they were good poker players just because they could rig online poker games, or if that made them solely computer geniuses. Either way, I didn't feel like I should bluff.

"They were taken from Mark's apartment the night he was killed."

"How do you know that?" Eric asked, suspicion in his voice, his eyes narrowed on me. He took a few steps to his left, putting space between himself and Jordan. Putting himself at a straight line to me. We formed a right triangle, with me furthest into the room and the two of them across from each other at the base. At the only exit.

"I saw them there," I said.

Eric scoffed and shared a look with Jordan. "You were too out of it. Even if you had noticed them in the short time you were conscious at his place, you wouldn't have remembered. I'm betting you don't remember the majority of that night."

"You'd win that bet," I said. And then the weight of what he said hit me. "Wait a minute. You *saw* me? Conscious and with Mark, I mean?"

Another glance between the two of them. Some silent agreement was made. I was afraid it was of the "might as well tell the truth; she's going to be dead soon anyway" variety. At least on Eric's end. I still didn't have a good read on Jordan. He was probably the poker-playing skill behind the whole operation.

"Yeah, we saw you," Jordan said.

"And you left me there? Roofied up and at Mark's mercy?"

"What roofie?" Jordan said. "It was just an Ambien. And by the time I left, you were passed out in bed and Mark said he was just going to crash too. I believed him or I never would have left you." He hadn't said "we" never would have left you. So was Eric in the apartment too? Or had Jordan pulled the trigger while Eric kept the Camaro running?

"Wait. Back up. So *you* slipped me the Ambien? At the Red Rock, right?" I asked Jordan.

He sighed and ran a hand through his floppy hair, though it fell right back in front of his eyes. "Yeah, it was stupid. I thought I was doing you a favor."

I was hardly one to rant at someone for slipping me a sleeping pill, was I? But I knew for a fact none of the college basketball players JoJo had visited ever ended up with a dead body beside them in the morning.

"Explain that to me," I said to Jordan, who ruffled his hair again and fidgeted in his chair, not unlike how he acted at GREET sessions.

"I could see how it was playing out—you were falling for the bullshit he was feeding you. You were going to go home with him. That was obvious in the book room."

I couldn't recall those conversations with Mark—that was about when the blackout started—but it played out the way Jordan said it would, so his instincts must have been spot on.

"And, what? You were jealous?" I asked. I hadn't picked up on Jordan being especially interested in me as anything more than a fellow gambler. Certainly not as a woman.

He scoffed at that, and I guessed I should have been insulted, but I just motioned for him to go on. I would have rolled my eyes at him, but that seemed an odd thing to do when there was a gun dangling from Eric's hand.

"Christ, no. I just thought Mark was playing you. And your resistance was low. I mean, shit, *all* of our resistances were low that night, obviously."

"Obviously," I said.

He leaned back in his chair and stretched, and I imagined him doing the same motion hundreds—thousands?—of times in the same chair as he played—cheated at—online poker.

He blew out a long breath and looked at me, slowly shaking his head. "I couldn't put a finger on it then, but something about Mark always rubbed me the wrong way."

"Because he was a fucking narc," Eric interjected, and Jordan nodded.

"Yeah, well, now we know what that hunch was, but earlier that night he'd been trying to get us all to talk about the illegal things we'd done because of gambling. Do you remember that?"

"Yes," I said. That conversation made a lot more sense now that Mark's identity was uncovered. I said a silent prayer that I hadn't opened up about JoJo. To an FBI agent.

"Besides, if you were going to go home with anyone that night, it should have been Seb," Jordan said.

I couldn't help but let out a tiny snort. "God, I wish I had," I said. Jordan nodded his agreement, looking up at Eric, who showed no sign of any emotion. Good poker face.

"He'd done the work earlier at Distill," Jordan said. "Was making his play, it seemed. I thought for sure you two would hook up later."

I shrugged. I wasn't going to throw out anything as derivative as the heart wanting what it wants. It was all chance and drugs that led to me going home with Mark. No heart involved.

"So, you saw what was coming and didn't like it," I said.

"Yeah, so I slipped an Ambien into your beer when you went to the john. I thought if you went home with him, you'd fall asleep as soon as you got there and at least wouldn't sleep with him."

"Or I could be date-raped," I said.

He shook his head quickly. "No. You wouldn't have been that out of it. Not with just one Ambien."

"But with a roofie as well?"

"What is it about roofies?" Eric said. "There were no roofies. I don't even know how to *get* roofies. Do you?" Jordan shook his head.

"It was in my system," I said. "The toxicology report showed it."

"Jesus, you were a sitting duck," Jordan said.

"Or a passed-out one," I said.

"So, who slipped you the roofie?" Eric asked.

"I'm guessing Mark," I said. "Maybe he really did intend on taking me home and…"

"Fucking asshole," Eric said.

Yeah, that had to be it. There was really no other answer, and I believed Jordan that he'd only slipped me the Ambien.

The irony was not lost on me that an FBI agent had horrific intentions toward me that night, while the criminal poker hackers had been trying to save me.

"I was right," Eric said to Jordan. Then to me he added, "When I picked Jordan up, he told me what happened. I said I didn't put it past this guy Mark to take advantage of you even if you had fallen asleep."

"That freaked me out, so we drove to Distill, just in case, and you and Mark were still in the parking lot, in his Prius. Making out a little," Jordan said.

Ugh. The idea of kissing Mark had at one time been attractive to me, but now, knowing what he'd intended? Double ugh.

"So we followed you to his place," Jordan continued. "We didn't really know what to do, but after about a half-hour I decided to go see if everything was okay."

He didn't know what he would be walking into, and Mark had about four inches and eighty pounds on slight, scrawny Jordan. "Thank you," I whispered. "Not for the Ambien," I added, and Jordan nodded. "But for being concerned for me enough to follow us. And to come to his apartment."

"You pulled me out of a bad situation," Jordan said. "I wanted to help, especially because maybe I'd put you in danger."

He'd been right: the Ambien alone probably wouldn't have been enough for Mark to overpower me if I'd been forced, but who knew? And Jordan hadn't known about the roofie or my incapacitated state.

"So I knocked on the door and Mark took a while, but came and let me in," Jordan said.

A memory of Mark's apartment the following morning came back to me. "Did you have a can of Monster with you?" Jordan shook his head. So, that can and smoothie cup had been Mark's after all. Frank's tests would surely confirm that at some point. And it would be less evidence to point to Jordan and Eric.

The more open they were with me, the more I was coming to believe I wouldn't be around to point the finger at them myself.

"He was already undressed, just in gym shorts. I couldn't see you, but I heard you stumbling in the bedroom."

I leaned forward in my chair, listening to Jordan's every word, letting him unveil what my failing memory could not.

"I said I wasn't leaving until I knew you were all right," Jordan said, then looked sheepish. "I told him I saw you take a sleeping pill just before you left, so I was worried."

"That *I* took the pill?"

Eric waved my words away—puny details in a much bigger game. He nodded for Jordan to go on, and I wondered if perhaps this was the first time Eric had heard this part of the story. Was he just the getaway driver in all of this? But why was he the one holding the gun now?

And quite naturally, too; it seemed like a perfect fit with his palm and fingers.

"He seemed a little freaked when I said you took a sleeping pill," Jordan said. Which pretty much confirmed that Mark indeed had slipped me the roofie—just a sleeping pill wouldn't scare him, but the possible effects of both combined might.

"I said I wanted to see you, so he led me to the bedroom. Your clothes were everywhere, and by then you were in the bed covered up, but with bare shoulders. Given the amount of clothes on the floor, I was guessing you were naked."

"You guessed right," I said.

"I said I'd take you home, but he said it'd be better not to move you. That he'd make sure you were okay."

"And you believed him?" I asked. It wasn't an accusation. Jordan's senses about Mark had been dead-on (no pun intended) so far. If he had felt I was safe, then he was probably right.

"I told him nothing had better happen to you. That I'd tell you about the sleeping pill the next morning and that I'd been there, and if he'd done anything to you, we'd know. That I'd be a witness."

I nodded. That was probably the best he could do under the circumstances. I was sure I would have been incapable of moving by that point. At least on my own.

He moved his chair from side to side, rocking a little in the swivel seat. "He said he was going to bed, leaving you alone, and to get out of his place. Then he did just that, climbed into bed with you, turned away, and threw a hand over his head like he was going to sleep."

My eyes went over to the table holding the sticky notes. "And you saw those as you walked out."

Jordan nodded.

"How did you know those were from his place?" Eric asked. That was what had started this whole thing—that I knew about the stickies coming from Mark's place. A fact that surprised them, and one they hadn't counted on.

"I'd been to his apartment before." Jordan's eyes got wide, and I quickly added, "With Seb. The three of us. When we first started hanging out. Seb and Mark talked about their setups, about the stickies. I mostly tuned it out."

"So you knew they were gone when you woke up that morning?"

I shook my head. "Not right away. Not for a couple of days after. Then I told the cops, and we…"

"What? You what?" Eric said, his gun rising from his dangling wrist to not quite aim at me, but closer than was comfortable.

"I thought it was Seb. Because of the interest he'd shown in them."

Eric and Jordan looked at each other, some puzzle pieces fitting together for them, some not.

I knew the feeling.

"So the cops think it was Seb?" Jordan asked. There was hope in his voice, which was quickly squashed by Eric saying, "Then why the hell did they raid our apartment last night?"

He motioned (unfortunately, not with his gun hand) at a small monitor in the corner of the room, and I realized it was coming from a security camera inside their apartment.

So, things had been hot for them since Mark's death, they'd been hiding out here, in their "office," and last night saw that indeed the cops had come looking for them.

"The Ambien," I said. No way was I going to tell them about seeing Eric's coworkers at the Excalibur. I had no idea how this game would play out, but I wasn't going to stack the deck against two guys who just happened to give me information.

If Eric and Jordan walked out of here, I didn't want their

next step to be to the IT department at the Excalibur.

"What? The Ambien?" Jordan asked.

"The cops told me last night about the toxicology reports and asked if I had any ideas about who would put a roofie and an Ambien in my beer. I said I had no idea. But I did remember that you'd used a sleeping aid of some kind that night I brought you to your apartment."

Eric looked at Jordan like he'd blown the whole thing for them both. I didn't point out that Eric not showing up for work—and most likely murdering Mark—had been a big misstep too.

"But wait," I said, "so you saw the sticky notes at Mark's apartment on your way out. What did that tell you?"

Another shared glance, then this time Eric answered me. "We knew someone was tracking us, electronically, that we were being *looked* at. The notes he made were way beyond what an average poker player would track on competing players."

"Seb seemed to think so too—he couldn't believe how thorough Mark was," I said.

"I wouldn't be surprised if Mark was feeling Seb out," Jordan said, "seeing his reaction to the players listed." He pointed to the stack of sticky notes on the table.

"If he suspected, somehow, that the person behind the cheating was in Monty's group, that would make sense." I still wasn't sure how that initial connection had been made by Mark, and guessing from how Frank talked about the lack of FBI cooperation, I would probably never know.

But he'd been right, Mark. The guilty party *was* in Monty's group, and had had quite a reaction when he saw the sticky notes. Poor Mark had just been in bed and not able to witness it.

"So, you what, grabbed all the sticky notes and ran?" I said. But no, then Mark would still be alive.

Jordan looked down at his feet, and Eric's grip on the gun tightened.

Ah. "No. You went out to the car and told Eric about the notes. And he, and his *pal*"—I motioned to the gun—"went back inside and took them. And made sure Mark's investigation went no further."

Jordan kept his head down, and Eric shrugged, like this was boring news. Old news, at least to him.

Then Jordan looked up, and it was the same expression of anguish that he had when I'd retrieved him from the poker table at the Venetian. Anguish, regret, and guilt. But something more.

"You didn't know," I whispered. Jordan exhaled loudly, like he'd been keeping something inside of him for days.

He had.

"You went out and told Eric. He said he'd go get the notes—you probably even made sure the door was unlocked, knowing Eric would go back inside to get them."

Jordan was shaking his head, but not looking at me. "But I didn't think…"

"You thought he was just going to get the notes and come back," I said. Some level of Jordan believed that. The same voice that told him his next hand would be the big winner had told him over the past few days that he didn't know, that Eric was just going to get the notes.

And I felt for the kid, I really did. It was that voice, and what it said, that got you through. That allowed you to at least get out of bed in the morning, if not quite look at yourself in the mirror.

Some part of him, the part that cropped up the minute after he placed a bet, knew what would happen if Eric went into Mark's apartment.

And he still told Eric about the notes.

"So when did you find out that Mark had been shot?" I asked Jordan, speaking as though it was a foregone conclusion what Eric had done when he went to retrieve the notes.

And it was. There was no doubt. If there had been, it would

have been erased by the look of resignation in Eric's eyes.

"The next day when the cops called," Jordan said in a voice barely above a whisper.

"So at least your surprise would have been genuine," I said. There was a tiny bit of venom in my voice, and Eric took one step toward me.

And then I had an idea. A way to play myself out of this hand.

It would take some bluffing, some reading of tells, and a whole lot of luck.

Forty-One

SOMETIMES WHEN PLAYING POKER, I'D GET IN A POT just to play two chip leaders against each other. It didn't always work, and usually not against really good players, but sometimes I'd be the buffer that would allow two players to bully each other. Get the pot nice and big and knock one out with a stack I couldn't have matched. Sometimes it ended with a player out and the other that much stronger, doubling up.

But occasionally I could sneak in with a crafty bet or a well-timed re-raise and steal the whole damn thing.

"So, Jordan," I said, leaning forward. "You did nothing wrong." His eyes darted across the rows of computers—the evidence of his wrongs. "*You* didn't kill Mark. You had no idea he was going to be killed. You just thought Eric was going in to get the stickies."

Eric snorted, but his was not the response I was waiting for. The wheels were turning in Jordan's mind, and I nearly held my breath to see which wheel would pull the cart.

"Right," he said, and I pulled my poker face tight as inside I breathed a huge sigh. Not quite one of relief, not yet, but perhaps there was a light at the end of the tunnel. A rope being thrown over the cliff as I dangled beneath.

"Bullshit," Eric said. He kept the gun at the ready, but not pointed at anyone, as he turned to Jordan. "You knew *exactly* what was going to happen when you got in that car and told me about his information."

Jordan started to crumble, and I jumped in. "But you didn't have to kill him. Take the notes so he'd have to start over. Trash his machines." I waved an arm at their computers. "That would give you enough time to get back here and dismantle your stuff, cover your electronic tracks. Surely you had an escape plan in place for that."

They did; I could tell by their looks—Eric's seething and Jordan's questioning.

"All he'd know in the morning is Jordan stole his damn sticky notes. Sure, he'd suspect you, but Jordan could say he'd taken them to help himself when he played. Stealing an advantage. It's not a felony to steal pieces of paper."

"He'd know it was us," Eric said. There was no questioning in his voice. Whatever guilt or remorse he had—if any—about killing Mark, he'd resigned himself to long ago.

"Maybe. But again, if you shut it down, covered your tracks, he couldn't prove it." I pointed at the stack of paper that had figures and dollar amounts on it. "You had a good run, made a nice profit. You could use that for a fresh start. Or your next stake."

Jordan was playing that out in his head, a scenario where Mark was still alive, he and Eric were no longer cheating, and they had money for—probably in Jordan's fantasies—infinite gambling.

I knew, because that often played into my fantasies. Not the never having murdered part, but lots of other sins washed away, and the infinite gambling part.

"She's playing you," Eric warned Jordan. "Trying to play us both. Against each other."

That was not news to Jordan, I could tell. Which gave me even more hope. He knew the cards I was holding and still wanted the action. Either he wanted to be on my side, believe me, or he was holding pocket aces and was going to bleed me dry.

"Maybe I am," I admitted. "But I'm not wrong." I looked directly at Jordan and waited until he met my eyes. "Am I?"

His eyes dropped, and though he didn't speak, we all knew he agreed with me.

Mark didn't have to die. And no matter if Jordan had known, deep down, what might happen if Eric went into that building, he had not pulled the trigger, nor known about it beforehand.

Not for sure.

"They'll cut you a deal," I said to Jordan. Eric raised his arm, pointing the gun at me, but I went on. "You give them the man who killed one of their own, show them how this whole poker thing worked… The FBI will work with you, Jordan."

"Shut. The. Fuck. Up," Eric said, lifting his arm higher.

I debated standing to make my point, but thought I made a smaller target in the chair, so stayed sitting. I still spoke to Jordan, but I swiveled in the chair to face Eric. Best to keep an eye on that gun. And the man attached to it.

"It's like Oxygen, Jordan," I said. "But we're talking about real oxygen this time, not just the feeling. The oxygen of not being in prison for a crime you didn't commit."

"Don't listen to her," Eric said.

"You told me yourself," I said, not looking at Jordan, keeping my eye on the silencer on the gun. The gun that had killed Mark as he slept.

The gun that would likely soon end my life.

"You *need* that oxygen, Jordan," I said. "You told me yourself you can't live without it. He's going to make you do that, when you only did some petty computer crimes."

"Stop it." From Jordan this time, but it was soft and unconvincing. I tried to glance his way and saw he'd swiveled the recliner toward the row of tables. So he wouldn't have to see me as I told him what he wanted to hear? Or so he wouldn't have to watch as Eric put a bullet through me, just like Mark?

"How are you going to live the rest of your life without oxygen, Jordan?" I said, louder now. Urgency. Indecision. It was what made players with bad cards bet when they should fold.

"No oxygen, Jordan. Think about it. For something you didn't even do!"

"Stop it," Jordan yelled as Eric screamed, "Shut the fuck up!"

And then the room was silenced by the sound of a gunshot.

Forty-Two

THE FIRST THOUGHT I HAD WAS I'D BEEN SHOT IN the ass. How was that possible? The second thought was shouldn't a gun with a silencer be quieter than that?

Shaking my head, I realized I was on the floor, having slid down on my butt when I heard the gunshot.

And I wasn't shot at all. The gun with the silencer was not that one that had gone off. It had been the one that Jordan was now holding in his lap, cradling it like a newborn kitten.

Eric lay on the floor between us, having fallen forward when Jordan had shot him.

Had killed him.

For it was obvious Eric was dead. Lifeless, with blood beginning to seep out from under his body.

Still, as I got to my feet and walked toward Jordan, I toed Eric's gun away from him, then kicked it under one of the tables.

"Breathe," I said to Jordan as I neared him, reaching out slowly for the gun. "Just breathe all that oxygen," I said. He nodded and handed me the gun. I looked to the low table beside him, where he'd obviously had the gun stashed. Nothing else there. I stepped back and looked around the room for a phone of any kind. No landline anywhere that I could see, and I had no intention of leaving the room.

"Phone?" I asked. Jordan looked up at me, his eyes hollow

and lifeless. I was willing to bet not as lifeless as Eric's. Slowly he pulled a phone out of his pocket, entered the security code to unlock it, and handed it to me.

I should have called 911, but I knew Ben and Jack would be frantic, so I called Jack first.

I told him where we were and that I was safe. He said nothing more and disconnected. I knew he'd take care of it from there.

I put Jordan's gun in the back of my pants like I'd seen cops do on TV, checking that the safety was on first.

I went to Jordan's chair, sat on the fat, upholstered arm, and put a hand on his shoulder, both of us looking straight ahead at Eric's body.

"No way will they give me a deal now, right? They won't have Eric to prosecute, so it will all fall on me."

I gave his shoulder a small squeeze. It felt like Ben's shoulder, small and bony. "I heard Eric admit, basically, to killing Mark, and that you weren't aware of it."

He looked up at me, knowing that it wasn't exactly the truth. Or not all of it, anyway. "You saved my life," I said. "That counts for a lot."

He scoffed, as if not believing me. Maybe he was right and he'd take the fall for Eric killing Mark. It would be justice, in a way, for Jordan had surely been the instrument of Mark's death, if not the actual shooter.

And yet he could have let Eric kill me now, been complicit yet again. They would have had a head start, some funds, and could have maybe made a run for it. Fled the country.

I supposed all those thoughts had gone through Jordan's mind as well, and yet he'd chosen to shoot Eric.

"I'll tell them all I can to help you out," I said.

He nodded, then turned back to look at his friend's body while we waited.

♠ ♥ ♦ ♣

IT TOOK FOREVER. First the cops had shown up at the same time Jack had. He'd gone crazy when they wouldn't let him see me right away, blasting them with the fact that they would never have even found me if he hadn't called them.

Shortly after Frank and Faxon had shown up, I said I wasn't going to say anything until they let Jack in, so they finally did. Faxon hadn't liked doing it, and Frank had given Jack a warning look.

He held me by the arms, doing a scan of me, making sure I was all right. I gave him a nod, and he stepped back, letting me take the lead.

I told the story, making Jordan look like an unwilling accomplice in an online scam and an unknown accomplice in murder. Jordan, at my warning, didn't say a word. I told him I'd call a lawyer and have them meet him at the police station.

Then the FBI showed up just as they were putting a handcuffed Jordan in the back of a police cruiser.

Cue obligatory turf war between the FBI and local cops, and it took even longer for us all to go to the station, where I could tell the story again and again to both the cops and the FBI.

I made the case for Jordan to be tried only for the online stuff, not the murder of Mark. And reiterated several times how he'd saved my life.

I wasn't sure how much weight any of it held, but I would work with his lawyer, making sure Jordan got treated as fairly as possible.

I didn't forgive him for the role he played in Mark's death, but I didn't forget that it could have just as easily been me lying on that floor, a pool of blood seeping from my body.

♠ ♥ ♦ ♣

FINALLY, IN THE LATE EVENING, I was allowed to go home. Jack had stayed at the station the whole time and looked about as tired as I felt.

"Is Ben okay?" I asked when we were alone in the Lexus, driving toward Summerlin.

Jack nodded, but kept his head forward, eyes on the road. "He was scared to death for you. But he was unhurt. He got back into the casino, found Jimmy, and they called me. I went straight to meet up with Frank, and Jimmy and Gus brought Ben home."

"So you haven't seen him?" I was concerned about Ben spending the whole day worrying about me. And Jack.

"No, but I spoke with him once while we were looking for you. Tried to reassure him. And, of course, I called him while you were being questioned at that house. Let him know you were okay. But that we'd probably be a while."

I checked the clock on the dash. "We missed dinner," I said, and Jack chuckled.

"If I know Lorelei, there are some tremendous leftovers keeping warm."

"That's a safe bet," I said, and he snorted. "What?"

"Nothing's a safe bet with you, Johanna."

I smiled, and we rode in silence. I replayed the scene from the house over in my head, tried to do an emotional check-in, and was shocked at what I surmised.

But Jack… Jack, who knew me so well, who could see my tell like a neon Vegas sign, was way ahead of me.

"Hummer?" he asked.

"Like you wouldn't believe," I said.

He put his hand on my knee and drove us home.

Forty-Three

INDEED, THE SHEPHERD'S PIE WAS OUT OF THIS WORLD and still warm.

Lorelei insisted on serving Jack and me in the dining room so the whole group could join in as we rehashed the morning.

Gus and Jimmy were there, had apparently held vigil with Ben all day, and for that I was grateful, thanking both men when Ben wasn't in hearing range.

Raymond either wasn't working or had decided not to work, because he joined us too.

When I got to the part about how I'd been both roofied and Ambiened, he slyly smiled and said, "Is that what they call being hoisted by your own petard?" A lot of eyebrows went up, and he replied, "What? I'm one semester shy of a college degree. I can use terms like that."

Which caused us all to laugh, some of the nervous energy of the day for my boys falling away.

Me, I'd never felt more alive, the Hummer raging through my veins.

Too bad about Jack's shoulder not quite being up to… tangling levels. Though if the looks he was shooting me all through dinner were any indication, he might just work through the pain.

When Jimmy and Gus left, Jack took Ben to his room, and

Lorelei, Raymond, and I did the dishes and sat at the kitchen table talking until midnight.

It felt good to have my *family* safe and sound in my house. Just sitting around the kitchen table, chatting and eating cheesecake.

Kind of like the *Golden Girls*.

When I yawned, we all called it a night. Knowing I'd still need to unwind, and with Jack not making a reappearance with an offer to help me do just that, I walked with Lor as far as our office to grab one of my journals.

Not quite the outlet I was looking for, but I'd take it.

Lor followed me in, grabbing one of her tablets from her side of the desk as I went to mine and sat down.

She studied me, then sat down on her side. "I know this is probably the last thing you want to think about right now…"

"Monty's treatment center," I said, and she nodded.

Earlier, while we'd been in the dining room, I'd called Monty and let him know what happened. Shortly after that call came a group text from him to the GREET members that the session for the next day was canceled and he'd reach out to us all individually.

"It's a good program," I said. "I hope he keeps it going even after this mess."

She nodded. "I hope he does too. But if your financial man says it's too risky? Well, you have to do what's best for you, Jo."

"What's best for our family," I said.

"No. What's best for *you*."

I nodded, taking a deep breath. Then I saw my cigar box. Pulling it over, I opened the lid and took out the tickets from Friday night at the Red Rock. I handed them across the desk to Lor.

"Take these. Cash them. Use that money for an investment in Monty's center. It won't come out of any house funds or investments."

She flipped through them, her eyes widening as she read the amounts. She knew I played poker for large stakes at times, had put the entry money aside for me, but she probably had no true idea of how much I could spend sports gambling.

Especially when done on a binge.

"This is a little more than what we thought about investing."

I waved at the pieces of paper like they could leap across the desk and bite me. "Then bank the rest. Or put it into finding a better place for GREET meetings. Or hiring help. Just… I don't want it."

She nodded, tucking the betting slips into an envelope and then sliding that envelope between the pages of her tablet.

It seemed like good karma that the ill-gotten gains from a gambling binge would be used for opening a treatment center for compulsive gamblers.

She tidied up her area, tapping the tablet against the desk, readying to leave. "Anything else you need?" she asked.

I shook my head, but my words came out differently. "Yes. If you could."

She seemed to notice the hesitancy in my voice, putting down the tablet, taking a pen in her hand, and watching me with patient, understanding eyes.

I thought about the work we'd done in GREET. How I'd tried to find a replacement for the Hummer and failed. Maybe that was why I had gone off the deep end last Friday.

But now I knew that there *was* a way to feel the Hummer. And it didn't involve point spreads.

"If you have time," I said, hedging, already thinking it was a dumb idea. Lor nodded encouragingly at me, and I cleared my throat and continued. "Could you do a little research for me?"

Nothing I couldn't do myself, but Lor was so good at that sort of thing. Besides, I knew that I could chicken out of this at any time, and probably would. Give it to Lorelei to pursue, and at least I'd have the information I wanted.

Then I could make a decision.

"I'd like to know how you go about becoming a private investigator," I said. I waited for a laugh from her, a snort, a scoff, something. But when I looked at her, she was nodding and writing, her head down over the tablet, her red hair falling forward before she tucked it behind a pale ear.

"Like, I know there'd be classes and certifications. A license of some sort. I'm guessing gun training, too."

More nodding from her, her hand continuing to scrawl across the paper.

"I mean, it's probably stupid, but—"

Her head popped up, the red mane falling into place, her eyes laser-like on mine. "It's *not* stupid. I think it makes a lot of sense."

"You do?" I said, and she nodded.

"So do I," Jack said from the doorway.

Some private investigator I'd make if the likes of Jack Schiller could constantly creep up on me.

"Yeah?" I said, looking from Lor to him.

"I really do," he said. He took up a stance in the doorway, leaning on his good side, crossing his arms. "And I'll even throw my hat in the ring."

"What do you mean?" I asked.

"How would you like some help with that?" he asked.

Lor looked from him back to me with huge eyes and swallowing a "squee" I knew she wanted to let out.

"I usually work alone," I teased Jack.

He raised an eyebrow at me and a soft smile crossed his face. "So do I. But I'm betting we'd be a good team."

"I don't bet anymore," I said. Still with her back toward Jack, Lor shot me a "what, are you an idiot?" look, but I only winked at her.

I might have problems reading Jack Schiller, but I knew when I had him.

And I had him now.

"I think this is one last bet you might want to make," he said. He gave me another smile and walked out of the door.

No, the last bet I would make would be with myself. And it was that Jack was right now making his way to my room, not his.

Acknowledgments

Readers Holli Bertram, Liz Kelly, Colleen Gleason, and Patti Kearly were invaluable in their feedback. The editing at Twin Tweaks and Editing 720 was, as always, top notch. And a big thank you to my last-look editor, Margo Burrage.

Thank you to Tyler Kearly for a quick tutorial on online poker stat keeping. Much like Anna did when Seb and Mark explained it to her, I quickly tuned out. But I retained enough to help with this book - so thank you.

The treatment group—GREET—that Anna joins is one created by me. Though I admire the 12-step programs, for plot purposes I wanted to have more freedom in the type of group sessions Anna attended. There are some programs that are similar to GREET, where the emphasis is on being in control of your emotions and mindfulness. In no way should my made-up group be used for true compulsive gambling problems.

In other words: Kids, don't try this at home.

The Anna Dawson Series continues with

AGAINST THE GRAIN

ANNA DAWSON BOOK 5

Try Mara Jacobs's romantic mystery

BROKEN WINGS

Try Mara Jacobs's *New York Times* bestselling Worth series

Worth The Weight

Worth The Drive

Worth The Fall

Worth The Effort

Totally Worth Christmas

Worth The Price

Worth The Lies

Worth The Flight

Worth The Burn

Find out more at
www.MaraJacobs.com

Mara Jacobs is the *New York Times* and *USA Today* bestselling author of The Worth Series

After graduating from Michigan State University with a degree in advertising, Mara spent several years working at daily newspapers in Advertising sales and production. This certainly prepared her for the world of deadlines!

Mara writes mysteries with romance, thrillers with romance, and romances with…well, you get it.

Forever a Yooper (someone who hails from Michigan's glorious Upper Peninsula), Mara now splits her time between the U.P. and Las Vegas.

You can find out more about her books at **www.marajacobs.com**

www.ingramcontent.com/pod-product-compliance
Lightning Source LLC
Chambersburg PA
CBHW031703170626
46808CB00005B/1594

* 9 7 8 1 9 4 0 9 9 3 1 5 7 *